COMPANION TO THE BESTSELLING

RANGER'S APPRENTICE

BROTHERBAND

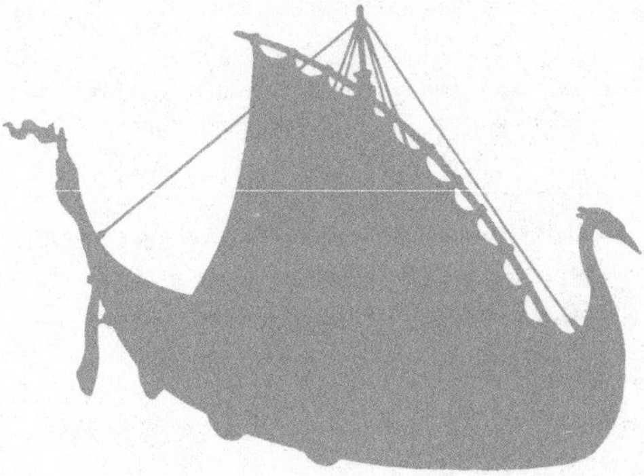

BOOK 9

THE STERN CHASE

JOHN FLANAGAN

VIKING

VIKING
An imprint of Penguin Random House LLC, New York

First published in the United States of America by Viking,
an imprint of Penguin Random House LLC, 2022

First published in Australia by Penguin Random House Australia in 2022

Visit us online at penguinrandomhouse.com.

Library of Congress Cataloging-in-Publication Data is available.

Printed in the United States of America

ISBN 9780593463819

1 3 5 7 9 10 8 6 4 2

BVG

Text set in Centaur MT Std

A Few Sailing Terms Explained

Because this book involves sailing ships, I thought it might be useful to explain a few of the nautical terms found in the story.

Be reassured that I haven't gone overboard (to keep up the nautical allusion) with technical details in the book, and even if you're not familiar with sailing, I'm sure you'll understand what's going on. But a certain amount of sailing terminology is necessary for the story to feel realistic.

So, here we go, in no particular order:

Bow: The front of the ship, also called the prow.

Stern: The rear of the ship.

Port and starboard: The left and the right side of the ship, as you're facing the bow. In fact, I'm probably incorrect in using the term *port.* The early term for port was *larboard,* but I thought we'd all get confused if I used that.

Starboard is a corruption of "steering board" (or steering side). The steering oar was always placed on the right-hand side of the ship at the stern.

Consequently, when a ship came into port, it would moor with the left side against the jetty, to avoid damage to the steering oar. One theory says the word derived from the ship's being in port—left side to the jetty. I suspect, however, that it might have come from the fact that the entry port, by which crew and passengers boarded, was also always on the left side.

How do you remember which side is which? Easy. *Port* and *left* both have four letters.

Forward: Toward the bow.

Aft: Toward the stern.

Fore-and-aft rig: A sail plan in which the sail is in line with the hull of the ship.

Hull: The body of the ship.

Keel: The spine of the ship.

Stem: The upright timber piece at the bow, joining the two sides together.

Forefoot: The lowest point of the bow, where the keel and the stem of the ship meet.

Steering oar: The blade used to control the ship's direction, mounted on the starboard side of the ship, at the stern.

Tiller: The handle for the steering oar.

Sea anchor: A method of slowing a ship's downwind drift, often by use of a canvas **drogue**—a long, conical tube of canvas closed at one end and held open at the other—or two spars lashed together in a cross. The sea anchor is streamed from the bow and the resultant drag slows the ship's movement through the water.

Yardarm, or yard: A spar (wooden pole) that is hoisted up the mast, carrying the sail.

Masthead: The top of the mast.

Bulwark: The part of the ship's side above the deck.

Scuppers: Drain holes in the bulwarks set at deck level to allow water that comes on board to drain away.

Belaying pins: Wooden pins used to fasten rope.

Oarlock, or rowlock: Pegs set on either side of an oar to keep it in place while rowing.

Thwart: A seat.

Telltale: A pennant that indicates the wind's direction.

Tacking: To tack is to change direction from one side to the other, passing through the eye of the wind.

If the wind is from the north and you want to sail northeast, you would perform one tack so that you are heading northeast, and you would continue to sail on that tack for as long as you need.

However, if the wind is from the north and you want to sail due north, you would have to do so in a series of short tacks, going back and forth on a zigzag course, crossing through the wind each time, and slowly making ground to the north. This is a process known as **beating** into the wind.

Wearing: When a ship tacks, it turns *into* the wind to change direction. When it wears, it turns *away* from the wind, traveling in a much larger arc, with the wind in the sail, driving the ship around throughout the maneuver. Wearing was a safer way of changing direction for wolfships than beating into the wind.

Reach, or reaching: When the wind is from the side of the ship, the ship is sailing on a reach, or reaching.

Running: When the wind is from the stern, the ship is running. (So would you if the wind was strong enough at your back.)

Reef: To gather in part of the sail and bundle it against the yardarm to reduce the sail area. This is done in high winds to protect the sail and the mast.

Trim: To adjust the sail to the most efficient angle.

Halyard: A rope used to haul the yard up the mast. (Haul-yard, get it?)

Stay: A heavy rope that supports the mast. The **backstay** and the **forestay** are heavy ropes running from the top of the mast to the stern and the bow (it's pretty obvious which is which).

Sheets and shrouds: Many people think these are sails, which is a logical assumption. But in fact, they're ropes. Shrouds are thick ropes that run from the top of the mast to the side of the ship, supporting the mast. Sheets are the ropes used to control, or trim, the sail—to haul it in and out according to the wind strength and direction. In an emergency, the order might be given to "let fly the sheets!" The sheets would be released, letting the sail loose and bringing the ship to a halt. (If *you* were to let fly the sheets, you'd probably fall out of bed.)

Hawser: Heavy rope used to moor a ship.

Way: The motion of the ship. If a ship is under way, it is moving according to its course. If it is making leeway, the ship is moving downwind so it loses ground or goes off course.

Lee: The downwind side of a ship, opposite to the direction of the wind.

Lee shore: A shoreline downwind of the ship, with the wind blowing the ship toward the shore—a dangerous situation for a sailing ship.

Back water: To row a reverse stroke.

So, now that you know all you need to know about sailing terms, welcome aboard the world of the Brotherband Chronicles!

John Flanagan

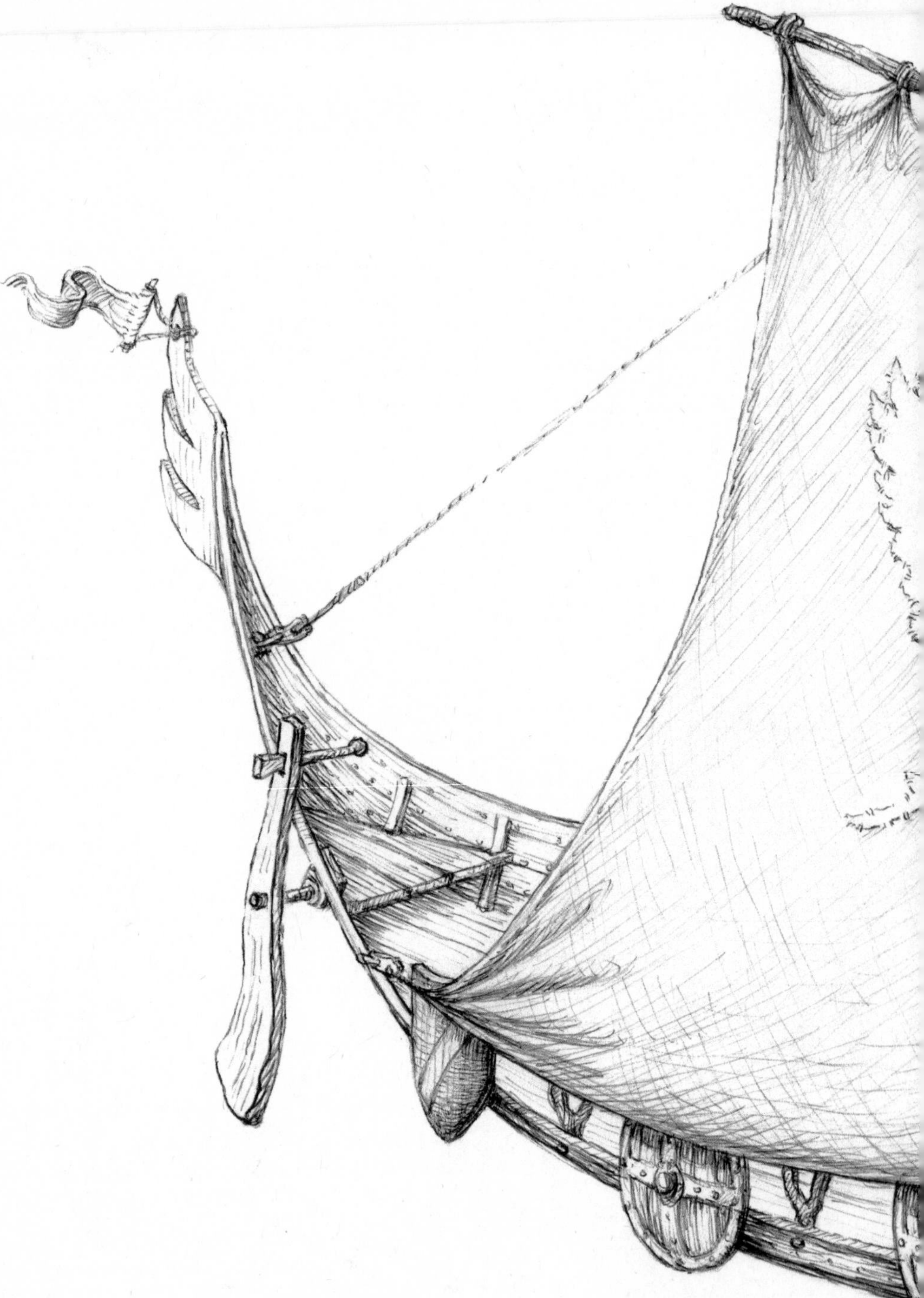

chapter one

Hal smiled to himself as the *Heron* cut smoothly through the water, rising and falling gracefully; swooping over the small, even waves and sending showers of spray high into the air on either side of her bows as she sliced down into the troughs.

It was good to feel the slight vibration in the tiller and the surge of the deck under his feet once more. He and his crew had spent the winter building this new *Heron,* and he was enjoying being back at sea, and in command.

They were off the Sonderland coast, well to the west of Hallasholm, carrying out final sea trials on the new ship.

"She's definitely faster than the old *Heron,*" he commented to Stig, who was standing close by, keeping an eye on the taut curve of the sail.

His first mate smiled. "That's only to be expected," he said. "She's two meters longer on the waterline."

Hal nodded. The extra length would make the ship faster through the water. But he had also had time to experiment with the cut of the sails—to shape them and reinforce them with extra seams so they formed a smoother, more efficient curve when the wind filled them. In addition, he had increased the height of the mast and yardarms, so the new ship carried more sail than the old.

All in all, he thought, it was a good result. But there was one thing that bothered him slightly, and that was one of the reasons they had put to sea—to test the new ship under a variety of conditions and see if she would deliver maximum performance.

"Coming about!" he called to Ulf and Wulf, who were crouched amidships by the sheets and halyards that controlled the sails.

Wulf signaled that they had heard him and were ready.

"Tack!" he called, putting the helm over and swinging the ship into the eye of the wind.

The twins brought the current sail down to the deck and hoisted its opposite number as the ship turned.

There, thought Hal, sensing a slight hesitation as the bow came around. But she had enough speed and momentum to carry her through the maneuver, and within seconds, the new sail had filled with a dull, booming sound and was driving her firmly on the opposite tack, the slight hesitation left behind. But, still, he thought, it had been there. He had first sensed it earlier, when the wind had been lighter than the brisk breeze that drove them now.

"Let out the sheets!"

The twins allowed the ropes that controlled the sail to loosen, and the sail to billow out somewhat, losing the tight, hard curve. As the pressure reduced, the speed fell away until *Heron* was coasting along, with the wind over her port side.

Hal waited, conscious of Stig's watchful gaze. Thorn, in his position by the fin keel, was watching as well. Both of his friends knew what was on his mind. They had discussed it earlier that day when they had set out on these final trials.

"She's griping still?" Stig asked quietly.

Hal nodded. "I'll try her again," he replied, then raising his voice, warned the sail handlers. "Coming about!"

Wulf signaled that he and his brother were ready, and Hal called out the executive order.

"Tack!"

The tiller went over and the bow started to swing up into the wind. But this time, without the same speed and momentum behind it, the movement was slower and more tentative. Hal felt the resistance that shuddered through the hull as the bow pointed up and tried to cross the wind's eye, then fell back to starboard, the sail shuddering violently and losing the wind so that *Heron* sagged off, away from the turn, and wallowed to a halt, sail flapping and sheets loose. Then the bow began to fall off further to starboard and the wind caught the sail, so that when Ulf and Wulf hauled in on the sheets, it filled once more and the ship steadied and slowly began to cut through the water, back on the original port tack.

Stig shook his head, a worried look on his face. "The old ship wouldn't have failed to come about like that," he said.

Hal shrugged. He was relatively sure he knew where the problem lay and it would be easy to fix. "Her bow is sitting too low in the water. It's causing resistance to the turn," he told Stig. "She simply needs re-trimming."

He called to Ingvar and Jesper, who were watching events, crouched in the rowing well on the port side, several meters astern of the mast.

"Move the cask back a meter," he ordered, and the two of them scrambled up onto the raised center deck, where a twenty-liter cask of water was standing on the center line, and where Hal had chalked a set of half-meter measurements.

They wrestled the cask back along the chalk line, settling it on the mark that Hal had indicated, taking a few seconds to make minor adjustments so the positioning was perfect. They knew that when Hal said *a meter,* he didn't mean a meter and a bit, or ninety centimeters. He meant a meter.

Satisfied that they had the cask correctly positioned, Jesper turned and signaled the fact to Hal, then the two of them dropped down into the rowing well, their eyes fixed on the young skirl at the steering oar.

Hal nodded, saying quietly to Stig, "That should do it."

The cask, full of water, weighed twenty kilograms. Moving it aft should have raised the bow slightly, altering the trim of the ship. Hal brought the ship up toward the wind. Ulf and Wulf, out of sheer habit, went to haul in the sheets and power up the sail, but he called out to stop them. He wanted to keep the speed and the power down to see if his slight adjustment had made *Heron* more responsive.

He glanced at the sail and at the wind telltale. The sail was full but bellying slightly. The wind was blowing over their port bow.

"Ready to go about!" he warned, then, "Tack!"

He shoved the tiller over and the bow swung up into the wind. This time, he didn't feel the hesitation as it crossed the eye of the wind. The bow continued to swing sweetly and under control as the sail shuddered and collapsed. Then Ulf and Wulf hauled it down and sent the starboard sail up in its place.

There was the familiar *WHOOMPH!* as the sail filled and the twins hauled in the sheets to set it in a firm, taut curve. The *Heron* surged forward on the new tack, gathering speed as she went. Hal allowed himself a satisfied grin.

"We'll try it again!" he called and they repeated the action—allowing the speed to drop off, then swinging the ship to starboard, across the wind.

And again, she completed the maneuver without hesitation, turning smoothly onto the new tack and powering away once more. Hal's grin grew wider as he moved the tiller slightly from one side to another. As ever, he enjoyed the feeling of the slight tremors passing through the tiller to his hands—tremors that told him the ship was a living being, not a lifeless assembly of timber, ropes and canvas. She was his, ready to do his bidding and to do it gracefully and smoothly. Gradually, the speed built up and she began to heel more to starboard as the twins held the sail taut.

"Loosen up a little!" he called, and the ship came upright.

The bow slashed through the water like a giant knife, sending spray high on either side. Contrary to expectations, releasing the sails a little so that the ship was more upright allowed it to plane, reducing the drag of the water on the hull so that she actually moved faster, sitting high out of the water.

It was an exhilarating feeling, but there was one aspect missing. On the old *Heron,* some fault or flaw in the hull or fin keel had created a slight vibration through the ship when she rose onto the plane this way, setting up a hum that resonated through the hull.

It had been a flaw, but Hal had always enjoyed it. Now that the hull didn't vibrate the same way, he found he missed it. He wondered if there was some way he could induce that same hum on the new hull and keel. He made a mental note to experiment when they returned to Hallasholm.

"Hal?" Stig said quietly.

He came back to the present. Planing like this was exhilarating. But it also had its dangers. The ship was very close to being out of control, and to signal this, she began to roll from side to side, the roll becoming more pronounced with each movement.

If this continued for too long, the roll would take over, so that the helmsman was always behind the movement, unable to check it. When that happened, the motion became more violent and more rapid, until the ship spun out of control or capsized.

"Slacken off!" he called to the twins, and they quickly spilled wind out of the sail so that the ship sank down off the plane and the rolling ceased, leaving *Heron* sailing smoothly and docilely on her way.

Stig shook his head. "I never enjoy that feeling," he said.

Hal nodded. "No wonder they call it death roll."

Sensing that the experiment was over, Thorn made his way aft to join them. He gestured at the cask, sitting on the central deck.

"That seemed to do the trick," he said. "But are we going to have to sail with a barrel of water sitting amidships?"

Hal shook his head. "I'll rake the mast back a little when we get home," he said. "That'll put enough weight aft to keep the bows up."

Thorn nodded. He was an experienced sailor and he knew the feel of a ship. As a result, he had also noticed that she was crabbing slightly during low-speed tacks. But having the technical skill and know-how to fix it were beyond him. Those things he would happily leave to his young skirl.

"Whatever you say," he replied.

Seeing that the experimental maneuvers were done with and *Heron* was heading for home, Stefan had resumed his normal lookout position on the masthead. His voice reached down to them now.

"Sail ho!" he called. "Sail on the port bow!"

chapter two

All eyes swung to follow the direction of his pointing arm. But from the deck, nothing was yet visible. A few seconds later, Stefan corrected his initial warning.

"Not one, but two ships! Close together!" he called.

Hal and Stig exchanged a quick glance. It was not unheard of for two ships to be sailing in company, although as a general rule ships traveled alone. But to be close together indicated something more sinister.

Stig moved to the starboard bulwark and sprang lightly upon it, steadying himself with one hand on a stay. "I see them!" he called, just as Stefan added more detail.

"Their sails are down! They're hove to!"

Hal felt his pulse quicken. Two ships close together, stopped in the water and with neither having a sail hoisted—Stefan's first warning of *sail ho* had been standard terminology for sighting a ship—usually spelled one thing.

Stig quickly confirmed that such was the case. "They're fighting!" he called. "The nearer ship is a raider, and she's closed alongside the other to board her."

Hal glanced down the length of the *Heron*. The crew were all turned toward him, watching him expectantly. "Arm yourselves!" he ordered.

There was an instant scramble for the rowing wells, where the Herons kept their personal weapons. Hal gestured to Edvin as the healer emerged with his sword slung round his waist. The crew's shields were ranged along the bulwarks of the ship.

"Pass me my sword," Hal requested, and Edvin moved aft to retrieve Hal's sword from the skirl's personal locker. Hal took it and, while Edvin steadied the helm, whipped the sword belt round his own waist and buckled it firmly in place. Then he took the tiller again with a nod of thanks.

"Ulf! Wulf! I'm bringing her as close to the wind as she'll bear!"

The twins nodded their understanding and bent to the sail-handling sheets. The two ships were in the worst-possible position for a swift approach—almost dead upwind of the *Heron*. Hal teased the tiller around, bringing the ship up into the wind until the sail began to flutter along its leading edge. Then he let her fall back a degree or two as Ulf and Wulf adjusted the sail.

Thorn came striding back down the deck to confer with his skirl. He was the fighting commander on board the ship and he would lead the charge onto the enemy's deck. He was buckling on his massive club-hand as he came, having removed the wooden hook he used for day-to-day matters. He raised his eyebrows in a question as he looked at Hal, deferring to the younger man's judgment and seamanship.

"We'll reach her in two long tacks," Hal said, understanding the unspoken question. "We'll board her from astern, over the starboard quarter."

The grizzled warrior nodded assent. It was what he had expected. He looked at Stig, who had dropped down from the port bulwark and was swinging his ax experimentally.

"You ready?" Thorn asked.

Stig grinned back at him. "Lead the way," he said and, as Thorn made his way for'ard, followed in his footsteps. The others in the crew stood aside to make room for the two warriors who would lead them aboard the other ship. Jesper, Stefan and Ingvar would follow them. Edvin would go next, with Ulf and Wulf—staying in their sail-handling positions till the last moment—being last to board.

Hal would stay by the tiller unless he saw the need to join the fight on the enemy ship's deck.

Beside him, crouched on the deck, Kloof lay with her chin on her outstretched forepaws. Her eyes flicked from side to side, watching the preparations among the crew. As they took their positions and handled their weapons, she uttered a low, rumbling growl from deep in her chest. She knew what was coming. She had seen it before.

"Steady," Hal cautioned her. "You stay here."

The dog's reply was another growl.

It wasn't just a sense of righteousness that compelled Hal's decision to join in the fight. Some years back, Erak had signed contracts and treaties with the other countries bordering the Stormwhite Sea, setting up Skandia and her powerful fleet of warships as custodians of the sea-lanes. After a long history as predators, Skandian wolfships were now committed to stamping out piracy and providing a protective umbrella under which commercial traders could go safely about their business.

It was Hal's sworn duty, if he saw a trader being attacked by pirates, to go to the ship's aid and to sink or take the corsair.

"Stand by to go about!" he warned. "Tack!"

With the altered trim and with the ship sliding across the wind at full power, there was no hesitation this time. The bow swung smoothly through the wind. The starboard sail came sliding down while the port sail rose quickly to the masthead, taking the wind, billowing out, then steadying as the twins hauled in and set it firmly.

The ship necessarily lost speed in the maneuver, but within twenty meters on the new tack she had recovered and was heading obliquely toward the battle at full speed. Hal saw movement in the port-side rowing well, and Lydia climbed up on deck, moving across toward him. She was slinging her quiver of darts over her left shoulder. Her atlatl hung from her belt.

Her role in the coming fight was a long-distance one. She wasn't equipped or trained for close-in fighting—although she could defend herself quite effectively at a pinch. Instead, she stayed back and protected the backs of the Herons as they fought, picking off any threatening enemies with her well-placed darts.

"They haven't seen us yet," she remarked.

Hal gazed keenly at the two ships, locked together. Their crews were a struggling mass in the bow of the trading ship—a wide-bodied vessel with plenty of room for cargo, but a corresponding lack of performance. Lydia was right. The raiders were intent on their prize and the trading crew had retreated to the bow, where they were struggling to hold off the boarders. Neither group had eyes for the small Skandian ship bearing down on them.

"Let's hope they don't until it's too late . . . for them," Hal replied. Kloof growled again, and Hal looked down to silence the dog with a warning gesture. The last thing he wanted now was for Kloof to alert the enemy by barking a challenge at them.

"Settle, girl," he warned her, and Kloof lowered her chin to her paws again, emitting a series of frustrated growls and grumbles.

"Time to tack again," Hal said, judging the speed and the angle with his eye. He wanted to slide *Heron* in alongside the pirate, on her starboard side. Mindful of the warning he had just issued to Kloof, he gave a low whistle to alert Wulf and Ulf, then indicated the tack with a hand signal before putting the helm over once more.

The little ship came round smoothly and accelerated toward the two ships. Hal could see now that they were locked together by grappling ropes, thrown from the pirate to secure her prey alongside.

"Who are they?" Lydia asked.

Hal, assuming she meant the pirates, replied, "They look like Iberians. There are eyes on the bow."

He had noticed this detail on the previous tack. Iberians painted eyes on the bow of their ships. It was a tradition that went back to an ancient superstition. Their forebears had believed the eyes allowed their ship to see the way in unfamiliar waters. He shook his head grimly. Of all the seagoing nations Erak had originally approached, the Iberians had been the most reluctant to join in paying for the Skandian fleet's protection. That was because the Iberians had a much greater interest in piracy than the others.

Heron was sliding in closer now. There was only forty meters to go. He called to Ulf and Wulf. "Drop the sail!"

He didn't want to slam into the Iberian ship at full speed. The sail slithered down in an untidy heap as the twins released it, and instantly the ship began to lose speed. Hal saw that he had judged it nearly perfectly as *Heron* glided in beside the pirate, the last of her way coming off her as she nudged against the other ship's side.

Jesper and Stefan swung grapnels over the side, hooking them into the Iberian's bulwarks and heaving on the ropes to bring the two ships together. As they did, Thorn turned to the waiting group of warriors and shouted his time-honored battle cry:

"Let's get 'em!"

As he bellowed the command, he leapt nimbly onto *Heron*'s railing, then up onto the pirate ship, his massive club swinging in small arcs, seeking a target. Stig was half a pace behind him, fanning out to his left, his battleax ready. The rest of the crew scrambled aboard in their turn, yelling their own versions of Thorn's battle cry.

They swarmed across the Iberian ship's deck. All her crew were aboard the trader, which accounted for the *Heron*'s being able to approach unnoticed. In a matter of seconds, the yelling Skandians had crossed the empty deck and were dropping down onto the trader.

It wasn't until they were almost upon the pirates that they were noticed.

chapter three

Thorn charged into the rear rank of the Iberian crew. His massive club smashed into one man, hurling him to one side, then he swung back again and took another in the chest as the startled pirate turned to face him.

A third Iberian tried to back away from the huge, heavy weapon, but Thorn caught him with the small, bowl-like shield he favored, slamming it into the side of his head and dropping him like a stone.

Maintaining his momentum, he plunged forward into the startled Iberians, dealing blows right and left with devastating force and power. The pirates, constricted by the narrowing space in the bow, tried desperately to avoid him. No shield could stand against that dreadful club, and Thorn simply mowed them down.

To his left, Stig saw a pirate preparing to stab at the one-armed warrior with his sword. Stepping forward, Stig caught the blade between the upper tang of his battleax blade and the spike on top of the handle. He twisted his wrist to lock the blade in place, then heaved with all the strength of his forearm and wrist to jerk the blade out of the other man's grasp. Unarmed, the pirate looked around to see the tall Skandian almost upon him. His eyes were fixated on the gleaming battleax blade.

Which was his undoing. Stig held his shield side on and drove it into the man's ribs, putting all his strength and momentum behind the metal-rimmed shield. There was an ugly cracking sound, and the pirate screamed in pain as he fell to his knees. Then, gripping his injured side with both arms, he toppled over.

On Thorn's right, Ingvar was engaged with a pirate who had tried to attack Thorn from that side. Ingvar's long voulge snaked out and the hooked blade snagged the mail corselet worn by the pirate, catching it at the shoulder. Ingvar heaved back with all his massive strength and the pirate was jerked off his feet and sailed several meters through the air toward the Skandian. As he did, Ingvar released the hook and reversed his weapon, bringing the hardwood shaft whistling round to slam against the man's helmet.

The helmet held, but the force of the blow was transmitted through the metal, setting the pirate's ears ringing and his eyes rolling, unfocused. He, too, fell to the deck.

Behind their leaders, Stefan, Edvin and Jesper were wreaking havoc on the pirates as well. The three Herons, trained by Thorn, were all expert swordsmen. Their razor-sharp blades darted in and out, constantly drawing blood and causing serious injury.

In the constricted conditions of the fight, they followed what Thorn had taught them, using the points of their blades in economic thrusts rather than swinging wild, undisciplined cuts with the edges.

On a crowded deck, Thorn had taught them, *three centimeters of point is better than a meter of edge.* Events now proved him right as the darting, biting swords constantly found their mark and left their opponents gasping in pain, clutching at wounds in their bodies and legs.

Startled by the unexpected ferocity of the attack from behind, the pirates were thrown into confusion. Some turned to face the new threat. Others tried to continue to force the trader's crew back into the narrow confines of the bow.

But now the defending crew gained new heart at the sight of the small group of deadly, determined Skandians.

"Come on!" yelled their captain, as he leapt forward, bringing his long-bladed sword down onto the helmet of the pirate captain who had been facing him. Caught unprepared for the sudden show of aggression, the pirate failed to counter the blow. The sword blade sank deep into his helmet, cleaving a deep cut in the metal. The pirate's last conscious thought was that he had dropped his own sword and was now unarmed and at the mercy of his former prey.

Then everything went black.

The Iberians were caught between two forces. And the shock of the surprise attack from the *Heron*'s crew was decisive. Half of the raiders were cut down or smashed to the deck by Thorn's massive club and Stig's sweeping ax. Others fell to the scything blows of Ingvar's voulge or the deadly jabbing strikes of the other Herons' swords. At least two, intent on escaping, were brought down by

Lydia's darts. Seemingly within seconds, the decks were littered with Iberian bodies.

The survivors began to throw down their weapons and call for mercy.

The Skandians drew back a few paces, while the crew of the trader moved among their erstwhile attackers, shoving them into a line and forcing them to kneel. Any who were slow in obeying drew instant kicks and blows from the liberated sailors.

The trader's skipper, his sword marked with the blood of the pirate captain, sought out Thorn, correctly identifying him as the leader of their rescuers.

"We owe you our lives, Skandian," he said. "And my ship."

Thorn nodded. He was breathing heavily—not from exhaustion but from the adrenaline surge of the battle.

"It's what we do," he said. Then he gestured toward the line of disarmed, kneeling pirates. "Better secure this lot. Tie their hands behind them, and we'll take them into port."

"Or we could simply hang them here," the captain suggested.

But Thorn shook his head. "That's not how we do it. They'll stand trial first."

The captain reluctantly backed down. His crew outnumbered the Skandians. He could see now there were less than a dozen of them. But he had also seen them fight and he knew superior numbers wouldn't count for much against these warriors.

"Seems a waste of time," he said, making one last attempt. "They'll be sentenced to hang anyway."

This time, Thorn said nothing. He simply held the other man's gaze in a steely glare. After several seconds, the captain dropped his eyes and turned to his men, standing ready.

"Get these animals tied up," he ordered brusquely. As his men moved to secure the surviving pirates, Thorn added another instruction.

"Leave four of them tied in front," he said. "They can row their ship into harbor."

Heron shepherded the other two ships into harbor at the nearest large town—some ten kilometers down the coast.

A group of curious onlookers gathered on the quay as the three ships tied up—the Iberian ship and the trader alongside the mole and *Heron* moored outboard of the trader.

The pirates, their hands bound behind them and secured in a line by a rope around their necks, were marched down the quay by the trader's crew. The Sonderlanders showed little respect for their prisoners, jabbing them with sword points and cracking the shafts of spears across their legs and shoulders to keep them moving. The pirates, knowing the fate that awaited them, shambled reluctantly along, moving as slowly as possible.

Piracy was a capital crime, and they had been caught red-handed. They could expect little mercy from a Sonderland court.

Hal, Thorn and Stig made their way down the quay, past the line of prisoners. Most of the Iberians continued with their eyes cast down, but one raised his head at the sight of the three Skandians and began to yell abuse at them.

"Curse you Skandians! You think you're so clever! Well, you'll learn your lesson soon enough! Wait till you see what we've got in store for you! You'll regret the day you ever saw an Iberian ship! We're going to—"

He got no further. Two of his companions shoved their way beside him, buffeting him with their shoulders and shouting threats at him.

"Shut your mouth, Miguel!" one of them snarled. "Just shut up!"

The pirate grew silent, glaring defiantly at his shipmates, but ceasing his tirade of threats.

Stig raised his eyebrows as he looked back at the man. "Now, what was that about?" he asked.

Hal shrugged. "Just bluster. He's not in any position to get revenge." He noticed a burly figure striding to meet them. The bronze medal around his neck identified him as the town's harbormaster. "And here's the man we need to see," he continued.

The harbormaster was a heavy-set, middle-aged man, obviously a former sailor himself. It appeared that his current position was a more sedentary one. His waist was thick and showed ample evidence of too much eating and too little exercising. His complexion was flushed and somewhat unhealthy. His long flaxen hair was parted down the middle and held to either side of his head in plaits. His beard was styled in a similar fashion. He shook hands with Hal and eyed the shambling group making its way down the quay, accompanied by jeers and curses from the townsfolk. Sonderlanders hated pirates, and word had quickly spread about their attack on the trader and the subsequent rescue by the Skandian ship.

"Nice work," said the harbormaster. He gestured to a tavern by the waterfront. "Will you join me for a drink?"

Hal shook his head. "We're in a hurry to get back to Hallasholm," he explained. "Let's do the paperwork, and we'll be on our way."

Looking a little disappointed, the Sonderlander led the way to his office, set at the foot of the quay. The doorway was low, constricted by the thatched roof that swept down steeply from the ridge line. But once inside, there was plenty of headroom in the well-lit, airy room.

Under the terms of the treaty Erak had put in place years before, *Heron*'s crew were entitled to a third of the value of the cargo they'd recaptured, and two-thirds of the value of the pirate ship. There was also a payment for each of the pirates captured and brought in for trial. All in all, it had been a profitable day for the *Heron* brotherband. They'd share the proceeds equally. Some skirls took a larger share of the reward, but Hal was content to be paid the same as his crew. After all, as he said, he couldn't do the job without them.

The exact sum owed would be calculated when the Iberian ship was sold and the trader's cargo assessed. Hal knew he could trust the harbormaster to give them an accurate accounting. Bitter experience had showed that anyone who tried to shortchange Erak and his men would soon regret the fact.

He signed the necessary forms that the harbormaster placed before him. Thorn signed as witness and the harbormaster countersigned, gathering the sheets together when he had finished, rapping them on the tabletop to make them even.

"You're sure about that drink?" he said.

But Hal shook his head once more. "Thanks. Another time, perhaps. We've got an engagement party to get to."

chapter four

Aided by a brisk offshore wind, *Heron* flew back down the coast toward the east. It took three days to sail along the coast to Hallasholm. There, Hal ran the ship into the narrow stream several hundred meters to the east of the harbor itself, where his boatyard was situated.

While the others prepared for the coming feast, for the next three days Hal and Stig worked on the ship. His first mate looked with interest at an innovation Hal added. He had constructed a rectangular timber shield two meters high by a meter wide, which slid into brackets set behind the steering platform.

"What's that for?" the tall warrior asked.

"In a sea fight, the helmsman is often targeted," Hal explained. "This will protect me, or whoever is steering, from arrows and projectiles shot from astern."

"I usually do that," Stig pointed out. In past engagements, he had covered Hal with his own large shield.

The skirl nodded. "That's what gave me the idea. This will leave you free for more important things."

He slid the shield out of the retaining brackets and stored it, ready for use, in the stern. Then he and Stig set about raking the mast back so that the ship sat level, and the keg of water could be dispensed with. Hal spent considerable time over this, tightening the backstays that held the mast and rowing around the ship in a small skiff to view her from water level.

Knowing that his skirl would continue to make minor adjustments until it was too dark to see, Stig finally called a halt. "Come on. It's as good as it'll get now, and we've got a party to get to."

At long last, Hal was satisfied that *Heron* was now trimmed properly and they dragged her into the boatshed on the creek bank and headed for the town.

The engagement party was just getting started.

The whole town had turned out—in fact, the evening had been planned as a major celebration, thanks to the popularity of the two principals, Ingvar and Lydia.

Ingvar had been born and raised in Hallasholm and the townspeople were delighted to see how he blossomed as a member of the *Heron* brotherband. Plagued since childhood by extreme shortsightedness, Ingvar's mighty strength had been underutilized until Hal equipped him with a pair of spectacles that allowed him to see beyond a meter's range.

Then Thorn had taken him in hand, training him and teaching

him, developing his motor skills, sense of balance and spatial awareness until Ingvar emerged as not just a powerful warrior but a highly skilled one.

Lydia had been born and raised far to the southeast. Orphaned at an early age, she had lost her one remaining relative, her grandfather, when pirates attacked her town. Lydia had been cast adrift in a sinking skiff during the fight. Hal and the Herons, in pursuit of the pirates, rescued her from the sinking boat and welcomed her into their crew.

A skilled tracker and hunter, Lydia was a valued addition. And her deadly accuracy with the atlatl and its meter-long darts had saved various members of the crew from attack on more occasions than they could count.

Adopted by a popular and well-respected widow in Hallasholm, Lydia quickly found the approval of her new neighbors. Her quiet, unassuming manner endeared her to the Skandians. And her position as a trusted member of the Heron brotherband cemented her popularity. The Herons were held in high esteem by the people of Hallasholm.

So, a month earlier, when Lydia and Ingvar shyly announced their intention to marry the following year, the reaction was one of universal delight and surprise.

Delight because the two young people were well loved and popular, and surprise because many had assumed that if Lydia were to choose a member of the Heron brotherband as her soulmate, it would be Hal, or even Stig.

But Hal wasn't ready to settle down with one girl, and Stig had withdrawn from romantic encounters since the death of his wife in the far-off western land. Besides, Lydia regarded the two of them as surrogate brothers, not as potential husbands.

Her relationship with Ingvar was different. As they traveled together and fought together against various enemies, a deep respect had grown between them—which gradually turned into an even deeper affection.

In battle, Ingvar was indomitable, except for his limited vision. Even Hal's ingenious spectacles left him with several blind spots. Lydia had taken to covering these—standing back from close combat and watching for enemies who sought to exploit Ingvar's weakness. Her deadly atlatl shafts took care of any who did, often without Ingvar even being aware that she had acted.

As the months passed, she grew to admire his courage and loyalty to his shipmates—particularly Hal. In spite of his massive strength and growing reputation in battle, Ingvar never put on airs or swaggered. Nor did he ever complain about his shortsightedness. He remained a simple, loyal and utterly dependable member of the brotherband, always ready to lend a hand if one of his companions was in trouble.

For his part, Ingvar simply adored the tall, quiet girl they had rescued. He held her tracking and hunting skills in awe. But most of all, he valued her quiet confidence and good humor. He would have happily laid down his life for her.

It was late afternoon and the sun had disappeared behind the high range of mountains north of Hallasholm. The town's main square was ringed by glowing braziers. Even though it was early spring, the evenings were still cool enough to make their warmth welcome. Strings of colored lanterns were hung across the open space of the square, and there were four cooking pits to add to the glow and the warmth. One bullock, a sheep and two boars were turning on spits over the beds of red-hot coals, which hissed and spluttered as fats and juices dropped onto them.

Ingvar and Lydia, as guests of honor, sat on two stools placed on the steps outside the Oberjarl's Great Hall. Unused to being the center of attention, they wore rather bemused expressions as they held hands, greeting friends and neighbors who passed by.

Long trestle tables had been set out in the square itself, laden with steamed vegetables, crusty pies and circular loaves of bread. A group of musicians had set up close by the young couple. They were filling the air with their rollicking tunes, and a dozen or so couples were dancing to the music. Several massive barrels of ale had been broached and were standing on their sides on low tables, so that revelers could fill and refill their tankards as they pleased. There was wine as well—a Gallican trader had visited Hallasholm only four days previously, and Erak purchased several dozen bottles for the party.

The Oberjarl was bearing the cost of the revels. Ingvar's parents were by no means wealthy, and the widow who had taken Lydia under her roof was even poorer. But Ingvar and Lydia were both members of the Herons, Erak's favored brotherband and the one he turned to whenever there was a difficult or delicate task to be carried out. Usually a man to count every coin he spent, he had thrown open his treasury for this event, telling his hilfmann, "Spare no expense. Spend whatever we must to make this a memorable night!"

Admittedly, he later added, in private, "We can always make it back by jacking up taxes on some of the wealthier jarls."

As far as Erak was concerned, if a jarl was wealthy, he had obviously not been paying enough tax to the Oberjarl.

The evening wore on. The shadows deepened as the last of the day's light faded away and the crowds in the square grew noisier and bigger. The fire pits and braziers cast weird and wonderful shadows over the square, and the music grew wilder and faster as more and more dancers took to the open space.

Thick slices of juicy, succulent meat were carved from the carcasses as they continued to turn. The spit handlers' faces shone with perspiration from the heat of the cooking fires. Vegetables were piled high on wooden platters to accompany the meat. Pies were cut open, emitting clouds of delicious-smelling steam, and loaves of bread were ripped apart to be stuffed with the roasted meat.

More and more barrels of ale were broached and some of the earlier arrivals crept off to fall asleep under the trestle tables. They would awaken later in the night and resume the celebrations.

Erak strode around the square, a beaming smile on his face, greeting the revelers. He held a massive tankard of ale in one hand and his staff of office in the other—a two-meter-long ebony rod surmounted by a silver ball and shod with silver as well. The silver ferrule on the base clacked loudly on the flagstones of the square as Erak tapped loudly in time to the music.

Kloof, a dark and determined shadow, followed the Oberjarl through the crowd, her eyes fixed on the gleaming black staff, waiting for Erak to lay it aside and take his attention off it. But the Oberjarl had made this mistake several times before and he kept a wary eye on the huge dog, occasionally shaking the staff in her direction and uttering dire threats as to what would become of her if she laid a single tooth on his treasured possession.

In truth, only the ball and the ferrule were survivors from his original staff. He had replaced the ebony rod three times after Kloof had managed to sneak it away on previous occasions, blissfully chewing the black-lacquered staff into several shorter lengths.

Erak stopped beside Hal and Thorn, who were watching events from a side table laden with food. Thorn was drinking ale, while Hal had a mug of fresh, sweet coffee in his hand. They nodded a greeting to the Oberjarl, who beamed back at them. Erak loved a party.

"Getting plenty to eat?" he inquired, and they nodded in the affirmative.

In fact, Hal was overburdened with food. The single young women of Hallasholm saw him as a valuable catch. And now that they knew he had no romantic interest in Lydia, they swarmed around him, bringing him plates of food, mugs of coffee and invitations to dance. Thorn watched with quiet amusement as they fluttered around him. Hal, it must be said, remained oblivious to the interest he attracted and was somewhat overwhelmed by the amount of food in front of him.

"Too much," he replied to Erak, indicating the heavily laden plate.

"Well, share it around," Erak said. He propped his staff against the table and seized a turkey leg from the plate, tearing at the delicious meat with his teeth, filling his mouth and chewing happily.

"You're welcome," Hal replied.

Behind Erak, a dark shape slunk out of the shadows, heading

for the unattended walking staff. Without turning his head, Erak sensed Kloof's presence and intention.

"Geddoudofit!" he roared, showering turkey meat in all directions.

Kloof, defeated, slunk back into the shadows. In truth, there had been plenty of time for her to snatch the black staff away. But that wasn't the game as she played it. She had to take the staff without Erak's noticing her doing so. Frustrated, she sank to her belly under a table, her eyes fixed on the staff.

She would wait. She had the patience of a hunter.

Erak stripped the last of the meat from the leg and tossed the bone to one side. Then he picked up the staff once more and shook it in Kloof's general direction.

"Touch my staff again, you shaggy fleabag, and I'll send you to dog Vallashal."

"Is there a dog Vallashal?" Hal asked, mildly amused.

Thorn nodded affirmatively. "Oh yes. There are bones to gnaw on and an abundance of walking sticks to chew. The dogs sit around a giant table and tell stories of their mighty deeds on earth, chasing cats and squirrels. It's actually quite pleasant."

"I'll give her pleasant," Erak muttered darkly.

Hal and Thorn exchanged a smile. Then a voice from the steps to the hall was heard calling, as the musicians ceased playing and the dancers paused for breath and to regain their balance.

"People of Hallasholm! Pray silence please for Jesper Swiftfoot of the Herons!"

The musicians' leader, who had called for silence, held out a hand to usher Jesper to the improvised stage.

"Oh no," Thorn said quietly.

"Good people!" cried Jesper. "Pay heed to me now, for I have a saga to relate!"

"Oh good. A saga," said Erak.

"Oh god. A saga," mimicked Hal.

chapter five

Four steps led up from the square to the entrance of Erak's Great Hall. Jesper strode to the top step now and smiled down at the expectant crowd. The musicians relaxed, settling down to sit and watch. They knew of Jesper's sagas and realized there would be no need for accompaniment. Jesper's sagas were anything but musical. They were more in the nature of chanted poems.

Although calling them poems was something of a stretch. Their meter was often suspect, and Jesper's concept of rhyme was, to say the least, unconventional.

He struck a dramatic pose now, his feet wide apart, his right arm stretched out and his left grasping the collar of his jerkin. He threw back his head and declaimed:

While Erak serves drinks, and some vittles to feed ya,
pay heed to the story of Ingvar and Lydia.

Perhaps *unconventional* was too kind a word. But the audience, full of the spirit of the evening, weren't in any mood to be critical. They whooped enthusiastically.

"Now here's the chorus!" Jesper told them. He began to clap his hands, setting a rhythm for them.

Ingvar the mighty and Lydia the bold,
listen to me while their story is told!

He repeated the chant several times, and with each repetition, more and more of the audience joined in, clapping, stamping and waving full tankards of ale in the air, often drenching their neighbors as they did so. Standing to one side at the rear of the audience, Hal and Thorn rolled their eyes at each other.

Once he was satisfied that they knew the chorus, Jesper launched into the body of the saga.

Ingvar was a mighty lad,
as tall as any tree,
The only problem that he had
was that he couldn't see.

"Oh my lord," Hal muttered. "He doesn't get any better, does he?"

"This is good stuff!" Erak yelled enthusiastically. "Who said we don't appreciate culture in Hallasholm?"

Jesper continued.

So Hal said you've a problem
that I think I'd like to tackle.
He took a piece of tortoiseshell
and made Ingvar his spec-tackles.

"Spec-tackles?" Thorn queried. Hal shrugged. Around them, the crowd boomed out the chorus once more.

Ingvar the mighty and Lydia the bold,
listen to me while their story is told!

Jesper launched into his second verse.

Lydia was born and raised
in a far-off foreign land.
She was rescued from a sinking ship
by the Heron *brotherband.*

This time, there were hoots and whistles of appreciation from the rest of the crew, who had moved through the crowd to stand at the base of the steps. Notably, Ingvar and Lydia were not among them. The two guests of honor made their way to the fringe of the crowd and stood by Hal and Thorn.

Erak, noticing them, shouted to them in delight as he beat time with his staff to another chorus. "This is great stuff! It's about you, you know!"

Lydia gave him a sickly smile. She leaned closer to Hal and asked him: "Can't you stop Jesper?"

Hal shook his head. "I've never managed to yet."

Ingvar growled deep in his chest, a sound that was reminiscent of Kloof. "I could stop him," he threatened, but Thorn laid a hand on his arm.

"He's doing it because he loves you both," he said, and Ingvar, realizing the one-armed warrior was right, subsided.

Hal grinned at him. "After all," he said, "it's not easy to come up with verses as bad as this. It takes a special kind of talent."

Kloof, sneaking in behind Erak, her eyes on the staff once more, let out a sudden yelp of surprise as he slopped ale from his waving tankard all over her. She scuttled back into the crowd.

Erak looked around curiously. "What was that?" he asked.

Nobody answered, and he shrugged, turning back to watch Jesper and snagging a full tankard from a passing serving man. Jesper was now well into the saga, recounting the Herons' most recent adventure against the raiding Temujai.

They fought against the Temujai chief,
a brave and fearsome warrior . . .

"Actually, as I recall," Hal said, "he was short and rather tubby."

"Poetic license," Thorn told him. Jesper continued.

Ingvar made him sorry
and then Lydia made him sorrier.

"Oh, that is so bad!" Lydia interjected. But there was worse to come.

Lydia shot a blunted dart,
from out of her atlatl.
It hit the Sha'shan in the head
and set his brains a-rattle.

Lydia threw her hands wide. Jesper was certainly playing fast and loose with the facts. She had knocked out a sentry with a blunted dart, but never the Sha'shan himself. The crowd roared with delight.

Ingvar the mighty and Lydia the bold,
listen to me while their story is told!

To her dismay, Lydia realized that, this time, Hal had joined in on the chorus as well. She glared accusingly at him.

Hal shrugged. "If you can't beat 'em . . ."

She snorted in disgust. "You should be ashamed of yourself." But in spite of herself, she found she was starting to grin. The next time the chorus came round, they all joined in, egged on by an exuberant Oberjarl. Jesper's tale was rapidly approaching a climax. The crowd grew noisier and wilder as he continued.

The Tem'uj swarmed round Ingvar
just like the rising tide.
He knocked the first one senseless

and a dozen more besides.
But the enemy kept on coming.
There were more than you could count and
They sailed the Heron *'cross the lake,*
then sailed her down the mountain.

"Now that's not bad," Thorn said. "After all, you did sail her down the mountain."

Hal nodded agreement. For once, Jesper had got things right. The imagery of sailing the ship down the mountain more than made up for the clumsiness of an atlatl making brains rattle.

Another chorus, then Jesper delivered his final verse.

The Temujai were defeated,
it was a fearsome fight.
"Marry me," said Ingvar,
and Lydia said, "All right."

The crowd hooted and cheered with delight, turning to raise their tankards and glasses to the young couple at the rear of the crowd. Jesper then delivered a triumphant coda to the saga.

The two of them agreed to wed,
and that's why we're here tonight!

The cheering intensified. The crowd surged around the couple, raising them onto their shoulders—in Ingvar's case, it took four men—and carrying them forward to set them down at the top of the stairs. Lydia hugged Jesper, who flushed with pleasure. Then Ingvar slapped him on the back and very nearly propelled him into the crowd.

Thorn and Hal watched with benevolent smiles from the rear of the crowd as the citizens of Hallasholm gathered around Lydia and Ingvar, cheering them, toasting them over and over and wishing them well. Hal glanced around for Stig, but there was no sign of his friend.

"Where's Stig?" he asked.

Thorn nodded in the direction of the house Stig shared with his mother. "He left when the saga ended," he said. "I think an evening like this has a few too many memories for him."

Hal nodded his understanding. He checked his coffee mug to find it empty. The blackened pot by the nearby fire was down to the dregs as well. He looked up at the sky. It was a clear night and the stars blazed down above them.

"Think I'll turn in as well," he said, yawning. It had been a long day. He had been up before dawn and spent the day working on the final adjustments to *Heron*'s trim. Suddenly, he was very weary.

"I'll stay awhile," Thorn told him. "I haven't had a dance with your mam yet."

Hal grinned at him. "I suppose you two will be next," he said.

Thorn raised an eyebrow. "Next?"

Hal indicated the square and the throngs of people celebrating. "To do all this," he said.

Thorn laughed. "Just as soon as she says yes," he replied.

Hal regarded him for a few moments. "I'd like that," he said, and turned away.

He trudged across the noisy, brightly lit square and out into the darkened houses beyond, heading up the hill to the eating house his mother ran. Kloof, finally giving up on Erak's staff, padded silently beside him.

The noise of the celebrations carried up the hill to him as he prepared for bed. He was asleep a few seconds after his head hit the pillow. He woke once, in the small hours of the morning. Kloof was barking at something. *Probably some late revelers heading home to bed,* he thought. Then he rolled over and slept again.

chapter six

Erak woke early the following morning.

It was a long-established habit of his, born of years spent as a wolfship skirl. Dawn was the time of most danger at sea, a time when the growing light could reveal an enemy who had approached and drawn close in the hours of darkness.

No matter how late the hour when Erak went to bed, instinct would awaken him as soon as the first light began to creep across the eastern sky.

That wasn't to say that he invariably woke bright-eyed and alert. This morning, he was decidedly dull-eyed and drowsy. There was an ache behind his eyes, and his mouth was dry as sawdust.

"Must have been something I ate," he muttered, swinging his

legs out of bed, then amending the thought, with unusual candor. "Must have been something I drank."

He pulled his clothes on and ran his fingers through his shaggy hair and beard, padding through his house to the kitchen, where a large jug of water was on the bench top. The cold night air had kept it well chilled, and he reached for it greedily, gulping down deep drafts of the refreshing cold water. His thirst satisfied, he poured the rest into a basin and plunged his face into it, gasping at the shock and splashing water over the bench top and floor.

He reared up and back, cascading more spillage from his hair and beard, and blew out through his mouth and nose.

"That's better!" he gasped. His head didn't throb so painfully now and his vision was clearer. He breathed deeply.

"Fresh air. That's what I need," he told himself. His sealskin boots were lying haphazardly by the door, where he'd stripped them off and left them the previous night. He sat on a stool and tugged them on. Then he rose and swung his bearskin cloak around his shoulders. Taking his staff in his right hand, he stepped out into the dawn light.

The cold air seared his lungs, and he felt his head clearing even further. Then he set out for the harbor, his staff clacking loudly on the flagstones of the square as he went.

There was nobody else stirring. The town had partied long and hard the night before, and its residents were warmly tucked up in their beds, resisting any urge to move. The sound of multiple snoring was evident as he made his way past the neat rows of houses. Skandians slept as they did everything else—with vigor and enthusiasm and a maximum amount of noise.

For a few moments, Erak contemplated returning to his own bed. But the fog was rapidly fading from his head, driven away by the cold, fresh sea air. He shook his head against the temptation. He was up now and awake. The sun was well above the horizon, and he could feel its rays warming his body, driving away the chill of the night.

Walking swiftly, in long strides punctuated by the rapid clack of his staff on the ground, he emerged from the last line of houses at the waterfront, turning left to walk along the beach to the harbor itself.

And stopped, puzzled.

Something was wrong. There were half a dozen ships pulled up on the beach. He frowned and looked at the nearest, secured by an anchor driven into the sand above the high-tide mark. The ship was canted to one side as it rested on its keel. But he realized that its mast was angled even farther.

And its yardarm wasn't secured at the top of the mast. Rather, it was lying across the hull, with the sail unfurled and flapping in ribbons.

The rigging had given way. The stays that secured the mast in its upright position were missing. He stepped closer, shading his eyes against the low-lying morning sun. The stays weren't missing, he realized. They had been severed, and lay untidily beside the ship.

He broke into a run, moving to get a closer look at the ship. The steering blade was gone as well, he saw. The twisted creepers that secured it to the starboard bulwark were a mass of frayed strands—the ends of which were clean-cut, not broken.

He looked back to the tattered sail and saw that it had also been slashed with clean cuts.

And the oars, which were normally stowed in brackets along the middle of the ship between the mast and the stern, were all missing.

He spun around and studied the next ship in line, seeing the same damage there: cut rigging, shredded sail, collapsed mast and cross yard, and missing oars and rudder.

As he began to jog along the beach, checking the other ships lying there, he saw the same signs of sabotage on all of them. Then a sense of panic seized his heart. His own ship, *Wolfwind*, was moored along the harbor mole—the stone wall constructed to shelter the harbor from wind and waves. Had she been damaged as well?

He looked toward the harbor, but from his position on the beach he couldn't see *Wolfwind*. She was hidden by the raised wall of the mole, set above the beach. Now he was running, angling up through the sand to the beginning of the mole. He clambered up the rocks onto the broad walkway and looked to see whether *Wolfwind* was undamaged.

A roar of rage sprang from his chest as he stopped to study the harbor proper. There were three other ships moored along the harbor front, all showing signs of the same damage as those on the beach.

But *Wolfwind* was gone.

There was an empty space where she had been moored. Not believing what he was seeing, Erak paced along the mole to where his ship had been. Then he saw a huddled shape farther along, toward the harbor entrance, and he broke into a run once more.

He dropped to one knee beside the figure. The man was lying facedown, his cloak covering him. There was no movement, no sign of life, and when Erak reached to turn the man over, he saw the blood-soaked front of his tunic and the lifeless, staring eyes.

"Tegar," he said softly. He recognized the man. Normally, the harbor and beach were patrolled by four guards during the night. But because of the party, the number had been cut to two. Tegar had been one of them. Erak rose swiftly and looked around. Where was the other guard? He racked his brain, trying to remember who else had been rostered on, but his racing, troubled mind couldn't focus on the question. Then he saw another still form lying ten meters away and ran to him. This time, there was no need to turn the guard over. He was lying on his back, staring unseeingly up at the sky. Like Tegar, he had been stabbed.

"Rogger," Erak said, recognizing him and kneeling beside him. He touched the dead man's face. It was cold. He had been lying here for hours.

A deep-seated rage began to burn in Erak's chest. He rose to his feet and looked around. Who had done this? Who had invaded their harbor, killing the guards and wrecking the ships, leaving them incapable of putting to sea?

Who had stolen *Wolfwind*? And why?

But there was no answer forthcoming. There was no sign of any stranger. Everything looked normal—except for the two dead guards and the line of crippled ships. Erak strode to the guardhouse, where a large brass alarm bell hung on a pole outside the door. He seized the rope and began pealing the alarm, the sound echoing across the sleeping, sun-drenched, peaceful streets of his little town.

Slowly, people began to emerge from their houses, shading their eyes as they peered at the harbor, and the lone figure of their Oberjarl sounding the alarm.

chapter seven

Gradually, people began to stream toward the harbor as Erak continued to ring the alarm bell. They were in various stages of undress but most of the men were carrying whatever weapons had been close to hand when the bell had roused them.

The alarm bell was a signal of danger, a sign that there was trouble brewing. And Skandians didn't face danger unarmed and unready for action.

They poured toward the harbor, stopping and exclaiming as they saw the crippled wolfships lying along the beach. Owners or crew of those ships diverted, running down onto the sand, cursing and shouting in dismay and anger as they saw the damage. Svengal, Erak's first mate and longtime companion, was among the first to reach the Oberjarl. He was wearing only a shirt and trousers. His feet were bare and his hair was wild and unkempt. A long sword gleamed in his right hand.

"*Wolfwind*'s gone," Erak told him. He decided that the town was well and truly alerted and let go the rope leading to the bell's clapper. The clanging stopped, the last peal echoing across the water and making the ensuing silence all the more acute.

Svengal gaped at the empty space along the wharf, not comprehending. "Gone?" he repeated. "Gone where?"

"Stolen," Erak said. "Someone came in the night, killed the harbor guards and stole my ship."

The families of the murdered men had made their way onto the mole now and they gathered in two sad little groups around the bodies. One of the women began to sob as she knelt beside her dead husband. Tegar's brother took several angry paces toward the burly Oberjarl, his face contorted in anger.

"Who did this, Erak? Who killed my brother?"

But Erak had no answer for him. "I don't know," he said. "Someone came in the night and killed him and Rogger." He gestured toward the empty mooring. "And stole *Wolfwind*."

Svengal seized Erak's arm and shook it to gain his attention. The Oberjarl seemed to be in a daze, Svengal thought, puzzled by the killing and the fate of his ship.

"We need to get after them!" he urged.

Erak turned hopeless eyes on him. "How?" he asked. "There's not a ship left that's seaworthy."

From the beach, cries of anger and despair continued as more and more of the villagers became aware that Hallasholm's fleet had been put out of action.

Svengal released his grip on the Oberjarl's wrist and studied the damaged ships still moored to the mole, then turned toward those on the beach. Now he could recognize the extent of the damage, he realized that none of them could put to sea. And that repairing the damage would take at least a day—possibly more.

"Curse them!" he said bitterly. "Who was it? Who could have done this?"

Erak could only shrug. There were several countries around the Stormwhite who felt little or no love for Skandia. But there was no clue as to which one of them might have done this.

Hal arrived, breathless from his run down the hill. His mother's house was one of the farthest from the harbor. A few minutes later, Stig followed him along the mole. Both were armed, Erak noticed—Hal with his sword and Stig with his heavy saxe.

Quickly, Erak explained the situation, and Hal's eyes narrowed as he repeated Svengal's question.

"Who did it?" he asked.

Once again, Erak could only shrug. "Maybe the Magyarans," he said. "They bear a grudge against us. Or the Hungassi."

Hal shook his head. "The Hungassi aren't seamen," he said. "They're river pirates, and they rarely venture onto the open sea. Whoever took *Wolfwind* obviously sailed her away, and they simply don't have the necessary skills."

"Whoever it was, we have to get after them!" Stig exclaimed. He was looking up at the few clouds scudding across the sky. Chances were that the ship thieves had taken the quickest and easiest way out, with the wind behind them. That would have taken them to the southwest.

"In what?" Erak demanded, and indicated the other ships in harbor and on the beach.

For the first time, Stig realized the enormity of the problem facing them. Even with a ship, it would be difficult to run the thieves down. The sea left no trails for them to follow. And Erak was right. There wasn't a ship left in Hallasholm that could mount a pursuit.

"There might be one," Hal said. Dropping the sword, he turned away and dashed down the mole, turning right when he reached the landward end and heading off into the houses that lined the harbor. Stig realized what he was thinking.

"Heron!" he shouted. "She's in the boatyard on East Creek! Maybe they didn't find her!"

And he too set off at a run after Hal.

He was gaining on his friend as they emerged from the last few outlying houses and started up the slight hill that led to a ridge overlooking East Creek and Hal's boatyard. Kloof bounded ahead of them, barking excitedly. If the thieves weren't familiar with the layout of Hallasholm, they may well have overlooked the fact that one ship lay outside the confines of the harbor.

And that was the fastest, handiest ship in the country.

They crested the hill and paused momentarily to look down at the large boatshed where *Heron* was moored. Then, without a word, they broke into a run once more, slipping and sliding on the long grass, stumbling over the uneven surface beneath it, but miraculously, both keeping their feet.

The open end of the boatshed, leading out into the creek, was facing away from them, so they had no way of knowing if their ship had survived the night unscathed. Hal tugged open the side door of the building, heaving it back against the protest of its old, rusting hinges, and dashed inside, Stig following on his heels.

They both stopped in the dim interior, hoping against hope. Gradually, their eyes became accustomed to the dimness. Before them *Heron* floated easily alongside the small timber dock. Hal stepped aboard her, an immense feeling of relief flooding through him as he checked rigging, sails, tiller and oars.

Heron was untouched. The raiders hadn't found her.

"Cast off," he said to Stig as his first mate joined him aboard the ship. "We'll sail her around to the harbor."

Heron rocked as Kloof bounded aboard, and the two young men moved quickly to release the bow and stern lines that held *Heron* fast. They each seized an oar from the rack that ran along her center line behind the mast and they began to pole her out into the stream, digging the oar blades into the muddy creek bed. The water was only two meters deep here, and *Heron* slid easily out of the boatshed. One final, massive shove sent her gliding out to the center of the creek. The tide was running out, and *Heron* began to move downstream with it, spinning slowly in the current.

Without a word, the two friends dashed to the halyards. Kloof settled on the deck by the steering board, her chin on her paws, watching them intently. Hal looked up at the wind telltale, glanced downstream, and came to a decision.

"Starboard sail," he said briefly. They seized onto the halyard, heaving the yardarm and sail up the mast until it clunked into position at the top. The canvas sail shivered and flapped as the wind caught it. The ship began to move a little faster with the extra thrust of the wind on the sail. Hal scrambled across the raised center decking and dashed to the tiller. Once Stig saw that he was in position, he began to haul on the sheet to tighten the sail.

Heron was side on to the wind as the sail filled. She began to drift to leeward under the increased force, heading up into the wind like a weathervane. Hal hauled on the tiller and her bow fell off to starboard as the rudder took effect.

Stig let the sail out further as she turned downstream, then hauled it tight again once her bow was pointing toward the open sea beyond the creek.

Hal's quick assessment of the situation had been accurate. They would make the mouth of the creek on this tack, as he had seen when he selected the starboard sail. Stig closed one eye and peered at the sternpost, lining it up with a tree on the bank. They were drifting to leeward, he saw. Hal would have to bring her head up to avoid another tack.

"Fin keel?" Stig called.

Hal nodded assent. "Let it down."

Stig scrambled up onto the center decking and grasped the top of the fin keel—a two-meter-long board that slid up and down through a gap in the bottom of the hull. He leaned his weight on it and shoved and felt it slide down against the resistance of the sheepskin lining that sealed the gap around it and held it firm. The keel bit into the water and the ship began to slip more easily downstream, the leeward drift curtailed by the steadying pressure of the keel.

Hal felt the bow rise and fall on the first line of rollers as *Heron* shot clear of the stream and into the sea proper. They were heading away from Hallasholm and they'd have to bring the ship round onto the starboard tack to head for the harbor. He waited to gain some extra sea room, then called to Stig.

"Wear ship! Go!"

Hal put the tiller over, swinging the ship to starboard, as Stig released the starboard sail and it came slithering down onto the deck. Quickly, Stig grabbed a trailing end where it threatened to fall into the water alongside. Then he scrambled across the deck to raise the port sail. As it filled with the wind behind it, it forced the ship further round to starboard. He trimmed it in and cleated the line to hold it.

Between them, two men could handle *Heron* in calm weather like this—although it helped that Stig was well muscled and powerful. She was running now at an angle to the line of the waves, rising and falling over them, rolling as she plunged down the back of each one, twin showers of spray fanning out on either side of her sharp bow as she reached the bottom of each trough. The low-angle early light caught each shower of spray, turning it to glowing drops of silver.

Ahead of them, they could see the entrance to Hallasholm harbor.

chapter eight

They made one further tack to turn into the narrow gap in the stone walls that formed the harbor entrance. Hal glanced at the mole and saw the crowd hadn't diminished. A low murmur of relief arose from those assembled as they saw *Heron,* whole and undamaged, slip through the gap.

Hal brought the ship up into the wind as they neared the empty berth where *Wolfwind* had rested. She spun on her heel, then began to lose way. He used the last of her momentum to bring her parallel to the mole. Several of the Heron brotherband were on the wharf and they threw ropes to Stig. He fastened them at the bow and stern and those ashore began to haul the ship in to moor her alongside.

Hal fastened the tiller as he felt the ship bump gently against the wicker fenders that lined the mole. He stepped up onto the port-side bulwark as Ulf leaned across the gap to give him a steadying hand.

"Thanks," Hal said briefly, then gestured to the untidy raffle of the two sails where they were piled on deck. "Will you and Wulf tidy up the sails, please?"

Stig followed him ashore, nodding to the twins as they set about folding and stowing the sails. Two men might be able to handle the ship, but it left no time to stow the gear neatly as they went.

Erak was appraising the little ship as she rose and fell gently alongside the mole.

"She's all right?" he asked. "No damage?"

Hal shook his head. "They didn't find her—whoever they were," he reassured the Oberjarl.

Svengal rubbed his chin as he looked at the crippled wolfship lying astern of the *Heron*. "What I don't understand," he said, "is why they didn't do more damage to the other ships." They all looked at him and he explained. "I mean, it's all pretty superficial, isn't it? We can set it to rights in a day or so. Why didn't they smash holes in the hulls? Or even burn the ships?"

For a moment, they all considered this. Then Hal grasped the reason.

"Noise," he said. "If they'd started smashing the hulls, someone might have heard them. And the flames could have been seen and the alarm raised if they'd burnt the ships. All this damage could be done quietly—slashing rigging and sails, cutting the fastenings for the rudders. It would have all been relatively silent."

"Good point," Erak said. "That's why nobody heard them."

"I think Kloof did," Hal said, a little shamefacedly. "She started barking at some time around the third hour of the morning. I should have got up to see what alerted her." He glanced apologetically at Erak. "Sorry about that."

But the Oberjarl brushed the apology aside. "You couldn't have known," he said. "And others must have heard her bark—but they didn't get up to see what was going on either."

"The good news is," Stig put in, "they don't know we've got a ship ready to follow them—and a fast one at that. They'd be expecting to have a clear run for at least a day. Instead, we've cut their lead"—he hesitated, looking at the sun to estimate the time of day—"to about five hours."

"More than that," Hal said. "We need to provision the ship and fill the water casks before we can set sail. That'll take a couple of hours."

"Then it's time we got started," Svengal said briskly. He was well used to stocking a ship for a voyage, and he turned and began yelling orders to the men grouped around them, sending some to the village to fetch sacks of flour and dried and salted meat and fish. Edvin, who served as the *Heron*'s cook, quickly joined in, seeking out the men and women in the crowd who provided bread and vegetables for Hallasholm's fleet.

Stig took a hand too, organizing a party of men to begin filling *Heron*'s casks with fresh water.

Hal spoke to the rest of the crew, who were all on the mole awaiting orders.

"Better get home and collect your gear," he told them. "We

could be in for a lengthy trip." As he spoke, he remembered that he had tossed his sword aside when he had set off running for the boatyard. He looked around for it now but saw no sign of it.

"Looking for this?" Svengal said, handing him the sword with a wide grin. "You really must stop throwing it away like that."

"Thanks, Svengal," Hal said. He went to slide it into its scabbard, and remembered that he had simply drawn the sword and dashed out the door when he heard the alarm bell. The scabbard was still at home, along with his charts, navigating instruments and seagoing clothes.

"I'd better get my stuff," he said. He took one last look around at the busy scene. The earlier confusion had given way to an organized effort to get the ship ready for sea, and there were plenty of people capable of supervising the work. He wasn't needed here.

"Me too," Erak said suddenly. He turned to Svengal. "Svengal, you're in charge while I'm gone."

Svengal raised his eyebrows. "Gone? Where are you going?"

Erak jerked his thumb at the *Heron*. "I'm going with Hal and the boys. *Wolfwind*'s my ship, and I plan to get her back."

Hal paused, eyeing the Oberjarl dubiously. "If that's the case," he said slowly, "we need to get one thing clear. You may be Oberjarl. And *Wolfwind* is your ship. But on board *Heron,* I give the orders. Not you."

Svengal turned away to hide a grin. "Oh, he'll love that," he said under his breath.

There was a long pause, while Erak and Hal locked gazes. The Oberjarl chewed the ends of his mustache. His face grew red and he glared at the young man in front of him. Hal faced him calmly.

On board a ship, there could only be one person giving the orders. And that person was the skirl.

Finally, Erak drew in a deep breath. "Agreed," he said. "Now let's get going."

Hal's estimate of the time it would take to have *Heron* ready for sea turned out to be pessimistic. In just over an hour, she was stored, her water casks were full and her stocks of firewood for Edvin's little stove were replenished. The crew reassembled, stowing their weapons and personal gear aboard in the lockers beside their rowing benches and hanging their shields on the pegs set along the ship's bulwarks.

Erak arrived with his seagoing bag and looked around, uncertain where he should stow his equipment. Hal pointed to his own spot—a tiny enclosed sleeping hutch under the port-side rear decking.

"You can take my spot," he said. "I normally sleep on deck when we're at sea."

Much as he trusted his crew and his alternate helmsmen—Stig and Edvin—he was never fully comfortable if he was too far from the tiller when they were at sea. He had a rolled-up sheepskin and tarpaulin in the stern, a few meters from the steering platform. He was accustomed to bedding down there. Besides, he found the enclosed hutch belowdecks to be a little claustrophobic.

Erak nodded his thanks and dropped down into the rowing well to access the space. Astern of the hatch that led inside was Lydia's screened-off sleeping space in the rowing well. She too preferred the open air.

Stig and Hal made a quick inspection of the ship, testing stays and fittings to make sure everything was properly in place and firmly fastened. Most of the crew's families had made their way to the mole and were ready to farewell their sons. The Herons, their gear and weapons stowed, made their way back ashore to say goodbye. Hal saw his mother was among those on the mole. That was unusual, he thought. Usually they said their goodbyes back at home. Then he shrugged. There was a great deal that was unusual about today. He stepped up onto the mole and walked to her, embracing her for a long moment.

"Take care, son," she said. Her voice was steady. She was used to seeing him leave. But at the back of her mind was the memory that she had watched his father leave many years before, and he had never returned.

"I will, Mam. Don't worry about me," he said, his voice a little husky. Then he released her and stepped back. He was aware of someone standing close behind him. It was Thorn, and when Hal stepped away from his mother, the old warrior took his place, embracing her and kissing her on the lips. It was a long kiss, and Hal smiled at them benevolently. He was glad they had found each other, glad that they had developed a special relationship.

A few meters away, Stig was embracing his own mother. Various other crew members were farewelling their parents and siblings. Ulf and Wulf stood by their own mother, who hugged her two quirky sons.

"Look after one another," she said, and they both chorused a reply.

"We will."

They turned away to step down into the ship and Ulf said softly: "She hugged me first."

"That's because she wanted to hug me last," Wulf told him. Overhearing the exchange, their mother rolled her eyes. They would never change, she decided.

To a chorus of farewells and good wishes, the rest of the crew detached themselves and boarded the ship. Erak was the last aboard. Svengal slapped him on the shoulder as he went.

"Don't expect me to hug you," he said with a grin.

Erak scowled at him. "Get the rest of the fleet repaired and get them to sea," he said. "I want *Wolfwind* found."

Svengal became serious and nodded. "I'll see to things, boss," he said, as the Oberjarl stepped down into the ship, dropping the last meter or so. In spite of his graying hair and his bulk, Erak was surprisingly light on his feet, adjusting his balance easily to accommodate the rocking ship, set in motion by the waves coming through the harbor mouth and the large number of people moving around on board.

Hal took one last look around to make sure everyone was aboard, and spoke to Stig.

"Let's get underway," he said, and Stig relayed the order to the rest of the crew.

There was no need to stipulate individual actions. The Herons knew their tasks. While Ulf and Wulf crouched ready by the halyards, Edvin and Stefan cast off the bow and stern ropes, and Ingvar used his mighty strength to pole the ship away from the mole.

Hal unlashed the tiller and checked the telltale. The wind was still blowing steadily down from the mountains.

"Starboard sail," he ordered, and the twins heaved on the halyards and sent the starboard yard and sail sliding up the mast. The ship drifted uncertainly for a few moments, still under the impetus of Ingvar's final shove. Then the wind caught the sail, and as Ulf and Wulf hauled in, the little ship surged forward, the tiller alive and vibrating in Hal's hand. As ever, he felt the quiet thrill of being in control, of harnessing the wind to do as he wanted. Thorn slid the fin keel down in its recess and the ship steadied, moving more purposefully and gathering speed as it slipped through the water toward the harbor mouth.

The stone buttresses either side sped by them and they were in the open sea, the bow rising to the first of the rollers, then sheeting spray high to either side as she came down into the trough behind it.

The people on the mole followed her with cries of farewell and good wishes, but already their voices were growing faint as *Heron* surged eagerly into her element.

chapter nine

With the wind almost dead astern, Hal ordered the twins to let the sail out to its fullest extent, and *Heron* accelerated. She swooped and rolled gracefully as she met the rollers, coming at her from a thirty-degree angle off the bow.

As she rode lightly over each crest, the morning sun caught each successive shower of spray, setting it alight and creating thousands of glistening droplets. There was even a momentary rainbow formed as the light struck through the fine mist, quickly dispelled as the water fell away, then reappearing as the next wave sent more spray flying.

The command group—Hal, Thorn, Stig and Erak—were gathered close to the steering platform. Hal looked at the others. It was time for a decision.

"Which way?" he asked.

There was a moment's silence. Then Thorn spoke up. "The wind's been out of the northwest for the past three or four days," he said. "I figure whoever did this would want to put as much distance between themselves and Hallasholm as possible. So, southeast."

A southeasterly course would have *Wolfwind* running directly before the wind, as they were at present. It would also be one of *Wolfwind*'s fastest points of sailing, with the wind dead astern of her big, square sail. Hal looked at the other two. They hesitated for a moment, then both nodded.

"Southeast it is," he said. "We'll goose-wing the sails."

He passed the order on to Ulf and Wulf. Stefan and Jesper moved to help them as they raised the port-side sail as well, letting it far out to port so that the wind was right behind it. With both sails raised and let out as far as they would go—goose-winged—they resembled a giant *M* and offered double the sail area to the following wind. *Heron* surged forward under the additional thrust.

Hal knew this course would suit Erak, who was still convinced that the ship had been stolen by Hungassi tribesmen. Their land lay to the southeast of Hallasholm, and *Heron* was heading pretty well straight toward it. But Hal still doubted that the river pirates were behind the theft.

They weren't seafarers. They were used to navigating the relatively calm waters of the Dan River and its many tributaries. Besides, what use would they have for a large ship like *Wolfwind*? She was too big to maneuver easily in the confined waters of a river and it would take too many men to crew her. The Hungassi were used to raiding downriver traffic in small, handy skiffs, either under sail or oar power. A big seagoing ship like *Wolfwind* wouldn't suit their style of operations.

The Magyarans were another possibility, although a lot of the same arguments could be made against them.

One thing was sure, both tribes hated the Skandians and objected to their role as maritime police and guardians. Erak had upset a lot of nations when he abandoned raiding and began suppressing piracy.

Hal frowned as he had the thought. There was something in the back of his mind but he couldn't place it. A memory was nagging at him—something that had happened, or something that had been said recently.

But, no matter how he tried, the thought eluded him.

They ran southeast for the rest of the day, with Hal spending most of his time on the tiller. When darkness fell, he ordered the starboard sail down. The goose-wing arrangement was a delicate one—prone to accidents and mishaps—and he didn't want to continue with it once the light had gone and visibility was reduced.

Speed fell away noticeably, although *Heron* was still moving fast through the dark water. Hal stayed on the tiller until the ninth hour, then handed over to Stig, yawning hugely as he did so. He'd started the day early, and they'd been on the go ever since.

He rolled himself gratefully into the sheepskin sleeping mat and pulled the tarpaulin over him. In spite of their reduced speed, there were still regular showers of spray drenching the afterdeck. The droplets rattled on the stiff oiled cloth of the tarpaulin and he sighed gratefully as he closed his eyes and began to breathe deeply.

Not that he was fully asleep. He never was when his ship was at sea. His body was attuned to *Heron*'s motion as she sliced through the water, riding up the back of one wave, then sliding down its face into the trough behind it, feeling the constant thrust, then the smooth deceleration as the water grabbed hold of the hull, its silky resistance washing off the speed of the ship's descent. Occasionally, an out-of-sequence wave would rock *Heron* to one side, and the change in the ship's rhythm would bring him fully awake.

He would lie there, tensed, until he felt Stig bring the ship back under control and the regular swooping movement was restored. Then he would relax and sink back into the half slumber, his senses alert for the next variation in the ship's movement.

The first gray streaks were lighting the eastern sky when he awoke. Edvin was on the tiller. During the dark hours, Hal had sensed the change of control as Stig handed over. There was a subtle difference to the way the ship behaved under different helmsmen. Stig was inclined to use brute strength to make course corrections when stray wind eddies or waves pushed the bows off course. Edvin had a lighter touch—easing the ship back to its proper course with less disturbance.

Hal sat up, yawning and tossing the sheepskin cover to one side. Edvin sensed the movement behind him and turned to greet his skirl.

"Morning," he said softly. "Sleep well?"

Hal grunted and rose to his feet. There was a small cask of fresh water set close to the steering platform. He thrust his hands into it and splashed some on his face. Then he took the pannikin that hung from the cask and scooped out half a pint of cold water, sipping it slowly and washing away the taste of the night.

He moved to stand beside the steering platform, glancing up to check the wind telltale streaming from the sternpost. It was still blowing straight out in front of them.

"Wind hasn't backed?" he asked.

Edvin shook his head. "It's stayed steady all night," he told Hal.

The light was growing stronger now and the ball of the sun was showing a narrow curved strip of orange light above the horizon. As Hal watched, the narrow strip grew larger, becoming a half ball, then the full orb of the sun climbed above the horizon, setting the dull gray sea alight.

As it climbed higher, the glare became less, and Hal could make out a thin dark line on the horizon.

"Teutlandt," he said, jerking his head toward it, and Edvin nodded.

"We've made good time."

Hal didn't answer. That vague feeling of uncertainty was back with him—a sense that everything wasn't completely right. He checked along the length of the ship. It was easier to see detail now as the sun rose still higher, bathing the decks with light. He looked up at the masthead. Lydia was perched on the lookout spot, turning her head slowly from side to side as she checked the ocean all around. He drew in breath to hail her and ask if she could see anything, then stopped. If she could, she would have announced the fact.

The crew had changed positions during the night. Stefan and Jesper were crouched by the halyards and sheets. The twins were not in sight. No doubt they'd be sleeping in the rowing well.

Thorn was a huddled figure at the base of the mast, wrapped in a tattered sheepskin that was more patches than original material.

Kloof was curled up beside him, with her tail wrapped round her nose in the way that dogs have.

Hal turned at a sound from the port-side rowing well and saw Erak clambering up onto the central deck.

The Oberjarl glanced up quickly at the wind telltale—a movement deeply ingrained in every skirl on first waking. Shading his eyes, he peered around the horizon, scanning a full 360 degrees, then joined Hal and Edvin.

"Nothing in sight," he said. It was a statement of fact, not a question, and Hal could sense the frustration behind it. Doubtless Erak had nurtured the hope that first light would bring a sighting of *Wolfwind*. The empty horizon surrounding them had dashed what slight hope he might have cherished.

Hal could sympathize with the Oberjarl's disappointment. With each passing hour, with each kilometer they traveled, the area in which *Wolfwind* might be grew larger and larger. They had selected a course based on guesswork and supposition. But if *Wolfwind* had taken a direction that varied by five or ten degrees from theirs, she would have been drawing farther and farther away throughout the night. The area in which they might hope to find her would have grown to thousands and thousands of square kilometers.

They might even have sailed past the other ship during the night, missing her by no more than a few kilometers. Right now, they could be sailing away from her—and she from them.

"Maybe we should swing farther east," Erak growled. He had undertaken to follow Hal's orders when they left Hallasholm, but it was proving difficult to keep his word. *Wolfwind* was his ship, and he felt her loss acutely.

Hal opened his mouth, framing a diplomatic reply. Then he hesitated. Perhaps Erak was right. Perhaps the ship had been stolen by the Hungassi river pirates. In which case, they might as well bear further to port. A wave of uncertainty washed over him. He felt Edvin's eyes on him as he waited to see whether his skirl was going to order a change in course.

Then the thought that had been troubling Hal through the night suddenly crystalized in his mind. He looked Erak straight in the eye.

"It wasn't the Hungassi," he said. "It was the Iberians."

chapter ten

"The Iberians?" Erak repeated. "What makes you think they did it?"

But Hal held up a hand to deflect the question. He glanced quickly around the deck. There was no sign of Stig. He'd had the helm during the night. Doubtless he was still sleeping.

"Thorn," he called. He hardly raised his voice but the old warrior was immediately awake. He rose to his feet and started toward Hal. But the skirl's next order turned him around.

"Wake Stig and come here, both of you," Hal said. He looked at Erak. The big man was obviously seething with curiosity and Hal gave him an apologetic smile. "May as well wait till the others are here. That'll save me repeating myself," he explained.

On board a warship, where danger could threaten at any

moment, people tended to move quickly in response to orders, without wasting time on questions. Stig was awake the moment Thorn's hand closed on his shoulder. His eyes were wide-open and he was already rising to his feet.

"What is it?" he asked.

Thorn indicated Hal and Erak waiting for them. "Hal wants us."

The two of them made their way aft, moving easily in time with the ship's rhythm. When they were within easy speaking distance, Hal addressed the two of them.

"Remember when we took those Iberians ashore in Sonderland?"

They both nodded, frowning slightly as they wondered where the conversation was going.

Hal continued quickly. "One of them was particularly vocal, remember? He kept shouting threats at us."

Stig pondered the question, then he nodded slowly. "I remember. He was going on about how we'd be sorry. How we'd get our comeuppance." He frowned as the memory grew. "You said it was just bluster," he pointed out.

Hal nodded. "At the time, that's what I thought. But I've been thinking. Remember how his companions tried to shut him up?"

This time it was Thorn who replied. "You're right. At least one of them tried to stop him. He hit him with his shoulder and swore at him." He paused and then added thoughtfully, "He seemed pretty keen to stop him talking."

Hal was nodding eagerly now. "That's right. As if he was afraid his shipmate was going to give away some sort of plot."

"Something the Iberians had in store for us," Stig put in.

"Exactly!" Hal exclaimed, as his friends' recall reinforced the suspicions he had been turning over during the night. "They'd hardly be so keen to shut him up if it was just meaningless threats. They knew there was some kind of plan underway—some way of making us pay."

"Pay for what?" Erak asked, his forehead creased in a frown as he tried to make sense of the conversation.

This time it was Thorn who answered. "Making us pay for cracking down on piracy. What was it he said? Something like *you'll regret that you ever saw an Iberian ship.* And *you'll learn your lesson.*"

"That's pretty specific," Hal said. "He definitely implied that they had something in mind, something planned. And that we wouldn't like it when it happened."

He had turned to Erak while he spoke, addressing the words to the Oberjarl. Erak stuck out his bottom lip in an expression of disbelief. "As you said, it was probably just bluster and empty threats."

But Hal was shaking his head in disagreement. "Then why were his friends so keen to shut him up?"

Erak went to speak, then stopped, a shadow of doubt crossing his face. Hal saw the hesitation and continued eagerly, his words coming faster as the idea grew in his mind.

"They didn't want him tipping us off that they had some sort of revenge planned. They could see he was about to give away some scheme or other and they wanted him to stop! What other reason would they have for shutting him up?"

And that was the crux of the matter as Hal saw it. The threats and the abuse meant little. But the fact that the Iberian's companions had hurried to shut him down indicated that there was something afoot—something serious that was aimed at the Skandians.

"You're saying . . ." Erak began slowly, as his mind grappled with the information.

Hal interrupted him. "I'm saying it was the Iberians who were planning to steal *Wolfwind*. After all, it's no secret that they hate us—probably more than the Hungassi or the Magyarans. Think about it: We've probably caused them more grief over the past few years. We've taken a lot of Iberian ships."

"So they stole *Wolfwind* to get revenge," Erak said, and the tone of his voice indicated he was beginning to accept Hal's theory.

"Or maybe it was more than that," Thorn put in. He'd been listening carefully to Hal, and he agreed that the behavior of the captured pirates indicated that there was something afoot. "Maybe they plan to use *Wolfwind* against us somehow."

"Either way," Hal said urgently, "we're heading in the wrong direction. We need to turn west, toward Iberia."

The Teutlandt coast was a distant dark line off their port side as they sped toward the west. The wind was steady out of the north, which put it abeam of *Heron*—probably her fastest point of sailing.

Hal had taken the tiller once more. After several hours, Stig offered to spell him, but he shook his head irritably. He thought bitterly about the hours they had wasted heading southeast, while *Wolfwind* had presumably been heading to the west. It had cost them hundreds of miles, he thought savagely. Then he had a sudden wave of doubt. Maybe his intuition was wrong. Maybe they were now heading *away* from the stolen ship.

The continuing uncertainty gnawed at him, setting him on edge as he leaned forward, peering to the west. The tiller was tucked under his right arm, the waves of spray hitting him in the face without his seeming to notice them. As the day wore on, the rest of the crew changed positions, spelling one another at the halyard and sheets and lookout positions. But Hal remained at the helm. In the early afternoon, Stig made a move toward him once more. But Thorn's quick shake of the head stopped him.

Kloof, sensing the uncertainty and the tension in her master, growled softly to herself, occasionally standing up against the bulwark, propping herself there with her front feet and staring out into the distance.

On one of these occasions, she suddenly stiffened and let out a short, sharp bark, just as Jesper, perched on the masthead, called to them.

"Deck there! There's something off our starboard bow!"

Instantly, those on deck were galvanized into action, moving to the starboard gunwale and peering out over the rolling waves. Only Hal remained in his original position, hunched over the tiller. He cupped one hand around his mouth. "Is it a ship? Is it *Wolfwind*?" he called.

Jesper hesitated, then replied, "It's not *Wolfwind*. I'm not sure if it's a ship. Just something in the water."

Hal snapped at Stefan, who was already moving toward the mast. "Stefan! Get up there and have a look!"

Stefan had the sharpest eyes in the ship. He nodded and sprang to the lines leading up the mast, climbing rapidly until he was beside Jesper, who pointed to something in the distance. Stefan peered intently for some seconds, then turned to call down to Hal.

"It's a wreck! Just the hull of a ship, barely afloat. She's dismasted and sinking."

"Is it *Wolfwind*?" Erak bellowed the question, the anxiety obvious in his voice.

Stefan shook his head. "She's not big enough for *Wolfwind*—" he called.

Then Jesper interrupted. "Someone's on her! They're waving!"

"Coming about!" Hal shouted, to warn them to hold on. He put the tiller over, and Ulf and Wulf heaved on the sheets as *Heron* turned to starboard, her bow rising, then plunging violently as she met the waves full on.

"A little more to starboard," Stefan called, and Hal adjusted his course until the lookout signaled that he was heading for the wreck.

Within a few minutes, the hulk was visible from the deck and more detail was discernible.

She appeared to be a trader. Her mast lay shattered alongside the swamped hull, held in place by the tangled web of stays and halyards. She was down by the stern, with the rear half of the ship submerged as she rose and fell sluggishly on the waves. Apparently, a pocket of trapped air in the bow was keeping the for'ard section afloat, and as they drew closer, those on *Heron*'s deck could make out two survivors clinging to the forepart. One of them was waving a shirt or some other article of clothing. The other was ominously still.

Without the need to be told, Stig scrambled for'ard, perched in the bows ready to board the half-sunken wreck as they came alongside.

Judging speed and distance with an expert eye, Hal waited, then ordered the sail down. *Heron* surged toward the wreck, the way coming off her, until she nudged gently against the smashed timbers.

Stig dropped lightly onto the half-sunken ship and made his way to the bow, where the surviving crewman was trying to rise to greet him.

"Stay there," Stig told him, seeing the bloodstains on the man's tunic. The sailor sank back onto the deck, still clutching the jerkin he had been waving. Stig quickly checked the second crewman.

"He's alive!" he called back to Hal. "But he's in a bad way."

Balancing on the sloping, sluggishly moving forepart, Stig lifted the man and shuffled back to where *Heron*'s bow nudged against the wreck, held in place by Ingvar with a long boat hook.

"Edvin!" called Hal, but the medic was already making his way for'ard to receive the wounded man. He and Jesper lifted him gently aboard, laying him down on the deck, then Stig returned to help the other survivor on board. Overcome by events, the man was semiconscious.

Stig passed him up to the waiting hands on *Heron,* then scrambled aboard himself. Ingvar released the boat hook and shoved *Heron* away from the semi-submerged wreck.

Hal let the *Heron* drift away from the wreck, then ordered the sail up once more. As the ship gathered way, he gestured for Thorn to take the tiller as he moved for'ard to where the two shipwrecked survivors were being tended by Edvin and Lydia.

"Now let's find out what's been going on here."

chapter eleven

With the sails unrestrained and slatting loosely, *Heron* turned up into the wind and drifted slowly away from the waterlogged hulk of the wreck.

Under Edvin's instructions, a space was cleared in the center of the ship, aft of the mast, and the two survivors were laid out there. Hal waited until he had the men settled, then moved to kneel beside them.

"They're Gallican," Edvin told him. "They were heading for east Teutlandt to trade when they were attacked."

"By who?" Hal asked.

"He said they were attacked by Skandians," Edvin replied.

Hal snorted in disbelief. "That's ridiculous! He must be mistaken."

The semiconscious man looked up in alarm as Hal leaned over him. He tried weakly to recoil away from the young skirl.

"It's all right," Hal said, in a reassuring tone. He laid a hand on the man's arm in an attempt to comfort him. The sailor cringed even further, muttering weakly in fear. Hal looked at Edvin, puzzled.

But the medic only shrugged. "He seems frightened of us," he said. "When we first got him on board and he saw us, he reacted in the same way. He recognized us as Skandians and he was afraid."

Hal frowned thoughtfully while he considered that piece of information. Then he checked the other survivor, who remained unconscious. His breathing was shallow and his face was pale. There was a deep wound in his upper torso. Edvin had bandaged it, but blood was already seeping through the fresh linen.

"How bad are they?" Hal asked.

Edvin paused before answering. He indicated the unconscious man. "He's the worse. He's lost a lot of blood and he's barely breathing. The other one isn't in great shape but at least he's conscious." He paused, then said sadly, "Both of them are beyond my skills. We need to get them to a proper healer as soon as possible."

Hal looked at him in surprise. As far as he was concerned, Edvin was an expert healer. If he felt he wasn't up to the task of looking after the two men, they must be in a bad way. Not that Edvin's skill—or lack of it—made any difference. They couldn't treat the two men on board *Heron* for any length of time. They'd have to put them ashore as soon as possible and find a healer to take care of them. In the meantime, the injured man's wild accusations needed to be addressed.

He leaned down by him once more and tried to make his voice as soothing and friendly as he could.

"Who did this to you?" he asked. "Who attacked your ship?"

The wounded man looked at him groggily. Edvin had given him a painkilling draft, and it was obviously affecting his senses.

"Skandians . . . ," he said weakly. "Skandians attacked us. Killed all the others . . ."

"Skandians," Hal said. "How do you know they were Skandians?"

"They were in a wolfship," the man said, his voice barely audible. "A big one." He raised his head, indicating *Heron*. "Bigger than this . . . square sail . . ."

Hal looked up and met Thorn's gaze. The others had gathered round the survivors where they lay on the deck. *"Wolfwind,"* he said grimly, and Thorn nodded. It had to be *Wolfwind*. There was no other Skandian ship at sea in this area.

". . . killed my crew." The man's speech faltered. "Left us alive to tell . . ." He shuddered and his eyes closed briefly. Hal resisted the urge to reach down and shake him awake. Eventually, the man's eyelids fluttered open.

"Left us alive . . . said for us to tell . . ." His voice faded away and his breathing became ragged.

"Tell who?" Hal urged, trying to keep his voice low and soothing, in spite of the questions raging in his mind. The man looked at him, his eyes unfocused. He waved a hand weakly at the figures surrounding him.

"Tell everyone," he said. Then, after a long pause, he added, "Tell everyone . . . Skandians are raiding again . . . like the old days."

The last few words seemed to exhaust his remaining strength, and he sank back down onto his pillow, his eyes closing. For a moment, Hal feared he was gone, then the man drew in a long, shuddering breath.

"So that's it," Hal said. "The Iberians are trying to discredit us—to set people against us."

"It'll take more than one ship sunk to achieve that," Stig said. "Besides, it's only luck that we chanced upon—"

"Never mind that," Edvin cut in with unusual forcefulness. "We can't stand here nattering all day. These men will die if we don't get them proper care."

Hal rose to his feet, considering the fact. "You're right," he said. "That's our first priority."

"So where do you suggest we take them?" Stig asked.

Hal considered the problem, then came to a decision. "There's a big trading port twenty kilometers to the west. Bolshafen, the Teuts call it."

"I know it," Thorn said. "It's a major town. There's sure to be a healer there."

"Then that's where we'll take them," Hal said. He gestured to Ulf and Wulf, who had been part of the interested circle of spectators. "Man the sheets, lads. Let's get her underway."

He strode quickly back to the tiller as the twins scurried to their positions. Within a few minutes, *Heron* was underway once more, driving southwest toward the Teutlandt coast.

The sun was slanting down as they came in sight of the trading town. They had been speeding along, parallel to the coastline and several kilometers out to sea, for some minutes when Stefan called out from the lookout.

"I see it!" he called, then added, with a note of curiosity apparent in his voice, "There's a fire of some sort. A big one."

Within a few minutes, those on deck could see what he meant. There was a thick pall of smoke hanging above the Teutlandt town.

"Looks like they've been in the wars," Thorn commented.

Hal remained silent. A worm of suspicion gnawed at him as he wondered if the fire in Bolshafen was connected somehow to the sinking Gallican trader and its shipmates. He nudged the tiller so that *Heron* was heading directly for the town. As they came closer, he could see the harbor entrance and surrounds. Like Hallasholm, the town had a stone wall surrounding the harbor to provide protection for ships inside. A narrow entrance was offset to one side, so that it wasn't facing directly into the prevailing wind and waves.

He could see several sources of the smoke that billowed above the Teutlandic town. Two were in the harbor and there were three more in the town itself—although they were all close to the harbor as well. As they surged closer still, he could see men running along the harbor moles, toward the entrance. Obviously, *Heron* had been sighted. The late-afternoon sun glinted off weapons.

"I don't like the look of this," he said, to nobody in particular. If they entered the harbor, they would come close to the two bastions that stood either side of the entrance—within easy spear-throwing range—and the running men seemed to be gathering on either side of the harbor entrance. He came to a decision.

"Shields!" he called.

The crew, who had been watching the harbor with similar

misgivings, hurried to fetch their shields from their pegs along the ship's bulwarks. Stig, once he had retrieved his own, unhooked Hal's triangular shield and passed it to him. Hal nodded his thanks and slipped his arm through the straps.

"Are we going in?" Stig asked.

Hal hesitated for a moment, then came to a decision. "Yes. Everybody get down and cover up as we go through."

Stig repeated the order and the crew slipped down into the rowing wells, where the sides of the ship would protect them. Hal strained his eyes, trying to see if there were any heavy projectile weapons deployed along the mole. He could see none. But many of the Teutlanders were carrying bows, and the remainder were armed with spears. He could hear them now. They were shouting angrily and many were brandishing their weapons at the fast-approaching Skandian ship.

"Maybe we should turn away," Thorn said quietly. He had moved from his accustomed position in the waist of the ship to stand beside Hal at the steering platform.

"I think you're right," said Hal, as he saw a man step forward and hurl a spear at *Heron*. It fell short, but it was a signal for half a dozen bowmen to loose shafts at the ship. Two arrows thudded into the rail three meters from where Hal stood.

"That's clear enough," he said. "Coming about!"

He heaved on the tiller, swinging *Heron* away from the harbor mouth.

Ulf and Wulf released the sail and scrambled across the central decking to raise its counterpart. *Heron* hesitated as she swung, then the sail filled and she accelerated away, passing less than twenty meters from the harbor wall and its angry occupants.

A hail of spears and arrows filled the air. Most of them missed, thrown off by *Heron*'s sudden about-turn and her rapid acceleration. But two arrows zipped through the taut fabric of the sail, and another slammed into Stig's shield, where he stood covering the sail handlers.

"Curse you Skandians!"

Hal heard the shout distinctly, then a chorus of abuse rang out as the ship sped away from the harbor. He glanced back and saw three half-sunken ships along the inside of the mole, and several fires burning in the warehouses that lined the harbor front.

"It seems we're not welcome in Bolshafen," he said heavily, as the town and its pall of smoke receded in their wake.

chapter twelve

The badly wounded survivor passed away that night. He went quietly, and it was some time before Edvin, who was catnapping close beside the two men, realized that he was no longer breathing.

Edvin took it hard. It was his mission as a healer to preserve life. To his mind, there was no higher calling, and he couldn't get rid of the thought that the Teutlanders' senseless refusal to allow *Heron* into their port was the cause of the man's death.

"It's so mindless," he said bitterly to Stig. "There was just no need for this to happen."

Stig laid a comforting hand on his shoulder. "You can't be sure," he told him. "Even if we'd got him ashore, he was pretty badly injured. Who's to say that he would have survived?"

But Edvin shook his head and stared silently out at the horizon. Lydia joined them, overhearing Stig's last remarks.

"If you're going to blame anyone, blame the Iberians who raided the town in *Wolfwind*. They're the cause of it," she said. "The sooner we catch up to them, the better."

When dawn came, they hove to and buried the Gallican at sea, wrapping him in a canvas shroud and weighing him down with several large rocks they took from the ballast stones in *Heron*'s bilges.

They lowered the cocooned body over the side and watched as it floated for several seconds, until the air trapped in the canvas shroud escaped, and the body began its last plunge into the depths of the Stormwhite. Hal wasn't familiar with whatever gods the Gallicans might pray to, and Skandians weren't a particularly religious group, regarding their own gods with a kind of affectionate disdain. Yet he felt something should be said over the man, and the other survivor clearly wasn't up to the task, lapsing in and out of consciousness as his condition deteriorated.

Awkwardly, Hal cleared his throat and stood up on the gunwale, staring at the swirl in the water that marked the spot where the Gallican had disappeared.

"May whatever gods you worship take care of you and see you safely in your own version of Vallashal . . . ," he said. The crew stood about uncomfortably, not sure if he had finished or if he had anything to add. He shrugged and looked about the deck.

"Somebody say amen," he said at length.

Ulf and Wulf obliged. "Amen," they intoned.

"Right then," Hal said, slapping his hands together. He had never officiated at a funeral before and wasn't sure of how they should proceed. But it seemed that everything necessary had been done. "Let's get underway."

• • • • •

Around the middle of the morning, Hal and Erak conferred, checking the angle of the sun and the contours of the coastline that was still a distant presence on their port side.

"I think we've crossed the border between Teutlandt and Gallica," Hal said. He pointed to a cone-shaped mountain rearing up about a kilometer inland. "That looks like Mount Gryphon to me."

Erak shaded his eyes and studied the landmark. He nodded slowly. "Could well be," he said. "Maybe things will be a little friendlier in Gallica."

"Well, if that's Gryphon, the next town is Leduc, a few kilometers west of here," Hal said. "We'll head for it and see what sort of welcome we get."

But the welcome at Leduc was much the same as it had been at Bolshafen. The entrance to the harbor was closed with a heavy chain boom, stretched between the two moles and sitting just below the surface. Any attempt to crash through it would splinter *Heron*'s timbers. Besides, the mole was lined with armed men and smoke was rising from fires in the township itself.

As before, they could see the wrecks of several ships in the harbor.

"Looks like *Wolfwind* has beaten us to it," Hal muttered, as he headed the ship out to sea once more.

He handed the tiller over to Stig and fetched a map of the area from the tiny chart cabinet in the stern. He spread it out on deck and studied it. Then he pointed to a small island off the Gallican coast.

"There's a fishing village here," he said.

Erak nodded thoughtfully. "They may not have a healer," he pointed out.

Hal shrugged. "If not, they can always take our man into Leduc. They'll have boats."

Erak nodded. "Good thinking. Unless *Wolfwind* has visited here as well."

"It's a small village. And a remote island. It'd hardly be worth their while to raid there. They want big towns where the word will spread quickly. At least we know we're on the right track," Hal added. "*Wolfwind* is definitely heading west."

They made landfall at the little island in the midafternoon. There was no harbor, just a stretch of rocky beach protected by two deep headlands. Half a dozen fishing boats were drawn up on timber racks that kept them out of the water at high tide. A small group of buildings huddled around the beach. Smoke rose from several chimneys, but there was no sign of the thick, heavy smoke they had seen at their two previous landfalls, and none of the fishing boats seemed to be damaged.

Nets were hung out on racks to dry and gulls wheeled around the beach, searching for scraps where the locals cleaned their catch.

"This all looks pretty normal," Stig observed as they sailed into the little bay. Hal had the twins let the sails loose when they were thirty meters off the shore. *Heron* gradually lost way and drifted, rising and falling with the waves, as all on board studied the shoreline.

Their arrival had been noticed, of course. But there was no sign of antagonism or panic among the fisherfolk on the beach. They gazed with some interest at the neat little ship drifting easily in their bay. One or two raised a hand in greeting.

"That's better," Hal said. "Lower the sail, boys, and run out the oars. We'll take her in to the beach."

While Ulf and Wulf gathered in the sails, the rest of the crew clambered down to their rowing benches, running out the long oars, and *Heron* was soon knifing through the clear blue waters of the bay toward the beach. Lydia came to stand beside Hal. He noted that she had a quiver of her long darts slung across her shoulder and was holding the atlatl—which usually hung from her belt—ready for action in her hand.

"Don't think you'll need that," he said softly.

She raised an eyebrow. "Then that'll be all to the good," she said. "On the other hand, if I do need it, it'll be good to have it ready."

"Easy all," Hal called, as the shore approached. The crew stopped rowing, raising their oars vertically as *Heron*'s prow grated onto the thick, coarse sand. She drove up a little way, then stopped, tilting slightly to one side.

Jesper dropped over the bow onto the damp sand and ran up the beach, carrying a fluked anchor. He drove it into the sand above the tidemark to hold *Heron* steady. As he did so, Lydia moved to the bow to keep an eye out for any hostility on the part of the locals. But her caution proved unnecessary. There were half a dozen people gathered on the beach and one of them, a big man with his beard arranged in two plaits, stepped forward and held out a hand to Jesper. His right arm was heavily tattooed.

"Greetings, stranger," he said. He nodded toward *Heron.* "What ship is that?"

"She's the *Heron.* She's a Skandian patrol ship," Jesper told him, and the man pursed his lips thoughtfully as he looked at the beached ship.

"She's small for a Skandian," he said. "And I see she's not a wolfship."

Wolfships carried a distinctive wolf's head on their bow posts. *Heron,* of course, was adorned with a carved bird's head, long-beaked and fierce, depicting the bird for which she was named.

"She may be small," Jesper told him, somewhat defensively, "but she's fast and handy and can sail rings around any wolfship."

The man smiled. "No offense intended, young man. I'm sure she's a fine craft. You're welcome to Isle de Plessa." He indicated the land behind him as he stated the island's name. "What brings you here?"

"My skirl would like to talk to you," Jesper said, and he turned and waved to Hal, who had by this time joined Lydia in the bows. At the signal, Hal vaulted lightly over the bulwark to the firm sand below and made his way up the beach. Lydia remained onboard, her gaze roaming constantly over the Gallicans on the beach, one hand resting lightly on a dart in her scabbard.

When Hal was within easy talking distance, he stopped and introduced himself. "I'm Hal Mikkelson, and this is my ship, the *Heron,*" he said.

The big fisherman nodded a greeting. "Welcome to Plessa, skirl Mikkelson. My name is Tyrell. What brings you to our island?" A smile spread across his face. "If you're after fish, you'll find we have plenty."

Hal advanced a final few paces and they shook hands.

"No fish today, Tyrell," he said. "We're looking for a healer. Is there one in your village?"

chapter thirteen

The smile vanished from Tyrell's face, replaced by a look of concern.

"You have sickness on board?" he asked. No island community would welcome a ship with any form of contagion on board.

But Hal shook his head. "We have a wounded man," he said. "A Gallican sailor we rescued two days ago from a sinking ship. My medic has done all he can for him, but he needs more skilled medical help than my man can provide."

Tyrell's worried look disappeared. "We have an excellent healer in the village," he said, and Hal breathed a small sigh of relief. Tyrell gestured toward the ship. "Bring him ashore and let's get him to the healer."

He turned toward some of the islanders standing nearby and

ordered them to bring a litter, while Hal walked back to the ship, where Edvin was waiting, watching proceedings anxiously.

"There's a healer here," Hal told him. "Bring the Gallican ashore."

Under Edvin's direction, Ingvar dropped to the beach and stood ready while Stig and Stefan carefully lowered the Gallican sailor over the gunwale. Ingvar took him in his arms and carried him a little way up the beach. The sailor was semiconscious and moaned softly in the big warrior's arms. As Ingvar reached the tidemark, two islanders came running down the beach with a canvas litter. They placed it down on the sand and Ingvar lowered the wounded man onto it. As the two men lifted the litter from the sand and headed for the village, Edvin accompanied them, pacing beside the wounded man. He looked at Hal as he passed him.

"I'll just see that he's all right," he said.

Hal nodded, then looked back to the tattooed fisherman. "My medic takes his job seriously."

Tyrell nodded approvingly. "Then he's a good medic," he said.

Hal was looking around the small village that huddled on the slopes surrounding the bay. He estimated that there were no more than twenty houses in the village. They were all one-story affairs built from unevenly shaped timber—most likely driftwood for the greater part—with thatched roofs. The gaps between the timbers had been sealed with mud and daub and the buildings seemed to cling to the slope of the hill—as if huddling there from the prevailing wind that would sweep the island in winter.

"It's a small village to have a resident healer," he remarked.

Tyrell nodded. "We're lucky. Fishermen are prone to accidents, so we have more than our share of injuries. And of course, there's a lot of sickness in winter when we're working in the cold and wet of the Stormwhite.

"The healer came to us some years back when the ship he was on was driven onto the rocks around the headland there." He indicated the northern arm of the bay. "He was on his way east, but liked it here and decided to stay." He paused, then continued. "What happened to the man you brought here?"

"His ship was attacked by a wolfship," Hal explained.

Tyrell looked at him in surprise. "A Skandian?"

Hal shook his head. "A renegade. She was stolen from Hallasholm harbor several nights ago—we think by Iberian pirates. Since then, she's been raiding along the Teutlandt and Gallic coasts. And attacking ships at sea."

The fisherman rubbed his chin thoughtfully. "We sighted a wolfship the day before yesterday," he said. "A big, square-rigged one—not like yours."

"That's her," Hal told him. "Did she come here?"

Tyrell shook his head. "We were at sea, maybe five kilometers from here on our normal fishing grounds. We saw her on the horizon. She'd already had a look into the bay here. She checked us out, but then she turned away."

"You probably weren't big enough to bother about," Hal said. "Which way did she head when she left you?"

Tyrell considered the question, frowning slightly as he remembered the encounter with *Wolfwind*. "West. Southwest actually," he amended, and Hal nodded.

"Back to the Gallic coastline," he said. "She's raiding large settlements—burning and sinking ships in harbor and destroying port facilities. When we tried to land that wounded man, we were driven off. That's why we came here. We hoped that word of her raiding wouldn't have reached a remote little settlement like this."

"So you're going after her?" the Gallican asked.

"She has to be stopped," Hal said bluntly.

Tyrell looked doubtfully at *Heron* where she was drawn up on the beach. "With that ship? She's a lot smaller than the square-rigger. And your men will be badly outnumbered."

"She's all we have. All the other ships in our fleet were put out of action when they stole *Wolfwind*. But she's a fast sailor and she's very maneuverable. We'll outsail the Iberians."

"You'll need to," Tyrell told him.

Hal said nothing for a moment. Then, beyond the big fisherman, he saw Edvin returning from the village. The medic approached them, and for the first time in several days, the concerned look on his face had gone.

"He's in good hands," Edvin said as he drew closer. He addressed Tyrell. "Your healer knows his business."

The fisherman nodded agreement. "That he does," he said.

Then Edvin looked back to Hal. "There are no serious wounds," he told his skirl. "But a lot of bruising and contusions. He thinks maybe there are a couple of cracked ribs. With bedrest and care he should be up and about in a week or so. Obviously, they wanted him to survive so he could spread the word."

"That's what he told us," Hal replied. He turned his attention back to Tyrell. "Thanks for your help. We'll get underway and see if we can catch up with her. Southwest, you said?"

"When we saw her last," the fisherman replied. "That should take her back to the mainland."

While Hal and Tyrell had been talking, several of the crew had come ashore to stretch their legs and greet the villagers. Stig had led a small party to the village, refilling several water casks from the village pump. Hal let out a shrill whistle now and they converged back on the beached ship.

"We'll get underway," he told them. "Tyrell here sighted *Wolfwind* two days ago. She sniffed around here, then headed back for the coast."

"Probably raiding more towns and ports," Stig said darkly as he handed up the last of the full casks to be stowed aboard the ship.

"Most likely," Hal agreed. Then, in a brisk voice, he began issuing orders for putting to sea. "Jes, bring in the beach anchor. Stig, you and Ingvar can shove us off." He glanced at the telltale on the mast. The wind was directly off the beach. There would be no need for oars. "Ulf and Wulf, stand by the sails."

Tyrell smiled as he heard the twins named. "Ulf and Wulf?" he said. "I'd wager that causes confusion."

Hal shook his head ruefully. "More than you might imagine," he said. He reached out and shook the fisherman's big, calloused hand. "Thanks for your help, Tyrell, and for taking the survivor off our hands."

"We seafarers have to look out for one another," the fisherman replied. "We'll take him back to the mainland when he's fully recovered."

Hal turned and heaved himself up over the ship's gunwale, then moved aft to the steering platform. Ulf and Wulf were already sorting their lines, he saw. "Port sail," he told them, as he passed. Without waiting for further orders, Stig and Ingvar set their shoulders against the bow of the ship, set their feet in the wet sand and heaved together. *Heron* stirred, came upright, then slid cleanly off into the water. As soon as she was afloat, Stig and Ingvar reached up to grab hold of the gunwale and hauled themselves aboard. Stefan and Jesper reached down to help them as they sprang upward.

Heron's momentum slid her smoothly back into the bay. Then, as Hal ordered the sail up, she began to swing slightly. The sail caught the wind and the movement increased, then she was slipping smoothly away from the shore as Ulf and Wulf trimmed the sail to catch the wind more efficiently. Hal kept her moving in a smooth curve until her bows were pointing out to sea. Then he ordered the sails trimmed and she accelerated away from Isle de Plessa, heading back toward the mainland.

"I'm wondering how long *Wolfwind* will keep attacking Gallican ports," Hal said as the command group gathered in the stern. Edvin had the helm so that Hal, Stig, Erak and Thorn could discuss their next move. During the remainder of the afternoon, they had seen three more towns that bore the mark of recent damage. They had approached the first, and had received a similar welcome—or non-welcome—as they had at the earlier ports. From then, Hal had decided they were wasting their time trying to enter the harbors. It was obvious that they would be repelled by the inhabitants.

"She's heading west," Erak said thoughtfully. "But where to exactly?"

"That's the question," Stig put in. "If we knew that, we could get ahead of her."

"And do what?" Erak asked.

Hal regarded him seriously. "We have to stop her," he reminded the Oberjarl.

But Erak snorted derisively. "How do you plan to do that? She probably has three to four times as many men as we do."

"True. But we have the Mangler," Hal said, indicating the huge crossbow mounted in the bow and covered by a tarpaulin. "That'll even the odds a little. Plus we can outsail her so we don't have to come to close quarters."

"You're not going to shoot that overgrown crossbow at my ship!" Erak said indignantly.

Hal shook his head wearily. "What do you expect us to do?" he asked. "You said yourself that we're outnumbered. We can't just sail up to her and board her—not with a dozen men. We'll have to use the Mangler to reduce their numbers. Or to disable to sink her."

"Sink her? You wouldn't dare sink her! She's my ship."

Hal regarded the angry Oberjarl calmly. Any skirl felt a deep emotional bond with his ship, and he could understand Erak's indignation, illogical as it might be.

"I'll build you a new one," he said.

chapter fourteen

Nearing the coast once more, they saw the familiar pyres of smoke rising from yet another coastal settlement.

"No point in looking closer," Hal said to Thorn and Stig. "We know what the reaction will be."

They continued west, seeing the evidence of *Wolfwind*'s passing at two more towns. But then the trail went cold. The next town was undamaged, with no sign of burnt warehouses or sunken ships. The next was the same. Hal and Thorn looked at each other, puzzled.

"He's stopped," Hal said. "Why?"

Thorn shrugged. Hal pointed the ship toward the harbor entrance. There was no sign of damage, but as in previous towns, an angry armed mob formed on the mole, brandishing weapons and yelling threats as they recognized *Heron* as a Skandian ship. Even though she wasn't a classic wolfship, the twin-sail *Heron* rig had become familiar throughout the Stormwhite in recent years.

"I'd say he's given up raiding coastal towns," Thorn said. "Word of the damage he's caused must have gone ahead of him, judging by the reception committee we just saw. Without the advantage of surprise, he'd find himself in trouble if he tried to enter the harbor."

"So where's he gone? What's he up to?" Hal asked.

There was a long silence. Then Stig, who had been a party to the conversation, spoke up.

"Maybe he's gone back to what he was originally doing," he said. "Attacking ships."

Hal considered the idea. "That makes sense," he said. "So I guess he would have headed north, away from the coastline. The news seems to have spread along here that he's raiding. If he's started taking ships, he'll want them to be unaware of what he's been up to."

"Northwest," Erak said, and when they all looked at him, he added, "If he does plan to take ships, he'll want a choke point—somewhere that shipping concentrates." He shrugged. "At least, that's what I did when I was raiding."

Thorn nodded. Like Erak, he remembered those days. "You're right," he said. "He'll look for somewhere the shipping concentrates. And that's the entrance to the Stormwhite—north of Cape Shelter. It's a narrow strait and ships come there from all directions—north, west and south. That's where I'd head if I were him."

Hal regarded the two older men. "Do I sense a certain nostalgia for the bad old days?" he asked.

Erak and Thorn looked back at him blankly.

"I have no idea what you're talking about," Erak said.

Thorn nodded. "Neither do I."

Hal sighed. But he suspected they were right, and their advice was born of long experience raiding and plundering in the Stormwhite. "Set a thief to catch a thief," he muttered, then gave orders to turn the ship northwest.

It was the following morning when they saw evidence that Erak and Thorn's theory was correct. Stefan was on the lookout perch and he called out a sighting of two ships to the north, heading toward them.

"Two sail!" he called, pointing in their direction. "Heading toward us . . . no, wait. They're turning away."

"Where are they heading?" Hal shouted.

Stefan hesitated before he answered, making sure he was right. "They're heading east," he replied. "Across wind."

It was their best move if they wanted to avoid *Heron*. The prevailing wind was still blowing steadily out of the north. Their change of course put it on their beam—usually a fast point of sailing for any ship. But *Heron* would be heading into the teeth of the wind if she were to intercept them.

Hal shaded his eyes and peered to the north. He could see them now—two vague, light-colored smudges on the horizon. That would be their sails, he knew. *Heron* was currently on a starboard tack, with the wind coming obliquely across her starboard bow. That meant she was heading away from the two ships. He shouted orders to bring her round to the port tack, then headed her to the east of the two ships. With *Heron*'s superior sailing qualities, that should let her intercept them.

"How are they rigged?" he asked. From his lower position, he couldn't see any details of their sail plan.

Stefan answered. "They're square-riggers," he yelled. Then he added, "Traders, by the look of them."

Hal nodded in satisfaction. If they were traders, they would be slow. Trading ships were built to hold as much cargo as possible. As a result, they were wide in the beam and heavy. In addition, they carried less sail area than an out-and-out warship like *Heron* or *Wolfwind*.

He closed one eye and studied the nearer of the two in relation to the port-side rigging. *Heron* was head-reaching on her. As the two ships moved, *Heron*'s path was drawing gradually ahead of the other ship. That meant, if everything else remained constant, they would intercept her within a few hours. He frowned thoughtfully. His instincts told him that *Heron* was not performing at her maximum.

"Sheet home a little," he ordered the twins. And, as they hardened the sail to the wind, he called, "Hold it at that." He sensed she was moving faster, and when he checked their progress against the other ship, he could see that they were still gaining on her.

Heron sped on, swooping up and over the rollers, then smashing down into the troughs behind them, sending spray showering high over the mast and sails to splatter down on the aft deck.

Within an hour, the ship was in clear sight from the deck. The second ship had born away to the north, seeing that *Heron* was heading for her companion.

Hal snorted. "Some friends," he said, as the further ship left their quarry to the mercy of the Skandian ship pursuing them so implacably.

"No sense in both of them being caught," Thorn replied, overhearing him. "It's the smart move."

They were closer now and could make out the pale blur of the faces on board the trader, as the crew watched the *Heron* bearing down on them. There were only four crew members and they had obviously decided that fighting wasn't an option. They were busy throwing stores and equipment overboard in an attempt to lighten their ship and squeeze a little extra speed out of her.

"They'll regret that when they find out we're friendly," Stig commented.

Hal shrugged. There was no way he could stop them doing what they were doing. But Stig was right. Once it transpired that *Heron* wasn't intent on taking them, the crew would regret jettisoning so much valuable material.

"Maybe they can collect some of it later," he said. Several objects could be seen bobbing in the trader's wake, although much of what was thrown overboard sank immediately.

Heron surged up closer to the trader. When they were twenty meters away, Hal brought her round to a parallel course and the twins spilled some of the wind out of the sail to bring her speed down, matching the other ship.

"Give them a call," Hal told Stig. "Tell them we're friends."

Stig moved to the port bulwark, stepped up onto it and called across to the trading ship. As he did, the men on board stopped jettisoning equipment—whether because they believed him when he claimed to be a friend or simply realized the inevitability of the fact that they couldn't escape from the trim little ship riding along-side them. Hal signaled for Edvin to take the helm and moved to the port side as well.

"Where are you going?" Thorn asked warily.

Hal indicated the other ship. "I'm going aboard her," he said.

Thorn glanced down critically at his belt. Hal wore only his saxe, which was as much a tool as a weapon. Hal saw the look, guessed what Thorn was thinking and forestalled any protest.

"If I go armed, they may well try to resist. If I'm unarmed, they'll see we mean them no harm."

"Or they'll see you're an easy target and they'll kill you," Thorn warned him, but Hal shrugged his caution away. Stig had tossed a line to the other ship, and on his orders, two of her crew were busy hauling the two craft together. They bumped lightly, rising and falling together on the swell.

Hal stepped up onto the port-side bulwark. The trader's railing was half a meter higher than *Heron*'s. He paused. "Permission to come board?" he asked.

The trader's skipper nodded curtly. "Come ahead," he said, and Hal stepped up onto the other ship. Stig followed a few seconds behind him, looking around warily, his hand on the hilt of his saxe.

"What are you doing?" Hal asked out of the side of his mouth.

"Keeping an eye on my foolhardy friend," Stig told him.

Hal shrugged. He didn't expect the trader's crew to show any sign of fight. But if they did, he decided he'd be glad of his big friend's presence. He glanced back at *Heron* and saw Thorn and Ingvar standing ready to board. A few meters away, Lydia fingered her atlatl, her left hand on one of the long darts, ready to load and let fly.

Aware that such preparations were obvious to the traders, Hal moved toward the skipper, standing by the tiller. He extended his hand in greeting. "Hal Mikkelson," he said. "Skirl of the *Heron*."

The other man took his hand. "Bryan Murtagh," he introduced himself. Then he indicated his own ship. "This is the *Faun*."

"Why did you run from us?" Hal asked. He kept his tone reasonable, without any hint of reproach.

The trader's skipper hesitated for a few seconds, then admitted, "We recognized you as a Skandian ship."

Hal tilted his head in inquiry. "So? Do you have any reason to avoid Skandian ships?" Over the past ten years, Skandian ships had been a welcome sight to traders on the Stormwhite. They were known to protect traders from predators and pirates.

But Murtagh pursed his lips, his eyebrows lowered into a scowl.

"We fell in with one yesterday," he said. "A big square-rigger. We let her come close and we soon realized that was a mistake."

chapter fifteen

Hal glanced at Stig. Erak and Thorn had obviously guessed right. *Wolfwind*, for it could only be her, had given up coastal raiding and taken to attacking ships. He looked back to the trading skipper.

"What happened?" he asked.

"There were four of us, out of Hibernia. We were sailing in convoy, with cargoes of leather, hides and some silver, bound for west Teutlandt. We came through the straits and sighted a ship, but as it was a Skandian, we let her come close.

"Before we knew what was happening, she had closed on the *Maid of Alourn*—the biggest ship in our convoy—and boarded her. There must have been fifty of the Skandians, and the *Maid* had a crew of only eight men. They were overwhelmed and their bodies thrown overboard. Once she was taken, the Skandians moved on to a second ship, *Fenian Lass*—"

"They weren't Skandians," Stig interrupted. "They were Iberian pirates."

Murtagh looked at him, disbelief in his eyes. "Whatever they were, we weren't staying around to argue the toss. The two of us . . ." He looked around for the other ship that had been with him. It was hull down on the horizon, and he sighed fatalistically before continuing.

"The two of us hauled our wind and headed south. It was late afternoon and the Skandians"—he gave Stig a challenging look—"or Iberians, if you insist, were busy ransacking the two bigger ships. By the time night fell, we had a handy lead." He paused, then added bitterly, "We saw flames in the night. Apparently, they burned both ships."

"Did you go back to look for survivors in the morning?" Hal asked.

Murtagh nodded. "There were none. We found a few charred timbers and a torn sail and yardarm floating nearby. The ships were gone—as were their crews."

"There was no sign of the wolfship?"

The Hibernian shook his head. "She was long gone. I have no idea where."

"Still, it took courage for you to go back and see. She could have been lying in wait." Hal gave the trader an admiring look, and the man shrugged.

"We were careful," he said. "We lowered our mast and sail and went under oars. That way, we were pretty sure we'd spot the wolfship before she saw us." He added angrily, "The men on those ships were friends of mine. We'd grown up together and sailed together for years."

Hal nodded. "Still, it took courage to do what you did," he said.

Murtagh regarded him with a stony gaze. He still wasn't convinced that the pirates had been anything but Skandians.

"You say they were Iberians?" he asked.

"We're pretty sure," Hal told him. "They raided Hallasholm several nights ago, wrecked the rest of our ships and stole *Wolfwind*—she was the one who attacked you. We're trying to track her down."

"I hope you do," the Hibernian said. "Although you'll have your work cut out taking her." He glanced meaningfully at the small ship tethered alongside his own.

"We'll manage," Hal said. "You have no idea where she headed after she sank the other ships?"

Murtagh shook his head. "As I said, it was dark by the time we got away, and we didn't see her again."

Hal paused, considering his next question, then asked, "Which direction did she come from when you first saw her?"

The reply was immediate. "From the north."

Hal rubbed his chin. "And you didn't see her when you doubled back the next day, so she didn't keep heading south."

Murtagh considered the statement. "She might have. We might have missed her in the dark. There was no moon last night."

"True. But we've come from the south and we didn't see her today. So the chances are she went back north." He was speaking to himself, but the trader chose to answer.

"Or east. Or west," he pointed out.

Hal sighed ruefully. "True. But I have to start somewhere. Thanks for the information, Bryan. I'm sorry about your friends. Is there anything we can do for you?"

"Just catch them and stop them," Murtagh told him. "Sink them or burn them. That's what they deserve." He added the last in a vengeful tone, and Hal nodded.

"I'll do what I can," he promised. He glanced around the ocean, where several of the abandoned cargo items could still be seen floating. "Maybe you should collect up as much of your cargo as you can," he suggested.

Murtagh followed his gaze and shrugged. "Didn't do much good throwing it overboard," he said. "You still caught us easily."

"*Heron*'s a fast ship," Hal told him. Then he gestured to Stig and turned toward the railing. "Let's get back aboard. We've still got hours of daylight, and we might catch sight of *Wolfwind*."

The Hibernian skipper accompanied them to the railing and shook hands again before they reboarded their own ship. Stefan and Jesper unlashed the rope that had held the two ships together. Ingvar fended off from the *Faun*, and Hal took the tiller once more, turning away from the trader in a long curve as *Heron* gathered speed. Thorn and Erak joined Hal at the steering platform while he outlined the conversation he had with the Hibernian.

"So you think he's gone north?" Erak asked.

Hal paused, then answered. "It's as good a guess as any."

The Oberjarl frowned. "But still a guess," he declared.

Hal regarded him with frustration. "It's an educated guess," he said. Then, seeing the Oberjarl was still unconvinced, he added, "What else can we do? We have to pick a direction and north is as good as any."

"Possibly better than most," Thorn said, and they all turned to look at him. "North puts him near the strait that leads from Cape

Shelter into the Stormwhite. And it also puts him close to the Sonderland coast."

"Is that a good thing?" Stig asked.

Thorn regarded him evenly. "I think so. After all, he'll need a base somewhere."

"A base? What sort of base?" Hal asked.

"Well, he'll hardly want to stay at sea indefinitely. He'll want to give his men a chance to relax. And he'll need to unload the cargoes he's stolen. On top of that, he'll need to carry out the usual repairs to the ship—frayed rigging, sprung planks, that sort of thing.

"So my guess is he'll want to set up some sort of permanent camp along the Sonderland coast. It's pretty well uninhabited, with dozens of coves he could put into. But it's close to the Stormwhite entrance and the trading ships coming through the strait."

"That makes sense," Erak said, pondering the idea. He looked at the younger men. "That's how we used to do things in the old days."

Hal raised his eyebrows at Stig. "It's handy having two former pirates in the crew, isn't it?"

Stig merely grinned in reply.

Yet in spite of Hal's cynicism, the more he thought about Thorn's idea, the more reasonable it became. Crews did make long journeys on wolfships, often staying at sea for weeks at a time. But there was no denying that a wolfship wasn't the most comfortable of vessels. They were built for speed and dash, not comfort. So it made sense that the Iberian captain, whoever he was, would organize some form of land base where his men could relax and recuperate in between raids.

And they would need to unload the plunder they took from the ships they intercepted. After all, wolfships weren't designed to carry large amounts of cargo.

"So . . . ," he said slowly, "you think somewhere along the Sonderland coast?"

"That's the most logical place," Thorn said.

Erak grunted agreement. "It'll be a big camp. After all, there are forty or fifty crew on board *Wolfwind*, and they'll probably have others in support—or even spare crew members. If they're here for a long stay, they'll have their women with them as well. And craftsmen to carry out running repairs on the ship."

They all knew that ships were in constant need of repair. Ropes broke or frayed, masts split. Sails blew out. And skilled craftsmen were needed to keep them all in good shape.

"So we're not just looking for half a dozen tents on the shore?" Stig asked.

Thorn shook his head. "Far from it. We'll be looking for a settlement of at least a hundred people. Maybe with huts as well as tents. And a secure anchorage to keep *Wolfwind* safe and hidden from sight."

"All we have to do is find it," Hal said.

chapter sixteen

But before they discovered her base on the Sonderland coast, they found *Wolfwind* herself.

The bright sunny weather of the past few days had changed to a misty overcast. Rain squalls chased each other across the gray, sullen rollers, and the wind had veered from due north to northeast. *Heron* continued her smooth, swooping passage, heading north. It was early in the afternoon when Lydia, who was taking a spell as lookout, called a sighting.

"Sail!" she shouted from the masthead. "Off the port bow." She paused, then added, "I think it might be *Wolfwind*!"

The crew had been relaxing at their sailing stations but the sudden call brought them all to their feet, peering over the port bow in the direction Lydia indicated.

But the ship wasn't in sight from the deck. Hal gestured to Stefan, who was standing by the foot of the mast expectantly.

"Get aloft, Stefan," he said. "See what you think."

It was no slur on Lydia. Stefan had the keenest eyesight on board the ship. And he had more experience than Lydia when it came to recognizing ships in the distance. He nodded once and scrambled up the lines to the lookout position at the top of the mast. Lydia moved over to make room for him and pointed out over the port bow, at an angle of forty-five degrees.

"She was over there," she told Stefan. "She's hidden by a squall at the moment. No! There she is!"

Stefan cupped his hands round his eyes to concentrate his vision. A tiny, dull white rectangle swam into sight through the haze, on the very edge of the horizon. "I see her," he said softly. Then, after some seconds, he came to a decision.

"Looks like *Wolfwind* all right," he called to Hal, glancing down at the upturned faces on deck below him, then returning quickly to his scrutiny of the distant ship. In truth, his identification of the ship was half instinctive. There was little detail visible and only her sail showed above the uneven, broken line of the horizon. But *Wolfwind* was a familiar ship to him. He had seen her and recognized her scores of times over the past years, and something about that sail was familiar. Exactly what it was, he couldn't have said. But he was a skilled and experienced lookout and he had learned to trust his instincts.

"What's her heading?" Hal shouted.

Again, Stefan took a moment or two to decide before he answered. "Looks like she's heading north of northwest. She's got the wind on her starboard beam."

On deck below, Hal considered the situation. He didn't want

Wolfwind to sight them. If the bigger ship knew she was being tailed, she might alter course to evade them. Worse still, she might turn back and charge downwind at them. And while Hal fully intended to engage her eventually, he wanted to do it on his own terms. He wasn't quite ready for an all-out battle with the bigger ship yet.

Stig moved to join him, guessing what was going through the skirl's mind.

"Lower the sail?" he suggested. "We can keep after her under oars . . ."

Hal thought for a few seconds more, then shook his head. "No. We're smaller than she is, and our sail is a good deal smaller as well. If we can just see her, it's a good chance she hasn't seen us yet. All the same . . ."

As he spoke, he leaned on the tiller so that *Heron* bore away to starboard, on a diverging course from the wolfship. He braced the tiller with his elbow and cupped his left hand round his mouth to call to the masthead.

"Tell me when she's out of sight!"

Stefan, his eyes fixed on the distant sail, waved a hand in acknowledgment. Then, after a pause, he called out. "She's gone! Still on the same course, but she's dropped below the horizon."

Hal nodded to himself, then turned to Stig. "We'll hold this course for five minutes, then swing back until she's in sight again."

After he judged five minutes had passed, he eased *Heron* back to port and she surged after the wolfship. Some ten minutes later, Stefan and Lydia both called a warning.

"Sail! She's back!"

"Still on the same course?" Hal asked. Stefan replied in the affirmative. Hal called an order to the twins, telling them to ease the sheets so that *Heron* lost speed. After several minutes, Stefan confirmed that *Wolfwind*'s sail could no longer be seen.

Hal kept *Heron* plowing after *Wolfwind* at her reduced speed. Then, after another wait, he called to the twins to sheet home again and accelerated after the other ship. Ten minutes later, he was rewarded with another sighting from the masthead. Again, he immediately reduced speed and let the other ship sail out of sight.

"We'll play cat and mouse with her while daylight lasts," he told Stig.

His first mate nodded agreement. "And when it's dark?" he asked.

"We'll move closer. It looks like she's staying on one consistent heading, so we should be able to keep in touch with her during the night."

"You're not planning to attack her?" Stig asked. He knew that sooner or later, they would have to fight the other ship. To his mind, sooner was better.

But Hal pursed his lips and shook his head. "Not yet. She'd see us coming and be ready for us. When we do fight her, I want to take her by surprise."

"That makes sense." Stig grinned at his friend. Hal was a planner, he knew. A tactician who appreciated the value of surprise in battle—unlike his first mate, who shared Erak and Thorn's tendency to go bullheaded at the enemy at the first opportunity.

And so the day went on, with *Wolfwind* drifting in and out of sight as *Heron* alternately slowed and sped up again. After the initial excitement of sighting the bigger ship died away, the crew gradually relaxed, their interest only stirred by the regular calls from the masthead as *Wolfwind* appeared and disappeared on the horizon. After several hours, Jesper and Ingvar relieved the twins on the halyards and braces that controlled the sails. The twins, who had been on duty for three hours, relaxed on the benches in the rowing wells. Edvin served them a cold meal—Hal had forbidden his lighting a cook fire.

As the routine continued, and with nothing to do, Ulf and Wulf became bored. And, as ever when they were bored, they began yet another of their meaningless conversations. By now, the rest of the crew knew that they only began these conversations in order to disagree with each other. As Ingvar had once observed: "I swear, Ulf only says, 'It's a nice day,' so that Wulf will say, 'It's night and it's raining.'"

"Who do you think Ingvar will ask to be his best man?" Ulf asked.

Wulf, finishing his meal, thought for a few seconds. "He might ask me," he said, and his brother frowned at him.

"You?" he said. "Why would he ask you?"

"Because I am," Wulf said smugly.

"You are what?"

"The best man. Mam said so." Wulf enjoyed telling his brother that, as far as their mother was concerned, he was the favored son.

"I never heard her say that," Ulf told him.

"Of course not. She didn't want to hurt your feelings. She asked me not to tell you, as a matter of fact."

"But you just did," Ulf pointed out.

Wulf shrugged. "You tricked me into it."

His brother seized on the statement triumphantly. "How could I trick you if you're the best man?"

"Actually, if we're talking about just the two of us, I'm the better man," Wulf told him, sliding off the point, as he was wont to do. Ulf snorted, and Wulf continued. "It's only if we're talking about the whole crew that I become the best man."

"So you're saying you're the best man in this crew?" Ulf wanted to know. When Wulf said nothing, he went on. "Better than Hal? Better than Stig?" He paused, then delivered the ultimate challenge. "Better than Thorn?"

"No. I'm not saying that," Wulf said, and when Ulf snorted derisively, he amended: "I'm saying Mam said it."

There was silence between them for several minutes. Then Ulf picked up the subject once more. "So if you're saying you're the best man—"

"I'm not saying it. I'm saying Mam says it," Wulf corrected him.

Ulf glared at his twin and tried again. "So, if Mam says you're the best man . . ." He waited to see if Wulf would challenge that statement, and when he didn't, Ulf continued. "Why hasn't Ingvar asked you?"

"He probably doesn't want to offend Hal. Hal probably expects to be best man—even if he's not," Wulf said quickly. He'd had that answer ready for some time.

Ulf seized on the statement. "But Hal will be conducting the ceremony. After all, he's the ship's skirl. He can perform weddings."

Wulf shook his head. "Skirls can't perform weddings. That's an old wives' tale."

"Who says?" Ulf challenged, but again Wulf was ready with the reply.

"Several old wives," he said. "Presumably ones who weren't married by a skirl."

Ingvar had been leaning back against the bulwark a few meters away, waiting for Hal's next order to reduce speed. Much as he would have liked to avoid listening to the conversation, it had been impossible to ignore. He turned to glare at the two brothers.

"Any moment now, Hal's going to want to slow down again," he said.

The twins looked at him, frowning.

"So?" Wulf asked after several seconds.

"So when he does, I'm planning on using one of you as a sea anchor," Ingvar told him pleasantly. And since previous experience told the twins that it was more than possible he would carry out the threat, they decided it might be better if they fell silent.

For now, at least.

chapter seventeen

Night fell, and as darkness spread over the sea, Hal moved *Heron* a little closer to their quarry.

Wolfwind lay to the west of them, which meant she held the dying light a few minutes longer than *Heron* did. *Heron* was in the relative darkness to the east and he reasoned there was small risk of being seen if they moved closer.

His intention was to verify *Wolfwind*'s speed and direction—to ascertain that she was continuing to head north, and doing so at the same speed. Some ships, he knew, tended to slow down at night—although he doubted that *Wolfwind* would do so. It was a practice generally confined to trading ships, not warships. However, he needed to make sure.

He had spent the last few hours alternately slowing and speeding up to keep the other ship under periodic observation, so he had no accurate idea of the other ship's speed. Now he planned to maintain a constant gap between them for several minutes to determine how fast she was traveling. Once he was reasonably sure of that, he would drop back a little, maintaining that speed and course while he remained out of sight, and keep pace with her through the night.

Wolfwind's skipper made things easier for him by having a small lantern lit on the aft deck. It was normal practice for a ship traveling at night, although, of course, Hal wasn't about to do it. Small as it was, the light was clearly visible in the growing darkness, reflecting off the big square sail in front of it. Hal watched it carefully, calling instructions to the twins, who were back on sail-handling duty, until the two ships were moving at the same speed and *Heron* was maintaining a constant distance from the big square-rigger.

Then he slowed for a few minutes, allowing that dim distant light to disappear over the horizon. Once that happened, he increased speed to match the wolfship once more. After some time, Thorn came aft to relieve him on the wheel.

"So long as she maintains her course and speed, we should be able to catch up with her again tomorrow," Hal said.

Thorn nodded. "Don't forget we'll have the light behind us at dawn, and she'll still be in darkness," he said. When the sun came up, of course, their positions would be reversed, with *Heron* catching the light first, while *Wolfwind* remained in shadow.

In the hour after midnight, a light rain began to fall and the wind dropped. Hal, who had been napping under his sheepskin and tarpaulin, woke instantly as the ship's motion changed. He threw back the covers and rose, moving to stand by Thorn, who had the tiller. The moon was low in the northeast, its light haloed and diffused by the moisture in the air.

"What do you want to do?" Thorn asked.

Hal peered ahead through the darkness. He could make out the shapes of Stefan and Jesper in the sail-handling positions. They too had sensed the alteration in *Heron*'s speed and were alert for any changes he might order.

He looked up at the telltale. It was stirring slightly in the reduced wind, but the wind direction was the same as it had been.

"We'll keep her as she is," he said, coming to a decision. "The wind will be the same for *Wolfwind*. So if we change nothing, we should maintain our relative position."

"More or less," Thorn said. They both knew that the two ships would react differently to the reduced wind speed. Chances were that *Heron*, being the lighter of the two, was overtaking and creeping up on *Wolfwind*. The uncertainty formed a tight ball of apprehension in the pit of his stomach.

"More or less," he agreed. "We'll heave to an hour before dawn, just in case. Wake me then," he said and turned back to his bed.

Not that he would sleep, he knew. The fear that they might well be creeping closer and closer to *Wolfwind* loomed large in his mind. Yet there was little else he could do. If he slowed down or hove to, there was a good chance that they would lose touch with the stolen wolfship. The more he thought about it, the more he realized that the course he had chosen was the correct one. It was risky and it depended on a lot of guesswork. But it was still their best choice if they were to stay in contact with *Wolfwind*.

The light rain pattered down on his face as he lay on his back, staring up at the sky. Only a few stars were visible, showing dimly through breaks in the cloud cover. He was conscious of a low mutter of conversation.

"I asked Erak," said Ulf. "He told me Hal."

The two brothers were off duty and, by rights, should have been sleeping. But they too had sensed the change in conditions and were expecting to be called to the halyards and braces any moment.

"He told you Hal what?" Wulf said, a little testily. He had a good idea what his brother was talking about and he was always annoyed when Ulf found an alternative source of information. It made it so much more difficult to bamboozle him.

"He told me Hal is going to be best man. Hal and Stig."

"How can you have two best men?" Wulf queried. "Only one can be best. The other has to be second best."

"Well then, Hal is going to be best man, and Stig is going to be second best."

"If you ask me, that's just plain greedy," Wulf said. "Most people are happy with one best man. What's Thorn going to be?"

"He's going to give the bride away."

"Who's he giving her to?" Wulf demanded.

Ulf grinned in the darkness. He always enjoyed being able to correct his brother. Wulf could be so pedantic, he thought. "You mean, *to whom is he going to give her,*" he said, adding in a lofty tone, "You can't end a sentence with a prepojunction."

"I can end a sentence with anything I choose," Wulf declared belligerently. He sensed he was losing ground in this conversation but couldn't see how to regain the initiative.

"I assume he's giving her away to Ingvar," Ulf said.

"But he doesn't own her, does he? How can he give her away if he doesn't own her?" Wulf challenged.

"It's just what people say," Ulf said. His voice was uncertain. He sensed he was on shaky ground. But Wulf sensed the doubt behind the statement and pounced on it.

"Are you saying people say Thorn owns Lydia?" he challenged.

"No. He's going to give her away. It's what people say about the bride's father. And Thorn is standing in loco parentis."

"Hah!" Wulf snorted derisively. "You'd better not let Lydia hear you saying her parents were crazy! She mightn't like that."

"I'm not saying her parents were crazy. *In loco parentis* is an old Toscan term. It means . . ." He hesitated, not sure what it meant, then improvised, "It means *the parent who gives her away.* I guess because you'd have to be crazy to give away a girl like Lydia."

"And what about Lydia herself?" Wulf asked, changing tack. He knew that was an effective way of confusing his brother.

But for once Ulf was up to the trick. He allowed himself a superior smile. "I believe she's going to be the bride," he said.

Wulf shook his head, irritated. "I don't mean what's she going to be. If Ingvar has two best men—"

"A best man and a second-best man," Ulf corrected him.

Wulf gave an annoyed gesture that pushed the correction aside. "What is Lydia going to have? Aside from loco parents?"

"Well," said Ulf, then hesitated. He hadn't asked about that. "Usually a bride has bridesmaids."

"Who would they be? She doesn't have any close friends. Not girlfriends, anyway."

He was right, Ulf realized. Lydia hadn't grown up in Hallasholm, so she didn't have any girls who were longtime companions. She wasn't a particularly gregarious type—her time spent as a hunter and tracker made her a somewhat solitary person. And her position as a member of the elite Heron brotherband and her reputed warrior skills made her a figure held in some awe—even apprehension—by the young women of Hallasholm. As a result, her friends tended to be limited to the Herons.

"That's right," Ulf agreed. Now that he thought about it, he couldn't think of any of the girls in Hallasholm whom Lydia might ask.

"So, maybe we could do that," Wulf said.

Ulf frowned, now thoroughly confused. "Do what?"

"Be her bridesmaids. I'd hate to see her go without," Wulf said.

And to that suggestion, Ulf couldn't find a reply.

chapter eighteen

Fog.

During the night, the wind had veered further, until it was from the south, bringing warmer air with it.

The rise in temperature reacted with the moisture-laden atmosphere so that when daylight came, *Heron* was moving slowly through a dense white fog. The wind had dropped to a gentle whisper that wasn't strong enough to disperse the clinging white mantle surrounding them.

Hal was at the tiller. He had taken up the position an hour before dawn, although in these conditions, there was no sign of sunrise—just the gradual lightening that spread through the glaucous mass enveloping them.

Overside, the sea was an oily black. The weight of the fog seemed to press down on the ocean surface and suppress the waves, although Hal knew that was a false impression. It was more due to the lack of wind.

The sails flapped and slatted as the wind came and went. Moisture condensed on the sail and spars and rigging and fell to the deck in heavy drops. From the tiller, Hal could only just make out the forward third of the ship, and the shadowy figures who moved on the deck.

Naturally, there was no sign of *Wolfwind.*

A faint gust stirred the sail, and *Heron* surged forward, suddenly emerging into a patch of clear water, surrounded by the drifting fog on all sides. Then she was back in the all-embracing whiteness again, the water gurgling softly down her flanks.

And so it continued. They would grope their way through the fog for several kilometers, then emerge into a clear patch, only to plunge into the next bank of translucent vapor, which would close quickly about them, obscuring all vision.

Tension on board *Heron* grew, with the entire crew, even those off watch, lining the rails and staring into the thick whiteness that enclosed them. Then, as they emerged into clear water once more, all eyes would scan the surrounding ocean, anxiously seeking the first sign of the ship they had pursued through the night.

"Of course," Thorn said to Hal as they came out into clear water for the fifth time, "*Wolfwind* may well be behind us. We could easily have gone past her in the night."

Hal spun quickly at the words to scan the clear patch of water behind them. His breath came more freely when he saw nothing there. He was also bedeviled by the realization that they may have strayed off course during the darkness. There was no way of checking their direction now, as the sun was invisible. They could be sailing on a diverging course from *Wolfwind* and never know it. The only way he had of controlling their direction was to keep the wind—what little there was of it—astern of them.

The tension wasn't eased by the fact that they had virtually no warning as to when they would emerge into the clear. One minute they would be enshrouded by the fog, the next, they would sail out into open water, with visibility suddenly expanding to a wide area on all sides. The sudden emergence into the light hit them like a physical force. Each time it happened, they scanned the surrounding ocean nervously, looking for a sign of *Wolfwind*.

And each time, they were disappointed.

"How long do you think this will keep up?" Hal asked Thorn. The old sea wolf had taken up a permanent position by the steering platform, and Hal readily deferred to his years of seagoing experience.

Thorn shrugged. "Depends on the wind. Until it freshens, this muck is going to stay with us. And if it stays like this, gusting and stopping, gusting and stopping, the fog will . . . There she is!"

The cry came as they emerged from the fog into open water.

Thorn threw up his left arm, pointing to a dim shape off their starboard bow as it slipped between two banks of fog. It was only there for a few seconds, then the gray-white mass swallowed it.

"She's under oars," Hal said. He had noted that *Wolfwind*'s mast was bare and she had six oars deployed on either side, keeping her moving smoothly through the water.

"Wind's too light to move her beyond a crawl," Thorn said.

They kept their eyes glued to the spot where the ship had disappeared, straining for another glimpse of her. But there was nothing, just the rolling bank of fog coming ever closer to them. From the crew forward, a low murmur of conversation told them that the rest of the Herons had spotted *Wolfwind* as well. Jesper, perched on the forward gunwale behind the bow post, turned to relay the news. But Hal waved a hand to indicate that they had seen the other ship. He didn't want Jesper shouting out a sighting. Sound traveled a long way through fog, and he didn't want to take the chance that the crew of *Wolfwind* might hear them and become aware of the lithe shape sliding along behind them.

"Think she saw us?" Hal asked.

His friend shrugged. "She was only there for a few seconds. And we're a lot smaller than she is. I doubt it."

"She's head-reached on us during the night," Hal commented. The previous night, *Wolfwind* had been off their port bow. Now she was lying to starboard. Their relative positions had changed during the hours of darkness.

"She may have changed course," Thorn said. "Or we drifted off ours."

"Well, we've found her again," Hal said. He eased the tiller so that *Heron*'s bow swung to starboard, heading for the last spot where he had seen *Wolfwind*. When he judged she was more or less directly ahead, he brought the ship back to port. Once more, the white mass closed around them as they slipped into the fog bank.

"This is eerie," Thorn said uncomfortably.

Hal glanced at him. It was unusual for Thorn to show any sign of tension, he thought. But this slipping in and out of the fog, never knowing what they were going to find waiting for them, was nerve-racking in the extreme.

They glided on through the dimness. This bank of fog was one of the largest they had experienced so far. Hal's imagination worked overtime. He kept feeling they were catching up to *Wolfwind*—that any moment now they would run upon her in fog—although common sense told him that, under the impetus of twelve oars, she would be moving faster than they could.

Nevertheless, he set the crew to listening at the bow, and he and Thorn ceased their own desultory conversation in order to hear.

Once, he thought he heard a man's voice calling out, and he looked quickly around his companions. But nobody else seemed to have heard the sound. Then he was sure he could hear the sound of oars grinding in rowlocks. But again, he seemed to be the only one who had heard it and he shook his head dismissively.

For once, the transition into clear air was not as sudden as it had been. The fog thinned around them, and they slipped out into clear water and bright light. Blinking at the brightness, Hal was horrified to see *Wolfwind*, barely four hundred meters away and directly in front of them. She was a good fifty meters from the next bank of fog as *Heron* emerged into the open water behind her.

There was no time to turn or retreat back the way they had come. They could only continue on, hoping against hope that the crew on *Wolfwind* hadn't seen them.

Heart in mouth, Hal watched as the big wolfship slowly slipped into the next wall of fog, her shape gradually dimming until she had disappeared.

"Heave to," Hal called quietly to Ulf and Wulf, and they

released the sheets, spilling the faint wind so that the ship slid quietly to a stop. He glanced at Thorn. "We'll give her a chance to get ahead of us again," he said.

The one-armed warrior nodded agreement.

"Think they saw us?" Hal asked for the second time.

Thorn could only shake his head uncertainly. "If they didn't, their lookouts need keel hauling," he said.

Belatedly, Hal realized that all their attention had been focused on what lay ahead of them. He took a quick glance over the stern now to make sure there was no danger lurking behind. Thorn noticed the action and frowned. He had been just as guilty as Hal—and his years of experience meant he had less excuse for the mistake.

"Not that we thought anyone was following *us*," he said.

But Hal shook his head angrily. "It's the enemy you don't see that gets you."

Thorn raised his eyebrows and agreed.

Several minutes passed as they lay rocking on the gentle, oily swell. Then, when he judged *Wolfwind* had regained her lead, Hal signaled to the twins to sheet home and *Heron* ghosted smoothly forward once more, slipping into the dampness of the fog.

As before, they set to listening. This time, Hal thought to himself, If I think I hear oars up ahead, I'll act on it.

But he heard nothing, just the creak of the ropes in the blocks, the gurgle of water down their sides and the slatting sound of the sail as it alternately caught and spilled the uncertain, fluky wind. Once, he thought he felt the breeze freshen slightly and he squinted up at the telltale, just visible in the gloomy white light.

It streamed out once, then drooped as the gust of wind took it, then let it fall. He cursed under his breath. They needed the wind. Under oars, *Heron* was no match for a full-sized wolfship.

Bright light flooded over them as they sailed out of the fog bank into a large stretch of open water. The sun must be burning the fog off, Hal thought. At the same time, he cast a nervous glance at the next bank of fog, a kilometer away. There was no sign of *Wolfwind*. His ruse of heaving to for several minutes must have allowed her to regain her lead. He relaxed, letting out a long-held breath as he checked the telltale once more. He thought the wind might be freshening and . . .

"There she is!"

Several voices echoed the warning from the bows, and he looked down in time to see *Wolfwind*, oars thrashing the water to foam, as she burst out of the fog bank, heading straight for them.

chapter nineteen

There was no time to turn back into the fog behind them. They were in an open patch several kilometers wide, with nowhere to hide. *Wolfwind* was slightly off their port bow, charging down on them with a bone in her teeth. Spray flew from her oars as they beat the water.

Hal threw the tiller over and swung *Heron* to starboard, away from the oncoming wolfship. *Heron* moved a little faster as the wind came abeam, her best point of sail. But the bigger ship was still outpacing her. Hal hoped he'd been right, and that the wind was picking up. It might disperse the fog, but it would give them the speed and maneuverability they needed to avoid *Wolfwind*.

He looked up at the sail, checking to see whether it was set for maximum performance. He half opened his mouth to call to the twins to sheet home further but he could see that they needed no such urging. *Heron* was moving as fast as she could in the light wind that blew from the south.

But that wasn't fast enough. *Wolfwind* was moving faster and narrowing the gap between the two ships. She had swung to port to intercept *Heron* and the two ships were racing to converge at an invisible point on the ocean.

Out to starboard, Hal could see a ruffle of wind on the water. He prayed it was more than a momentary gust, that it signified a strengthening wind. He looked back at *Wolfwind*. She was closer than before, barely two hundred meters away. It was going to be close. If they could reach that patch of wind, and if it remained constant, they would have the speed they needed to escape. *Wolfwind*'s crew had been rowing through the night and they couldn't keep up their current muscle-numbing pace indefinitely. If *Heron* could just stay ahead of her for a few more minutes . . .

If, if, if.

"She's getting closer," Thorn warned him—unnecessarily.

"I know," he replied, his voice tight. His eyes darted between the ship pursuing them and that ruffle of wind on the water. Then to the spot on the sea where their two courses would intersect. He thought *Heron* was going to reach the point first. But he couldn't be sure.

The ruffle was still there. And it seemed to be growing stronger.

But *Wolfwind* was now only fifty meters away and he could see the crowd of armed men in her bow, waving weapons and shouting threats and abuse at the little ship in front of them.

Stig had ordered the crew to unsling their shields from the pegs that held them along the ship's sides. They crouched in the rowing wells, covered by the big, round shields. An arrow zipped overhead and hit the tip of the yardarm, spinning off and dropping into the sea.

"Hope they don't have too many of them," Thorn muttered. He fetched the man-high rectangular wooden shield Hal had constructed. He slid it into the brackets that held it in position and Hal crouched behind it.

None too soon. He heard another arrow thud into the shield and instinctively winced. It was a common tactic to aim for the helmsman in a pursuit, and he was glad he had thought to construct the big shield.

"You'd better take cover," he told Thorn. The old sea wolf didn't have one of the cartwheel-sized shields that the other crewmembers used. In battle, he depended on a small, bowl-sized shield on his left hand, relying on his reflexes and hand speed to ward off attacks. In this situation, that wouldn't give him any protection.

Another arrow zipped overhead. Thorn watched it skate off the mast and fly into the sea. He moved into the stern and crouched down by the sternpost. From there, he was covered from the archers behind them.

Now a volley of arrows rained down on *Heron*. Hal heard two more strike the shield behind him while others slammed into the deck farther forward, by the mast. He could see Jesper and Stefan covering the twins with their shields as Ulf and Wulf crouched by the sheets, ready to respond to Hal's orders. Stefan's shield was already bristling with three arrows. As Hal watched, he snapped them off and tossed them overboard.

Hal chanced a look behind, peering out from beside the large shield that protected him. His heart rose in his mouth as he saw how close *Wolfwind* had come. She was barely twenty meters behind them, the bow wave fanning out on either side as she cut through the water. He made out at least four men armed with bows in the bow of the ship, with others crammed around them, yelling defiance and threats at the Skandians.

He looked to starboard. The patch of disturbed water was still forty meters away. It was going to be close.

Lydia was crawling aft in the port-side rowing well. She had her quiver slung over her shoulder and stopped just short of the steering platform, protected by the side of the ship and the big timber panel behind Hal's position.

"Do you want me to take some of those shooters out?" she called softly. She started to rise, ready to move onto the raised central deck. But Hal took one hand from the tiller and waved her down again.

"Stay under cover!" he warned her. "At this range, they'd be almost certain to hit you!"

As deadly as the atlatl was, it had one major drawback. To launch a dart, Lydia would have to expose herself entirely to the archers behind them. Hal wasn't ready to let her risk her life that way. The arrows were a problem, but not an insurmountable one. For the moment, the crew were safe behind their protective shields.

Another volley of arrows struck the timber behind him. The increase in their force, and the louder noise as they struck, told him that *Wolfwind* had closed the range even further. He risked another look and panic nearly seized him. *Wolfwind* was barely ten meters away from *Heron*'s stern, rising and falling in her wake, with the water between the two ships seething. The shouting, threatening crew on her bow saw him and redoubled their insults and battle cries. He ducked back into cover and an arrow sped past, flashing through the space where his head had been only seconds before.

He ground his teeth in frustration. If only they could hit back, he thought. But their major weapon, the Mangler, was useless in this position. It covered an arc of 180 degrees around the bow. With the enemy dead astern, there was no way he could bring it to bear.

There was a loud clatter, followed by a scraping sound, from the deck beside him. He looked across and saw a three-pronged grapnel sliding back toward the stern, with a hemp rope trailing from it. Obviously, one of the Iberians on *Wolfwind*'s bow had thrown it.

As he watched, one of the sharpened prongs caught in a cleat on the deck and held fast. The line grew taut as their pursuers began to haul it in. He sensed a slackening in *Heron*'s speed as the extra drag came on. Catching Thorn's eye, he gestured to the grapnel. Thorn nodded and scuttled out from his hiding place, his saxe in his left hand. The blade flashed once and the line sprang loose, recoiling over the rail as the tension was released. Hal felt a corresponding surge in *Heron*'s speed.

An arrow flashed down at Thorn, grazing his arm and leaving a bloody welt. He cursed and scrambled back into cover, at the same time as he hurled the grapnel overhand back toward the ship behind them. Hal heard a cry of pain and risked another quick look. Thorn's blind throw had been effective. A man tumbled off the bow of the big ship, falling into the sea and being driven under by her plunging forefoot.

"Are you all right?" Hal called.

Thorn shook his head in disgust. He was busy wrapping his scarf around the wounded arm, pulling it tight between his hook and his teeth. He released the grip with his teeth for a second to call back.

"A scratch. Nothing more."

Hal felt a sudden surge under his feet as *Heron* sailed into the patch of disturbed water and found the freshening breeze. The sail *whoomph*ed out, filling suddenly and then hardening as the twins hauled in on the sheets. The effect was instantaneous. *Heron,* her sail full and drawing, leapt forward like a spurred horse. From for'ard, he heard a cheer from his beleaguered crew as their ship pulled away from the straining wolfship behind them.

Hal risked another glance. *Wolfwind* was falling back. The gap between the two ships was widening as *Heron,* the wind abeam, accelerated briskly. Twenty meters, then fifty. Almost at the same time, he saw the ship's rowing rate falter, then slow, as the exhausted oarsmen realized they had lost their chance.

Belatedly, the crew of *Wolfwind* began to raise her square sail, but it was too late. *Heron* was gathering speed as the wind freshened, leaving the wolfship in her wake and powering across the clear path of water toward the distant fog bank.

For a moment or two, Hal considered going about and running down on *Wolfwind* so he could punish her with a few shots from the Mangler. He could still remember the feeling of panic and the sense of helplessness as the bigger ship had moved ever closer to them, and the temptation to make them pay for that fear was strong.

But he discarded the idea. They had come within a centimeter of disaster and they'd been lucky to escape. It would be foolish to chance their luck now for the sake of doing some damage to *Wolfwind* and her crew. The wind was steady enough, but who knew how long that would hold? If he turned back, the wind could drop or die completely and he could easily find himself becalmed once more, and at the mercy of the other ship.

In such a case, he knew, the exhausted rowers would find new heart and new energy, and the *Heron* and her crew would be overwhelmed.

No. It was better not to tempt fate now. Better to wait until conditions were in their favor and they could be certain of the wind and weather while they used *Heron*'s speed and agility to defeat the other ship.

Better to wait till he had a plan of action, not an improvised attack that could go belly-up in an instant.

He looked over his shoulder at the fast-receding wolfship. Arrows had continued to clatter down on *Heron* as she made her escape, but now he saw the final volley fall into the sea twenty meters behind them. Gradually, the crew emerged from their hiding places, grinning and slapping one another on the back. Lydia rose from the rowing well and moved to join Hal at the steering oar, as Thorn made his way from his refuge under the sternpost.

"That was close," Lydia said. She reached down and untied the rough bandage around Thorn's arm, refastening it more securely and neatly than he could manage with his hook and his teeth. He nodded his gratitude to her.

"Too damn close," Hal agreed. He looked astern, to where *Wolfwind* continued to fall behind. The strengthening wind was finally dispersing the fog, blowing it to shreds that drifted across the water, then dispersed. In these conditions, they could easily outsail *Wolfwind,* and eventually the pirates realized it. When Hal looked again, the captured wolfship had turned away and was heading back the way she had come.

An hour later, she was out of sight.

chapter twenty

Hal continued to steer *Heron* south for an hour after *Wolfwind* disappeared, then he turned and cruised west at a reduced pace. The fog had dispersed, banished by the sun and the freshening wind, and the sea was clear of any other shipping.

Eventually, he handed the tiller over to Edvin and called a council of war with Thorn, Stig, Erak and Lydia. They sat on the deck by the steering platform. Hal had fetched a chart of the western section of the Stormwhite and it was rolled up on the deck beside him.

"So, what do we do now?" Thorn asked. There was a pause while all eyes turned to Hal. He was the skirl, after all. He was also their best tactician and planner. He looked around the circle of faces and took the lead.

"*Wolfwind* was heading northwest when we first sighted her, and she continued on that course when she gave up the chase this morning. I suggest we head in the same direction."

"And try to take her?" Erak said scornfully. "How do you propose we do that? Her crew outnumber us by at least four to one."

Hal nodded agreement. "I certainly don't want to run into her again until we can come up with a way to reduce the odds against us," he said. "What I had in mind was to look for her base on the Sonderland coast."

"And then what?" Stig asked.

"Then I suggest we go ashore down the coast a little and go back overland to reconnoiter. Presumably, her crew must go ashore at some time. That would give us the chance to retake her. Otherwise . . ." He paused, knowing how his next statement would be taken by the Oberjarl.

Erak looked at him suspiciously. "Otherwise what?"

Hal continued reluctantly. "Otherwise, we might have to sink her, or burn her."

Erak leapt to his feet, his face flushed. "Burn her? You're not burning *Wolfwind*! She's my ship!"

Thorn reached up and placed a hand on Erak's arm, pulling the angry man back down to the deck. "Sit down, Erak. And calm down. That'd be a last resort. Nobody here wants to burn *Wolfwind*."

Erak resumed his seat on the deck. But he remained glaring at Hal. "She's my ship," he repeated, and the younger man nodded. Hal remembered the heartbreak he had felt when he lost his former ship, the original *Heron*.

"I know how you feel, Erak," he said in a conciliatory tone.

"And I promise that would be the last resort, as Thorn says. But we can't allow her to go on raiding and marauding. And as you say, her crew outnumbers us by at least four to one."

"I'm sure Hal will find another way," Stig put in.

Once again, all eyes turned on Hal. He sighed inwardly. Their faith in him was touching, he thought. He knew he had a reputation as a tactician and planner and he could see that the others all assumed he would come up with a way to redress the difference in numbers. But he had to admit that, at the moment, he had no idea how his little ship could defeat the mighty *Wolfwind.* He addressed Erak directly with his next remarks.

"You've got to accept that we'll have to damage her if we do fight her," he warned. "Our main advantage will be to use the Mangler against her and that'll mean we'll damage her—perhaps seriously."

Erak nodded reluctantly. He could see that it would be impossible for his ship to emerge unscathed from a battle with *Heron.* "Just don't talk about burning her," he warned, and Hal made a small gesture of agreement.

Lydia spoke for the first time. Usually, she was quiet during these meetings. But when she did speak, she showed a great deal of common sense. "All that is beside the point," she said. "The first thing we have to do is locate this base. How do you propose we do that?"

Hal reached forward and unrolled the chart of the Sonderland coast. He used his saxe to keep the chart from rolling up again, and Stig placed his own on the opposite side.

"First thing, we head northwest. That's where *Wolfwind* was going most of yesterday and again this morning when she broke off the chase." He leaned forward and traced a line on the chart with his forefinger, heading northwest to the Sonderland coast.

"There are cliffs all along the coast here," he said. "And plenty of unoccupied bays and inlets where the pirates might have set up their camp. All we have to do is find the right one."

"A little bit like looking for a needle in a haystack," Stig observed.

Hal looked at him. "Not really. After all, we know the rough direction *Wolfwind* was heading. Assuming she maintained that course, she'll hit the coast around here." He pointed again, indicating a spot on the Sonderland coast that seemed remote from any towns or large settlements. "The area is pretty sparsely inhabited, so I suggest we stay out to sea in daylight, then come in closer at night, looking for this base Thorn and Erak say they will have set up."

"Why by night?" Stig asked. He shrugged. "I mean, I can see that'll make it harder for them to see us. But won't the reverse be true as well?"

It was Lydia who answered, before Hal could speak.

"Fires," she said. "They'll have campfires and cook fires alight. And since we know where any towns or villages are"—she indicated several marked on the chart—"if we see the glow of fires in any other place, that'll probably be what we're looking for." She glanced at Hal. "Am I right?"

Hal nodded. "Spot on. The fires from a big camp will show up for miles around. It'll make our job a lot easier. And, as Stig points out, we stand less chance of being seen from the shore."

They were all staring at the chart, seeing in their mind's eye the way a large campfire would appear from the sea—and how far it would be visible.

"So, let's say we locate their base," Thorn asked. "What do we do then?"

"We find an inlet close by where we can put ashore without being seen," Hal replied. "Then three or four of us trace our way back along the coast to take a good long look at the campsite. And from there, we come up with a plan of action."

And from there, *I* come up with a plan of action, he thought to himself.

There was a long pause while they all considered this, then Thorn spoke. "Sounds fair enough to me. How about the rest of you?"

There was a chorus of agreement from the others. Then Erak was heard to say in the ensuing silence: "Just so long as you don't burn my ship."

They sailed on for the rest of the day, maintaining the same northwest course that *Wolfwind* had been following when they first sighted her. By late afternoon, the coast of Sonderland, rugged and bare, was in sight. There was, however, no sign of *Wolfwind*.

Hal glanced at the sun, sinking toward the horizon in the west. He estimated there was less than an hour of daylight remaining. Then they could begin to search in earnest. He swung *Heron* about, heading her out to sea until the land had sunk below the horizon. Stefan, in the lookout perch, confirmed that he had lost sight of the coast, which meant that the ship was no longer visible from the land. Hal kept circling while the sun went down. As night spread across the sea, he turned *Heron*'s bows toward the coast once more.

"Now let's see what we can see," he muttered to himself, as the shadowy outline of the shore crept closer.

chapter twenty-one

They cruised toward the coast until they were a kilometer offshore. The coastline was a dark, amorphous mass rising out of the sea ahead of them; here and there, the lights of farmhouses shone through the night. Hal gave a grunt of satisfaction. If individual houses showed up so clearly, they should have no trouble spotting the lights of a large camp.

"East or west?" Thorn asked beside him as the coast came closer.

"West," Hal said immediately. He had already thought this through. "In fifteen kilometers or so, the coast curves back to the north. I doubt that our friends would want a site so far from the sea-lanes. We'll eliminate this part of the coast first, then head to the east." He took note of a large hill a few hundred meters inland. It rose in a symmetrical shape for two-thirds of its height, then one side sloped steeply to form a sharp, uneven peak. "We'll use that hill as a reference point so we'll know where we started," he told Thorn.

Heron swung smoothly under his urging until they were cruising parallel to the coast. After several minutes, the moon rose over the landmass, creating a silver light path across the sea. Thorn studied it for a few minutes, then turned to look down moon. They would be invisible from the landward side. But if another ship was following them from the sea, they would be silhouetted plainly against that brilliant moon path. There was no sign of another ship to the south, however.

Hal saw his friend looking to port. "Nobody in sight," he said quietly.

Thorn shifted uneasily. "Still, we have no idea where *Wolfwind* has got to," he replied. "We could have passed her or she could have been lying in wait for us."

"Unlikely," Hal said. But as a precaution, he called quietly to Stefan. "Stefan, keep a lookout to seaward as well as watching the land. We don't want any nasty surprises."

"Will do," Stefan replied from his position high above the deck.

They ghosted on. After some time, Hal saw the loom of light above a tall headland. Then, as they passed the headland, they saw the source of the light. It was a large town built on a river mouth, and the lights of the houses showed that it sprawled up the hills either side. If the Iberians had set up a camp, chances were it would be spread out on level ground, not climbing the hills.

"Hekberg," Hal said. Knowing how risky it would be to approach the coast so closely, he had spent some time that afternoon studying the chart and making a note of landmarks and the towns and villages that spread along the shore.

Gradually, they left the lights of the town behind them and continued to make their way along the darkened coast. They had traveled another ten kilometers when Thorn gripped Hal's arm, pointing to a glow in the sky that had appeared above the coastline. It was smaller than the town they had passed, and as it came into their direct view, they could see neat lines of lights radiating out from a central point.

"That could be it," Thorn said. For'ard, they could hear a stir of comment from the crew as they spotted the lights on the shore.

"Hal?" Stefan called from the lookout position.

Hal waved an arm in acknowledgment. "We see it. Keep your eyes peeled."

He felt a surge of excitement stirring in his stomach—the familiar tensing of muscles that so often presaged action.

The closer they came, the more it looked like a settlement for one to two hundred men. It was on level ground, with an elevated promontory at the western, or farther, end. The lights were arranged in neat, symmetrical rows, as they would be if they marked the tent lines of a camp.

Stig left his position in the waist and walked back to join them.

"You're sure there's nothing on the chart?" Hal queried.

Thorn ducked down behind the chart table, where a shaded lantern was burning low down. There was a brief spill of light across the deck as he unshuttered the lantern to study the chart, then the light went out and he reemerged.

"Nothing marked," he said. "Nearest village is Jalkerk, and that's several kilometers away."

"If the chart is accurate," Hal said. He never fully trusted a chart unless he had sailed over the waters it represented. Mapmaking was an uncertain skill. *Heron* sailed on for several more minutes, with every eye trained on the lights on shore.

"I'll take her in closer," Hal decided, and heaved on the tiller to send the ship swooping over the small rollers and heading directly for the coast. He glanced quickly around to make sure there was no light showing from the ship, but all was in darkness.

The lights onshore grew closer. He began to think they might have found the pirates' secret base already, although there was a doubt gnawing at him.

"There's no big central campfire," he said.

Thorn shrugged. "Plenty of smaller ones."

They were closer now, close enough that Hal could make out the occasional dark shape of a person walking past the fires. All seemed peaceful, he thought. It didn't *seem* like a pirate camp. Then he reconsidered. There was no reason why pirates should carry on carousing and celebrating every night. Those onboard *Wolfwind* would be tired after their long journey—particularly those who had been called on to row after the little ship that had been dogging them.

"Any sign of *Wolfwind*?" he breathed. They were still several hundred meters offshore, but he had the ridiculous feeling that he might be heard if he spoke in a normal tone.

Stig obviously had the same fear. "Not so far," he said. "I can see some kind of ship tied up along the pier but I don't think it's her."

Hal kept the little ship ghosting along the shoreline, straining his eyes to see more detail. The site was flat and wide, which fitted his expectations. And it was the right size—suitable for between one and two hundred people.

And yet?

"What do you think?" Thorn asked impatiently.

Hal turned to look at him. As he did so, he caught sight of a yellow rectangle of light suddenly visible on the hill beyond the suspected tent rows. It was there and gone in a few seconds, as though someone had opened and closed a door to a lighted room. He stared into the darkness and gradually made out more detail.

Then he swung the ship away from the coast.

"That's not them," he said briefly.

Thorn looked surprised at his definite tone. He glanced back over his shoulder at the mass of lights, now receding behind them as *Heron* headed out to sea. "Are you sure?" he asked.

Stig moved to stand beside him, equally skeptical of Hal's positive statement. Hal gestured to the building on the promontory—which he may well have ignored without that fortuitous flash of light as the door opened and closed.

"Look at that building on the headland," he said, and his two friends did so.

"Looks like a small tower," Stig said finally. "Could be a look-out position."

"It's got sails," Hal said. "Four big paddles. They've been trimmed for the night: the canvas covering has been furled. But you can make out the framework."

Stig and Thorn looked more carefully and finally Stig muttered, "Yes. I can see them now."

"It's a mill," Hal said. "A windmill. It's set up there so it can catch the prevailing winds." He looked from one to the other as he added, "I doubt our friends would bother building a mill if they're only there for a short time."

Thorn nodded several times. The tension he had felt when he thought they had discovered the pirates' camp went out of him.

"You're right," he said. "Well spotted. What do we do now?"

"We keep looking," Hal told him.

They continued on through the night, sighting several more lit-up areas on the shore. Each time, the lights came from an established town or village. There was no sign of a camp on the coast. They reached the hill that Hal had specified as a starting point when they turned west.

"We'll keep on for another hour," Hal told them, checking the eastern sky for the first sign of dawn. "Then we'll put back out to sea, where we can't be seen."

They continued to parallel the coast. They sighted two more light looms, which turned out to be long-established coastal towns, and a smaller set of lights that, on investigation, came from a minor fishing village. The sun was beginning to show its first light over the eastern horizon when Hal decided to call it a night. He marked down a deep, curving inlet, with a small copse of pine trees on its western end, as a start point for the following night.

"We'll come back tomorrow night," he told the crew, "and start from here."

Then, with the fiery ball of the sun rising above the horizon and casting an orange glow over the sea to the east, he turned *Heron* south and headed out to sea.

chapter twenty-two

It had been a long and sleepless night while they searched for the Iberians' base camp. In addition to the loss of sleep, the tension of never knowing when and if they might sight the enemy added a mental strain to the physical deprivation.

Once the coastline was safely over the horizon, Hal gave his crew the opportunity to rest. There was little else to do during the daylight hours, so he set a minimal watch and hove to, lowering the sails and streaming a canvas drogue as a sea anchor over the bows to keep *Heron* from drifting too far in the southeast-setting current.

The day passed slowly, with the crew sprawled asleep on the decks and on the rowing benches. They had long ago learned the lesson of taking rest whenever the opportunity arose, and they could sleep anywhere, anytime.

The only diversions during the day were the changing of watch and the meals served by Edvin. Hal was grateful the calm seas allowed Edvin to light his small spirit stove so that he could boil water for coffee. In the midafternoon, he made a fresh pot—the fourth of the day so far—and handed Hal a mug of the heavily sweetened brew.

Hal sipped appreciatively, and glanced toward the sun, which was beginning to lower in the western sky.

"Three hours to dark," he estimated. Stig, who was hunched up, leaning against the port bulwark with his watch cap pulled down over his eyes, replied without moving.

"Time we started moving back toward the coast?"

Hal considered the idea, then discarded it. "We'll give it another hour," he said. "No point in getting there too early and having to wait for darkness."

He would still need a little daylight to find the spot where they had finished their search the previous night, so it would be a finely judged matter to return to the coast in time to do that, before the dark of night masked their approach.

Unlike the others, Hal found it impossible to sleep. The possibility that *Wolfwind* might suddenly appear over the horizon, coupled with the uncertainty of their entire situation, kept him on tenterhooks throughout the long, uneventful day. With nothing to occupy his mind while they drifted, he began to doubt their current course of action.

What if there was no pirate base along the coast? After all, he had only Thorn's and Erak's opinions that such might be the case. They could be wasting hours, even days, here, searching for a nonexistent camp, while *Wolfwind* continued to prowl the ocean, sinking ships and killing innocent sailors.

The fact that they were the only ship available to hunt down the rogue wolfship weighed heavily on him. If their theory was mistaken, there was nobody else to intercept *Wolfwind.* She could continue to ravage and plunder unhindered, while he and his crew twiddled their thumbs in a useless search.

Finally, the inactivity became too much for him. He stepped down into the rowing well and shook Stig by the shoulder. The first mate was instantly awake. Unlike his skirl, he had no difficulty falling asleep. By the same token, when roused, he wasted no time or energy in stretching or yawning. He shoved his cap back and looked quickly around the surrounding ocean.

"What is it?" he asked, seeing no sign of an enemy.

Hal gestured for'ard. "Get the crew on their feet. It's time we were moving."

Stig cast a quick glance at the sky, taking in the position of the sun. His sailor's instincts told him that an hour had not passed since he and Hal had discussed returning to the coast.

"We're a little early, aren't we?" he asked mildly.

"No. We're fine," Hal snapped back at him. "Get them up."

Stig studied his friend for a few seconds. He knew that Hal's mind rarely relaxed and he sensed that a situation like this—waiting for time to pass with nothing to keep him busy—would serve to make him anxious and irritable. Accordingly, he took no offense at the skirl's waspish reply. The weight of responsibility for their success or failure was on Hal's shoulders. Stig didn't have to make decisions or plot their course of action and for that he was grateful. All he had to do was obey orders and supervise the crew.

He stepped up onto the central deck and moved for'ard, stopping to wake the crew members where they lay sleeping on the deck. Thorn, he noted, was already awake, his eyes following the first mate as he moved around the deck. He seemed to have a sixth sense that woke him when action was imminent.

Under Stig's direction, Jesper and Stefan hauled in the sea anchor, stowing the dripping canvas drogue over the gunwale at the bow. Ulf and Wulf hauled the port sail up the mast. Complying with Stig's order, they took a reef in the sail so that it wouldn't show its full area to the wind—there was no point in sailing full speed for the coast as they were still early.

If Hal noticed his second-in-command's order to reef the sail, he made no comment on it. He knew that there was plenty of daylight left and he appreciated Stig's ability to read his mind and adjust to the situation.

Under the reduced sail, *Heron* began to glide smoothly to the north. Now that they were moving, now that he had something to occupy him, Hal felt the tension in his gut easing. He held the tiller lightly, feeling the tremors that ran through it as they rose and fell on the slight swell, and as random currents twitched at the rudder. He adjusted and corrected automatically so that *Heron* maintained a straight course, without deviating. He glanced over his shoulder to check the wake. It ran arrow straight behind them.

Satisfied that the ship was moving efficiently, Stig returned aft to the steering platform and grinned at his friend.

"That feels better," he said.

Hal returned the smile. "I hate having nothing to do," he said, with an air of apology for his previous behavior.

Stig shrugged it aside. "Don't we all?" he said. "D'you think we'll find that camp tonight?"

Hal noted the positive tone of the question and realized that his old friend must have sensed his own previous uncertainty and soul-searching. As far as the first mate was concerned, the existence of the pirate camp was a reality. It was good to know that Stig—practical and reliable as he was—had no doubt that they were on the right track. Hal smiled in gratitude at the first mate.

"Let's hope so," he said. "The tension is killing me."

"So I'd noticed," Stig said, then added, "You need to ease up on yourself."

Jesper was on the lookout perch. They heard him call to signify that the coast was in sight. Hal looked westward. The sun was balanced above the horizon and the sea was turning from vivid blue to a steely gray. Approaching from the southeast as they were, they would be out of sight from the land, but there was still enough light for him to pick out the landmarks he had noted the previous night that marked the end of their search area. He ordered the port sail down, and the starboard raised in its place. As the sail crumpled to the deck, Stefan and Ingvar scrambled across to untie the reefing cords and furl the sail properly.

Heron was moving faster now under a fully set sail. Hal headed her inland and turned to run east. After several minutes, they reached the spot where they had finished their search the previous night.

"Eyes peeled, everyone," Hal called. The crew lined the port bulwark, peering intensely inland at the dark coastline. The sun had finally set and the sea and sky around them were dark. Erak joined Hal and Stig in the stern. He stooped to light the shuttered lantern in the chart cabinet, ready to check the chart if a sighting was made.

"Lights up ahead!" Jesper called from the lookout position.

"We see them," Hal replied. There was a large light spill over the horizon, and before long they were abeam of it. It was obviously a big port—far too big to be what they were seeking.

Erak crouched to check the chart. "That'll be Malmet," he said. "It's a trading port." He stood, and Hal could see his teeth flash in a grin. "I've raided there a few times in the old days," he added.

Stig glanced sidelong at him, detecting a sense of nostalgia in his voice. "The good old days?" he queried.

Erak shrugged. "You said it, not me," he said. But he turned to look at the mass of lights on the coast as they slipped astern, and Stig was sure he heard him sigh. He exchanged a quick glance with Hal, and the two of them smiled.

The lights of Malmet slid astern until it was no more than a glow in the sky over the horizon. Two more settlements came and went, but they were both too small and dimly lit to be what they were searching for. Hal felt the uncertainty of the day returning. Were they on a wild-goose chase? Would they find the camp? Did it even exist?

What if *Wolfwind*, even now, was hundreds of miles away, running down an unsuspecting trader, hauling alongside her and boarding her with a horde of screaming armed men, slashing and cutting about them as they overran the crew?

"Lights!" called Lydia, who was perched way for'ard on the gunwales at the bow.

They peered ahead. They could see the dark mass of a high cliff rising out of the ocean ahead of them, and the glowing loom of light that rose above it. Erak crouched down to study the chart once more, then emerged and said in a quiet voice, "There's nothing on the chart for ten kilometers."

Hal felt that now-familiar tightening in his gut. The glow of light was larger than they would see from a small coastal village that might have been ignored or gone unnoticed by the mapmakers. It signified a large settlement—although not as big as a town.

They sailed on, the indirect glow growing brighter as they neared the headland.

chapter twenty-three

So far, the high headland obscured any sight of the light source. Judging that they had a few more minutes before the interior of the bay beyond it was visible, Hal called for the sail to be lowered and for the ship to proceed under two pairs of oars.

"Less chance of being seen," he explained—the tall, light-colored sail would be more visible from onshore. Ingvar, Stefan, Ulf and Wulf took their places on the rowing benches. Jesper remained on the masthead lookout. Lydia was still in the bows and Stig, Thorn and Erak grouped around the steering platform with Hal.

Lydia was the first to see into the wide, deep bay as they passed the headland. "I can see cooking fires and tents," she called. "And a big central campfire."

The group around the steering platform exchanged meaningful glances.

"That sounds as if it could be the place," muttered Thorn, and the others nodded agreement. A few seconds later, as Jesper's view of the bay opened up, he added the definitive information.

"I can see *Wolfwind!*" he called. "She's moored close to the beach."

Hal heard Erak give a small growl of satisfaction. At the same time, his own spirits lifted, all doubts dispelled. The knot of tension and uncertainty in his stomach unraveled.

"I'll take her in for a closer look," he said, then he called to the four oarsmen, "Take it easy on the oars. Keep it smooth and don't splash."

He planned to close in to within two hundred meters of the beach, and while *Heron*'s sea-green hull would be virtually invisible, the white foam raised by any splashing or mis-stroking with the oars could reveal their presence to any watchers on the shore.

Slowly, the little ship crept into the wide bay. Now all on board could see what Lydia and Jesper had reported. There was a long, sandy beach along the inner edge, and inland from it—on an area of flat ground—they could see at least a score of tents grouped round a large central campfire. Individual cooking fires dotted the ground close to the tents, and against their light, they could see the dark figures of men moving around the campsite.

Wolfwind was moored at the western end of the beach, held by her anchors so that she lay with her bows facing the land. Another, smaller ship was moored next to her. She was wider in the beam than the lean, speedy wolfship—a trader or transport rather than a warship. Beyond the campsite, the ground rose gradually, the cleared area near the beach giving way to the wiry, stunted trees that grew along the windswept Sonderland coast.

"There are at least twenty tents," Stig observed after a few minutes. "Four men to a tent makes it at least eighty men."

"Not all of them would be crew on *Wolfwind*," Hal replied. "Some of them would be here to secure the campsite and unload any plunder she brought in."

"What do you make of the second ship?" Thorn asked.

Hal shrugged. "She might have transported the extra men here. Or she could have been captured."

They were approaching the western end of the bay. Hal glanced up at the approaching headland. He caught a glimpse of light at the top, and straining his eyes, he could just make out a low structure at the edge of the cliff. As he watched, he saw the light again and realized it came from a lantern being revealed momentarily.

"Jes!" he called softly. "There's some kind of building on top of the cliff. Have a look."

There was a pause before Jesper answered. "Looks like a low tower of some kind. Probably a lookout tower for spotting ships out to sea. Someone's up there with a lantern."

"Which means their night vision will be pretty well destroyed," Hal said to himself.

Thorn answered him. "They wouldn't be keeping a lookout at night. Too hard to spot passing ships. There's probably a few men camped up there so they don't have to climb the cliffs every morning."

"Makes sense," Hal said. "We'll run in close to the cliff so they don't see us heading out to sea. Go for'ard, please, Stig, and keep an eye out for rocks or reefs close to the base of the cliff."

Stig grunted agreement and moved swiftly to the bow, scrambling up onto the railing alongside Lydia and peering at the dark water ahead for any sign of breaking waves or spray.

Heron moved smoothly into the dark shadow cast by the headland, and Hal guided her in a curve round the cliff, ten meters from the rocks. Once, Stig whistled softly and pointed to port, indicating an exposed rock. Hal swung out to avoid it, then came back in, hugging the shore once more. Erak and Thorn peered upward, watching the top of the cliff for any sign of movement there, any indication that the ship might have been spotted. They were so close in now that they couldn't see the lantern Hal had noted before. All those on board held their breath, waiting for a shout or cry of alarm that would indicate they had been seen.

But there was none. They swept around the base of the cliff. There was a slight indent in the coast beyond it, and another rocky headland three hundred meters away. Hal steered the ship to parallel the coast, staying twenty meters away from the tumbled rocks. The lookout post on the headland was to seaward of them now, and the chances that they might be spotted were reduced.

They heaved a collective sigh of relief when they passed the next headland and Hal placed its solid bulk between them and the lookout tower. The coast here was sheer and rocky, with the small waves washing gently against it. There was no beach, no place to land. Hal called for the rowers to bring their oars in and for Ulf and Wulf to raise the starboard sail. Now that they were clear of the campsite, he edged out to sea a few hundred meters.

"What now?" Stig asked, returning from his position in the bows.

Hal indicated the shoreline to their left. "We'll look for a landing spot so we can go ashore. I want to take a closer look at that campsite."

They found a suitable site five kilometers down the coast. A narrow gap in the cliffs opened up into a small bay with a sandy beach at its end. The inlet took a turn to the right as they entered it. Under oars, Hal guided the ship in and ran her gently aground on the beach. He looked up at the low cliffs that protected the narrow bay.

"We should be safe here," he said. "We're well undercover and we're hidden from anyone passing by to seaward." He indicated the kink in the inlet that shielded them from view.

He glanced up at the stars, noting their position in the sky, and said thoughtfully, "Only a few hours to dawn. We'll have to wait through another day before we check out the Iberians' camp. There's not enough time to get there and back in darkness."

"So . . . hurry up and wait again?" Thorn observed.

Hal gave him a tired grin. "We seem to be doing a lot of that lately, don't we?" he said. Then he added, "At least now we've found what we've been looking for."

They opted to make camp ashore rather than to sleep another night on the ship. Ulf, Wulf and Jesper carried their camping equipment up the beach to a spot above the high-tide mark. Edvin unloaded his cooking equipment and found a convenient spot among the rocks, in a small gully where the smoke from his cook fire would be dissipated by the time it reached the top of the cliffs surrounding the little bay.

Lydia, after consulting with Hal, set about climbing the low cliff on the western side of the inlet, to scout around the immediate area and make sure there was no danger in the vicinity.

While all this was being done, Hal, Stig and Erak shoved *Heron* back off the beach into deeper water. Once she was afloat, Stefan and Stig took an oar on either side and turned her through 180 degrees, so that the bow was pointing out to sea.

"Never know when we might want to make a quick getaway," Hal said, as they backed the ship into the beach. Erak and Thorn dragged her ashore, then set an anchor in the sand above the high-water mark.

Hal and the others stepped ashore, and trudged through the thick sand to where the rest of the crew were setting up camp. Hal heard a rattle of small stones at the base of the cliff and turned quickly, his hand flying to the hilt of his saxe. But it was only Lydia returning from her reconnaissance.

"Nobody in sight. And nothing inland—had a good clear view from the top," she reported, and the last bit of tension ebbed away from him.

At the base of the cliff, he could see the small glow of Edvin's cook fire and he realized how ravenous he was. Edvin could make coffee while they were at sea, but lighting a larger fire for cooking was too dangerous on board ship. They had been eating cold meals for some time now, and the thought of one of Edvin's hot, nourishing stews set his mouth watering.

Ten minutes later, he was eagerly devouring a bowl of rich beef-and-potato stew—one that Edvin had prepared.

"'At's good," he mumbled, his mouth full. The rest of the crew echoed his verdict, and Edvin smiled to himself. He obtained great satisfaction seeing his shipmates enjoying the meals he prepared for them. He wasn't the fiercest fighter in the crew, but he was far and away the best cook.

Hal finished his bowl. Jesper collected it and those belonging to the rest of the crew, and carried them down to the water's edge to clean them. Hal glanced out to sea, looking to the east where the sky was beginning to show the first light of dawn. He yawned hugely. It had been a long day. Stig smiled at him and gestured to the tent that had been set up for the skirl.

"Why don't you turn in?" he said. "I'll post a watch at the top of the cliff."

Hal rose and stretched gratefully. "Have someone wake me in four hours," he said, and headed for the comfort of his small tent.

chapter twenty-four

The day passed slowly. Aside from the lookouts that Stig had set at the top of the cliffs, the crew mostly slept.

Lydia was the exception. Once they were back on dry land, her long-ingrained instincts as a hunter and tracker were roused. After consulting Hal, she set out to reconnoiter the way back to the Iberian camp, looking for any signs of danger or any trouble spots along the way.

She found nothing to alarm her. The ground was uneven and rocky, and covered with the twisted, coarse scrub that was native to this part of the world. Farther inland, away from the cliffs, she could see small stands of taller trees—mainly pines, as far as she could tell. In the far distance, she made out a small curl of smoke—as would be seen from a kitchen cook fire. Moving inland, she could see a group of small buildings, most likely those of a solitary farm. She saw no sign of any people and the farm was far enough away for it to pose no risk to their activities.

Heading west along the cliffs, she came within two kilometers of the Iberian camp. The watchtower they had sighted the night before was clearly visible, and now she could see the tent that was pitched alongside it. She saw movement at the top of the stubby wooden tower. It was now manned, presumably with a lookout keeping watch out to sea. Even though she realized the lookout would be preoccupied with keeping watch seaward, she moved more carefully once she had seen it, crouching below the scrubby trees to avoid being seen.

Shortly after that, the flat land at the top of the cliffs broke up, falling away into a rocky gully that, after a kilometer or so, climbed back to more level ground overlooking the campsite. She studied the broken terrain and could make out several paths twisting their way through the tumbled rocks.

"That might hold us up," she muttered to herself. The gully would be difficult to traverse at night. On the other hand, it would conceal the Skandian party from the watchtower.

She decided she had seen enough, and staying low, she retraced her steps to the inlet where *Heron* was moored. She was pleased to note that from the clifftops approaching the inlet, she could see no sign that *Heron* was there.

She nodded to Stefan, who was on watch at the top of the cliff, and made her way down to the beach to report her findings to Hal. Discovering that the skirl was sleeping, she shrugged and made her way to her own tent. There would be plenty of time to apprise him of the lay of the land before they set out that night.

She glanced at the sun. It was after midday and she could hear gentle snores coming from the other tents. But she wasn't tired and felt no need for sleep. Instead, she rummaged through her gear, took out her tools and a small pot of glue and began setting the vanes onto a new atlatl dart, using a template to mark the end of the shaft so the vanes would be set evenly around it.

She had completed the first shaft and glued a nock point on the end when she heard footsteps approaching. She looked up from her work and saw Ulf and Wulf a few meters away, evidently intent on speaking with her. She frowned slightly, wondering what was on their minds. Conversations with the twins could tend to be bewildering at times. They often had a roundabout way of approaching the subject they had in mind.

This time was no exception. Since they seemed to be hesitating, she prompted them gently.

"What can I do for you boys?" she asked. She expected them to seek information about her reconnaissance of the route back to the pirate camp, or even about details of how to construct an atlatl dart, since that was what she was presently doing. But their opening statement had nothing to do with her current activities.

"Your wedding . . . ," said Ulf.

She wasn't expecting that and she tilted her head to one side. "Ye-es?" she said uncertainly.

"To Ingvar," Wulf chimed in, as if she might need further elucidation.

She switched her gaze to him. "That is the only one I'm planning," she agreed.

The identical twins nodded, as if that fact had needed confirmation. They waited for her to say more. Eventually, she prompted them.

"What about it?"

"Stig and Hal are going to be Ingvar's best men," Ulf pointed out.

Wulf quickly corrected him. "Well, they're going to be best man and second-best man." He looked at his brother. "They can't both be *best*," he pointed out.

Lydia saw Ulf draw breath to contest this point and she realized that if she allowed him to do so, this conversation could spiral out of control—as so many of the twins' conversations tended to do.

"That's right," she said quickly. "Hal is best man and Stig is second best. They've been Ingvar's friends for a long time."

Wulf gave a satisfied nod, indicating that he was pleased his ranking of the two friends had been accepted as correct. Ulf glared at him for a moment. Then he made an obvious effort and let the matter pass. He didn't want to argue with Lydia.

"And Thorn is giving you away," he said.

"He's your crazy parent," Wulf added in a knowledgeable tone.

Now it was Lydia's turn to frown. Thorn was indeed going to give her away, but she had no idea what that had to do with his sanity or lack thereof.

"That's right." She addressed this comment to Ulf, not wishing to engage Wulf in a debate as to Thorn's mental acuity.

"And Erak is performing the ceremony," Ulf said in conclusion.

Again she nodded, wondering where all this was going. "Once again, that is correct."

There was a long silence as the twins seemed to contemplate how to raise the next subject. Finally, Wulf came out with it.

"And what about you?" he asked.

She regarded him quizzically. "I believe the plan is that I will be marrying Ingvar," she said. "I am to be the bride."

But the two of them were shaking their heads when she finished speaking.

"No, we mean who will be helping you? Supporting you?" Wulf said.

Before she could reply, and question what in Gorlog's name he was talking about, Ulf explained.

"Who will stand by you? Who will be your bridesmaids?" he asked.

Lydia hesitated. "I don't have any," she said. "I haven't asked anyone."

In fact, up until this moment, the idea hadn't even occurred to her. It wasn't that she disliked the young women of Hallasholm, or that they disliked her. It was more because there had been no real opportunity for her to make close friends with women her own age. On top of that, she was a somewhat solitary figure—one who didn't find it necessary to seek human company.

The twins regarded her with compassionate eyes. Finally, Wulf said:

"Well, we'd like to be them."

"We're volunteering," Ulf added, as if to make sure she understood.

Lydia, for a few seconds, was speechless. Then she found her voice. "One small problem," she said. "Bridesmaids are maids. You're not."

Wulf waved the comment aside. "Then we'll be your brides*men*," he stated firmly.

"Bridesmen," Ulf repeated, with a note of satisfaction.

Before Lydia could reply, Wulf added, "After all, we're uniquely qualified."

Lydia turned her now-thoroughly-puzzled gaze to him. "And how's that?"

He spread his hands in an explanatory gesture. "Well, most bridesmaids wear identical dresses, so they'll look alike," he said. "And so nobody will mistake them for the bride."

"I guess that's true in part," Lydia said. She had never really questioned the reason why bridesmaids wore identical outfits. Perhaps Wulf was right, she thought.

"And we already are!" Ulf said triumphantly.

"Are what?" she asked.

"Identical," Wulf told her. "So nobody will mistake us for you."

She regarded them critically for a few seconds. They were both tanned and muscular, and in the past year they had both grown short, blond beards. Their hair was long and gathered either side in rough plaits. They were handsome enough, she thought, but their looks were extremely masculine. Two more un-bridelike figures she couldn't imagine.

"I can see that," she admitted, and they grinned at her.

"So, what do you say?" Ulf asked.

For a moment, she was tempted to laugh off the suggestion. It was ridiculous, she thought. But then she hesitated. Was it, in fact? Her closest friends in Hallasholm were the members of the brotherband. Indeed, people had often commented, with some wonder, on the fact that she was a sister of the Heron brotherband.

This crew had rescued her and welcomed her into their ranks.

Stig and Hal were truly brothers to her. The rest of the crew were like close cousins. She felt relaxed and at home among them—more so than with any group in her life.

Now two members of that crew—albeit two *very* eccentric members—were offering to stand by her as she walked down the aisle to be married; offering their love and support on what would be the biggest day of her life so far.

Her eyes misted as she looked at the two eager, identical faces before her. It would certainly be unconventional, she thought. But then, what about her life *wasn't* unconventional? Bridesmen. They would undoubtedly make her wedding day a memorable one. And what bride didn't want her wedding day to be memorable?

"I'd be honored," she said.

chapter twenty-five

The reconnaissance party set out before sunset to survey the pirate camp.

"A little bit of light early on will be helpful," Hal told them. "And Lydia says there's no sign of people for the first few kilometers."

They moved in single file through the head-high scrub that covered the headlands close to the sea. Farther inland, as Lydia had noted, small clumps of scraggly pine trees rose higher above the ground, where the constant sea breeze abated.

Lydia led the way, followed by Hal, Ingvar and Thorn, with Stig bringing up the rear. Although Ingvar would be of little use in observing the enemy camp, there was always the chance that they might encounter an enemy patrol, and his fighting prowess would be invaluable.

There was a narrow path that wound its way through the scrub, staying roughly parallel to the coastline. Whether it had been worn down by people or animals was anyone's guess. There was no sign of any life, animal or otherwise.

That was the case until they reached the wide ravine that crossed their path. Lydia, who was some ten meters ahead of the rest of the party, stopped and pointed to the ground in front of her. The others caught up with her and stared down at the small, dark pile of matter on the ground.

She poked it with the point of an atlatl dart and it broke up, showing a moist interior.

"Droppings," she said softly. "Bear droppings. And they're fresh. Keep your eyes open."

The others looked warily around them in the gathering dusk, searching for any sign of a bear in the near vicinity.

"What kind of bears do they have in these parts?" Stig asked, his eyes darting from shadow to shadow among the scrub.

"Big ones," she answered succinctly. "Big, bad-tempered ones at this time of year. They'll be coming out of hibernation and they'll be hungry and cranky."

"Good to know," Hal said. "What do we do if we bump into one?"

"Try not to. Bears don't like to be bumped. For my part, I plan to run."

"Can you outrun a bear?" Thorn asked.

She regarded him with a level, unsmiling gaze. "I don't have to outrun a bear," she said. "I just have to outrun you."

There was a long pause while the full meaning of this sank in, then Hal gestured toward the ravine ahead of them.

"Let's get going," he said, and they started toward the rim. The watchtower was now in sight and they moved in a crouch, heading for the narrow, winding path down into the ravine that Lydia had discovered that afternoon.

They descended into the dark gully, slipping and sliding on the rocks underfoot, sending showers of small stones rattling down ahead of them. Ingvar used his voulge as a walking staff to steady himself. Turning to watch him descend a particularly steep section, Hal wondered if he might have been wiser to leave the big warrior out of the reconnaissance party. Then he shrugged. If they ran into any opposition, they would need Ingvar's massive strength and skill. And Thorn's constant training had made the big lad more at home on uneven surfaces. Hours of practice had taught him to trust his innate sense of balance, even in situations where he couldn't see the ground he was treading on.

It's a matter of confidence, Thorn had told Ingvar, *and of not tensing up when you feel an uneven patch of ground.*

Tensed, tight muscles would destroy a person's equilibrium more than anything on ground like this.

The going was easier when they reached the ravine floor. Lydia found a narrow path that snaked through the jumble of rocks and boulders and led them confidently toward the western side.

"We could chance a light?" Hal suggested.

She stopped to consider the idea, then rejected it. "Too risky. Anyone on the far ridge would see us coming. Better to move more slowly and make sure nobody sees us."

Hal acquiesced. Lydia was the expert in these situations and he was happy to defer to her. He noticed that she stopped several times to study more bear droppings, flicking them aside from the path with the point of a dart. He kept glancing around nervously, looking for the sight of a large, shaggy beast bearing down on them. Thankfully, the others hadn't seemed to notice her actions, and he realized she had flicked the droppings aside so they wouldn't see them.

"No sense in getting everybody all het up," she said softly as he caught up with her on one such occasion. "So long as we don't corner it, or get between it and its cub, it'll stay away from us."

"Has it got a cub?" he asked.

She shrugged. "Always assume that it has," she said. "Cubs are what make a bear most dangerous."

Hal nodded as if he already knew this. He noted that his mouth was a little dry at the thought of encountering a bear and its cub in this twisting pathway through the rocks and blind gullies.

Finally, they reached the far side and scrambled up another steep track to the top. Lydia signaled for them to stay low as they emerged from the ravine onto the level plain short of the headland and watchtower. They crouched in the scrub behind her as she pointed out the watchtower to Hal. He could see the tent where pirates who manned the watchtower spent the night. As they watched, the tent flap was pulled aside as someone exited, and the lantern inside flared briefly until the flap was lowered once more.

The shadowy figure who had exited from the tent strode across to the base of the watchtower and began to climb a ladder to the platform above.

"I thought Thorn said they wouldn't keep watch at night?" Lydia whispered as they watched.

Hal glanced over his shoulder, looking to the east. "It's a full moon tonight," he said. "It had set when we passed this way yesterday but it'll light up the sea like a lantern." He paused. "It'll light us up too. We should get under cover."

She nodded agreement and led the small party back into the head-high undergrowth that covered the headland. Fifteen minutes later, the moon rose, flooding the land and ocean with a silver light.

Moving stealthily, the small party made their way inland behind the watchtower, and then paused at the opposite edge of the headland overlooking the bay.

The camp was a scene of activity at this early hour of the night. They could smell the wood smoke from a dozen cooking fires, and the aroma of meat cooking over the flames. Voices raised in conversation carried to them on the evening breeze and they could see men relaxing and eating round the fires.

"There's a lot of them," Hal said.

Thorn grunted agreement. "Too many. No way we could mount a direct assault." He gestured with his left hand toward the wolfship moored at the far end of the bay. "No way we could take *Wolfwind* either. There must be at least twenty-five men camped close to her—and we'd have to cross the entire camp to reach her."

"Maybe we'll have to burn her. Lydia could throw some fire darts into her," Hal mused.

Thorn raised his eyebrows. "Erak will love that," he commented.

"Erak might just have to," Hal replied. "I can't see any other way we could get to her."

The answer came some thirty minutes later, while they were still lying on their bellies on the cliff edge, studying the camp and watching the pirates' movements. A horn blared from the watchtower and they craned around to look out to sea.

The moon was almost directly overhead, flooding the ocean with light. There, some half a kilometer offshore, appearing to be pinned to the ocean like a bug, a trading ship was sailing slowly toward the west.

One of the men in the watchtower scrambled down and ran to the cliff edge, signaling the camp with a lantern.

Orders were shouted and men began running toward *Wolfwind*, scrambling aboard her and bringing in the anchors that held her fast to the beach. They heard the rattle and clatter of oars being run out through the oarlocks, and then the long ship was sliding backward away from the beach.

Hal glanced out to sea again. The trader was barely a third of the way between the headlands, and now that her crew could see into the bay and make out the size of the pirate encampment, they had obviously realized their mistake. They had turned to head southwest, looking for safety out to sea. But the bright moonlight held the trader in its grasp, and within minutes, *Wolfwind* was stroking smoothly after her, her speed building as she swooped over the low rollers.

"She'll never get away," Stig muttered as they watched the uneven contest. Now *Wolfwind*'s crew were hauling up her big square sail, and as they watched, it filled and tightened and the big warship accelerated under its thrust.

Like a greyhound after a rabbit, *Wolfwind* surged out of the bay, heading in pursuit of the trader and eating up the distance that separated them.

Not wishing to see the trader's fate, and realizing that the attention of all onshore would be on the two ships, Hal turned to his companions.

"Let's get out of here," he said.

chapter twenty-six

One by one, the five observers crept back from the edge of the cliff and made their way into the cover of the low scrub. They stood in a half circle while they made sure they had not been observed. Then Hal gestured to Lydia.

"Lead on," he said. "Let's get back to the ship."

They headed off, pausing at a clear patch of ground two hundred meters wide. Hal glanced behind them, back toward the headland. The land here dropped away and they were in a patch of dead ground, shielded from the view of those who manned the watchtower.

Lydia, who had waited at the edge of the clear space for the others to catch up, now signaled the way forward. Confident that they were concealed from view from the watchtower, they stood upright and moved a little faster.

It was this confidence that proved to be their undoing. They were a few meters short of the end of the clear ground when a party of men appeared from inland.

For a moment, the two groups froze as they caught sight of one another. Then Hal heard a voice calling a challenge across the open space.

"¿Quién es?"

The fact that the challenge was in Iberian told Hal all he needed to know about the other party. There were about a dozen of them, he saw, all armed. That was too many for the five Herons to fight.

Lydia came to the same conclusion. "Run!" she hissed urgently. She grabbed Ingvar's arm to steady him and took off at a fast lope toward the cover of the scrub ahead of them. The others followed suit.

Behind them, Hal heard a shouted order, then the sound of running feet—multiple running feet. He risked a glance behind and saw the Iberians strung out in an uneven line as they followed across the clear ground. Then he was in the scrub, with branches whipping at him, his hands raised in front of him to protect his face and eyes. He blundered on, nearly losing his footing in the uneven ground, lurching from one scrubby tree to the next until he caught up with Lydia.

"This way," she told him, and he saw that she had discovered a narrow, winding path through the low bushes and trees. Vaguely, he saw the shadowy figures of his friends receding through the scrub. Lydia had waited for him, relinquishing the task of guiding Ingvar to Thorn.

She turned and sprinted off down the path and he wasted no time in following her. In spite of the track's winding and twisting, he was making better time without the need to force his way through the bushes. Lydia was a few paces ahead of him and they quickly caught up to the other three. They paused for a moment to catch their breath, and he heard the sound of bodies blundering through the undergrowth behind them. So far, it appeared, the group chasing them hadn't discovered the same clear path.

"Who the devil are they?" Stig asked.

Hal shook his head. "Maybe a patrol. Maybe a hunting or a foraging party. Whoever they are, they're Iberians. We can't let them discover *Heron*."

The crashing and shouting was growing closer, then the noise abated. Lydia was first to realize what that meant.

"They've found the path," she said. "Let's get moving. We'll lose them in the ravine. It's just ahead."

Thorn, Ingvar and Stig took off in the direction she pointed. She caught Hal's arm to stop him and spoke in a low, urgent tone. "Keep them moving. Get down into the ravine and keep heading west. I'll wait and slow them up a little."

Hal noticed that she had taken the atlatl from her belt and was fitting a dart to it as she spoke. For a moment, he was tempted to remonstrate with her, but then he stopped himself. Lydia knew what she was doing, he thought. He shook his head bitterly at the fact that he had left his crossbow back at the ship. With two of them fighting a rearguard action, they'd be better placed to slow the pirates down.

But it was no good wasting time regretting something that he couldn't change. He nodded briefly to her and set off after the others.

Lydia turned back to face the track behind them. She had a clear view for about twenty meters before the path doglegged and blocked her vision. Standing side on, she drew back the arm holding the dart and atlatl, hearing the running footsteps and shouting voices getting closer. She set her feet wider apart and waited.

She didn't have long to wait. A burly figure, dressed in the Iberian style in loose, baggy white trousers and a long, belted overshirt, emerged from the scrub behind her. He skidded to a halt as he saw the dim figure waiting at the far end of the path, then smiled.

He brandished the long, straight sword that he held in his right hand and began to pace slowly down the narrow track toward the person waiting for him.

He was beginning to speak when he saw the figure move, casting something toward him with an overhand movement of the right arm. "You should have kept running. It might have—"

Almost instantly, he felt a jolting impact in his right shoulder. The force of it spun him half around and the impact jarred the sword from his grasp. He staggered, staring in disbelief at the long, heavy shaft that transfixed his shoulder. Then his legs gave way and he sank to the ground, gasping as he felt the first waves of pain seizing his upper body.

Vaguely, through eyes blurred with pain and shock, he saw the slim figure turn and disappear into the undergrowth. Then two of his companions came crashing down the track behind him, stopping abruptly as they saw him on his knees, and noticed the dark blood staining his white upper garment.

"Santos!" one of them cried. "What happened?"

Santos, realizing that there was no sign of the dart thrower, gestured weakly at the empty track. "They stopped"—he groaned—"one of them . . . shot me."

They pulled him to one side of the track and leaned his back against a scrubby tree. In spite of their best efforts, the movement caused him extreme pain, and he blacked out for a second or two. He opened his eyes and realized one of his companions had laid hold of the dart and was trying to pull it free. He raised a weak hand to stop him, knowing that the bleeding would intensify if he succeeded.

"No!" he gasped. "Leave . . . it . . ." Four more of their comrades caught up with them and, seeing one of their number obviously struck down, stopped beside him, looking warily around at the shadowy trees and scrub.

"What happened?" one of them asked. The man who had first seen the wounded Santos on his knees in the middle of the narrow track answered him.

"Santos has been shot. They stopped and shot him as he came round the bend here."

In truth, it was only one person who had stopped, but Santos was weak and in shock and wasn't able to explain clearly what had happened. The Iberians were now thoroughly alarmed at the thought that multiple armed enemies might be stalking them through the undergrowth.

"Who are they?" one of them asked. "How many are there?"

"I counted five," another replied. By this stage, the remainder of their group had arrived.

The man who had spoken looked around at the group. "There are twelve of us—"

"Eleven, Juan," another man interrupted to contradict him, pointing to the sprawled figure at the edge of the track.

Juan replied angrily. "Very well, eleven! That's more than enough to deal with five bandits." He had no idea whether the people they were pursuing were bandits, but it seemed the most logical answer to the question of their identity.

The other speaker, a short, stocky figure, indicated the dart that transfixed the groaning Santos. "We may outnumber them," he said. "But do you want to walk into one of those?"

There was a general murmur of agreement from the men around him. None of them was willing to take the chance of being the unknown shooter's next target.

But Juan, who had assumed the role of leader, continued to urge them after the smaller group. "No. We'll go carefully. We'll make sure we don't expose ourselves to the shooter, whoever he is. But we have to find out who these people were. From the direction they were coming, they'd been spying on our camp."

"So? What could they see?" the short man challenged.

Juan singled him out. "Who knows? Who knows where they came from, or who they are. But do you want to tell El Despiadado that we saw people spying on our camp and let them get away?"

El Despiadado—the Savage One—was the chief of the pirate band and the skipper of the captured wolfship. He had a reputation for cruelty and ruthlessness. None of the men present were willing to risk his anger. A few of them stirred uncertainly. Juan seized his advantage. "We'll leave Santos here for the moment." He paused, then said with an obvious sneer in his voice, "You can wait here with him if you're too frightened to go on."

As he had expected, the shorter man bridled with anger at the insult. Before he could answer, Juan continued, addressing the other men.

"We'll keep our eyes open. No more blundering out into the open the way Santos did."

The group of men looked at their wounded companion. A few of them muttered agreement and Juan concluded.

"And when we catch up with them, we'll make them pay."

Ahead of them, the Herons had reached the lip of the ravine. Hal hurried the others on down the rocky track and turned to wait for Lydia to catch up. She emerged from the undergrowth after several minutes, looking back over her shoulder as she ran to join him.

"They're just behind us," she told him. "I slowed them down a little, but they're still coming."

"Then we'd better move," Hal urged. He led the way down the track, sending showers of pebbles and loose stones cascading down before him. Lydia was more sure-footed and kept pace a few meters behind him. They reached the bottom of the path and found Thorn, Ingvar and Stig waiting for them. Hal gestured for them to keep moving.

"Go! Go!" he hissed. "They're right behind us!"

Thorn took Ingvar's arm and started to lead him at a run through the rock-strewn path that wound its way among the boulders and gullies. The others followed, conscious that, at any moment, they might be sighted from the top of the ravine. They had gone no more than thirty meters when disaster struck. A loose rock under Ingvar's foot gave way and he tumbled to the ground with a sharp cry of agony.

chapter twenty-seven

Ingvar tried to rise, but sank back down again with a groan, clutching at his right ankle. The rest of the small party gathered around him. Thorn dropped to his knees and deftly moved Ingvar's hand away from the injured ankle to inspect it. He gently eased the foot from one side to the other. Ingvar's sharp intake of breath told him that the movement was causing him intense pain.

Lydia had moved to kneel on the other side of Ingvar, the concern obvious on her face. "Stop that!" she snapped at Thorn. "Can't you see you're hurting him?"

Thorn glanced up at her and released his grip on Ingvar's foot.

"Can you move the foot yourself?" he asked Ingvar.

Ingvar complied, waggling the foot. But the action was obviously painful in the extreme. He groaned, then replied. "Yes. But it hurts like the very devil when I do."

"Then don't do it!" Lydia told him, her voice rising in pitch.

Hal put a hand on her arm. "Take it easy, Lydia," he said. "Thorn's trying to help him."

Biting her lip, Lydia moved away slightly, realizing that Hal was right.

Thorn sat back on his haunches and looked up at Hal. "I don't think it's broken," he said. "More like a bad sprain."

"It feels like it's broken," Ingvar said, his breath coming in fast, shallow gasps as he continued to rotate the ankle. He smiled wanly at Lydia, who shook her head helplessly. It was tearing her heart to see Ingvar—big, powerful Ingvar—disabled this way.

But Thorn shook his head. "A bad sprain often hurts more than a simple break," he said. "You'll be fine in a day or two."

"We don't have a day or two," Hal pointed out, looking at the rim of the ravine above them, waiting for the first sign of their pursuers.

Thorn rose and reached down to put his hands under Ingvar's arms. "Let's get you on your feet," he said. With Thorn's assistance, Ingvar heaved himself up from the ground. Thorn steadied him for a few seconds, then took his hand away. "Will it bear your weight?" he asked. Ingvar gingerly tested it, swaying as he applied more weight onto the ankle. He winced as the ankle took on more of a load, and finally balanced evenly.

"Seems . . . all . . . right," he said hesitantly. He steadied himself, then took a pace forward with the injured leg.

Instantly, the ankle gave way. Lydia moved to support him, but Thorn was quicker, grabbing Ingvar under the armpits to stop him toppling over. Ingvar bared his teeth in agony, lurching as he took most of his weight back on his uninjured leg. He cursed quietly for a few seconds.

"I can stand on it. But I can't walk on it," he told Thorn.

The old sea wolf nodded. "All right, put your arm around my shoulder and I'll help you along. Ready?"

Ingvar nodded, and Thorn stepped off, supporting the injured warrior's weight. Ingvar took an awkward, hopping step, grunting in pain as he did so. Then he took another, and another, resting his weight on Thorn.

"Keep going!" Thorn encouraged him. "You're doing fine."

"You've . . . got a weird . . . idea of fine . . ." Ingvar gasped as he hobbled beside the older man. He stopped as he inadvertently put more weight on the leg than he meant to, inhaling sharply.

Thorn stopped with him. "Are you all right?" he asked, but Ingvar was already urging him on.

"I'm fine. Keep going."

Hal, Lydia and Stig watched, wanting to help but powerless to do so. The track was too narrow and uneven for one of them to take Ingvar's other side and support more of his weight. Hesitantly, they began to follow the other two as they inched painfully toward the safety of the far side.

Then they heard a shout from behind them. Instinctively, they all stopped to look back. But Hal waved for Thorn and Ingvar to keep going.

"Keep moving!" he called. "Don't stop!"

The two lurched off again as Hal, Stig and Lydia looked back apprehensively at the rim of the ravine. There was one figure there, obviously the person who had just shouted. But within seconds, he was joined by half a dozen more, all of them silhouetted against the starlit night sky. As the Skandians watched, they could see the pirates casting about for the track down into the ravine. Then one of them shouted and pointed, and the small group turned toward the direction he had indicated.

All the while, more and more were arriving.

"There's a lot of them," Hal said.

Stig nodded. "Too many," he said. Lydia, relieved that she could finally take some sort of positive action, was drawing a dart from her quiver and clipping the atlatl to its base. Without speaking, she stepped forward and hurled the dart at the line of figures making their way down into the ravine. The dart was visible against the night sky for a few seconds, then it disappeared into the dimness. There was a short pause, then they heard a cry of pain and fear as it found a target. The Iberians scattered, insofar as the narrow, steep track allowed them to, seeking shelter behind the tumbled rocks and boulders beside the track.

"That'll hold them for a while," Lydia said.

But Hal shook his head. "Not long enough. Come on!" He led the way after Thorn and Ingvar, who had disappeared among the rocks. Behind them, they could hear the Iberians shouting to one another, each of them urging his companions on after the fleeing Skandians. Luckily, none of them seemed anxious to comply with the suggestion.

In a disappointingly short time, the trio caught up with their two hobbling companions, shuffling along the narrow, winding trail. Hal and Lydia exchanged a look, each reading the other's thoughts: Ingvar was moving too slowly to escape. It wouldn't be long before the Iberians caught up with the small party.

"How close are they?" Thorn asked, twisting to look at the two of them.

"Too close," Hal said grimly. "And they're getting closer."

"They're already in the ravine," Lydia added.

Thorn pursed his lips. She didn't need to say more.

"Leave me here," Ingvar said abruptly. He shook off Thorn's arm and hobbled to sit on a nearby boulder.

"No!" Lydia cried immediately.

"She's right." Hal said. "There's no way we're doing that."

But Ingvar shook his head stubbornly. "I'm holding you up. If you stay with me, they'll catch all of us. Leave me. I'll keep them off you and you can make it back to the ship."

Lydia put a hand on his arm. "We're not leaving you," she said firmly, but Ingvar shook his head again in frustration.

"So it's better if we all get caught because of me?" he asked. "I'm telling you, go on without me. It's the only way."

"Not quite," Thorn said, and now they all turned to look at him. He jerked a thumb toward the jumbled rocks and boulders around them. "There's plenty of hiding places here. I'll stay with Ingvar and we'll lie low while you draw the Iberians away. Without us to slow you down, you should be able to shake them off."

Hal opened his mouth to reply, but Lydia got in ahead of him.

"Good idea," she said. "But I'll stay with Ingvar."

Her fiancé rose awkwardly from his seat on the boulder. "No you won't," he said firmly. "Nobody's staying with me."

"I am," Thorn told him. He turned his glance on Lydia. "You

can't do it. He's too heavy for you to support. And besides, we need you to slow the pirates down." He gestured to the atlatl hanging from her belt.

"He's my fiancé!" Lydia replied. "I'm staying with him."

Hal spoke over her. "Thorn's right. Ingvar's too big for you to help him over these rocks. Besides, if the Iberians catch up, it'll mean close-quarter fighting, and that's not your strong point. On the other hand, Thorn and Ingvar together could prove quite a handful for a bunch of raggedy-pants pirates."

He looked at Thorn. "Find a hiding place and hole up there. We'll come back for you in two days."

Ingvar, Lydia and Thorn all began to talk at once. Hal made a furious gesture for them to stop.

"Shut up, all of you! You're wasting time, and we don't have any to waste. Thorn, you and Ingvar find a place to hide in the rocks. Lydia, you're coming with us. That's an order!"

The three fell silent. They were all strong-willed individuals, but on the *Heron,* discipline was strict and the skirl's authority was absolute. Reluctantly, Lydia and Ingvar fell silent. Thorn nodded approval at his leader.

Hal let his gaze run over the other two, challenging them to continue the argument. But each of them dropped their eyes. "Now let's find a place for you two to hole up."

Thorn hauled Ingvar back to his feet and they set off, shuffling as fast as they could, scanning the rocks to either side of the path for a potential hiding place. The others followed, Lydia turning from time to time to pace backward, watching the trail behind them. She had another dart ready, fitted to her atlatl.

They went another forty meters before they found a likely spot. The track they were following forked into two, the side trail leading down a gully whose steep walls were formed by a tumble of large boulders. Thorn jerked a thumb toward it.

"This looks like a good spot," he said.

Hal nodded, and stepped closer to clasp hands with the two of them. "Stay out of sight," he ordered. "We'll lead the Iberians away. And we'll be back for you two days from now."

He unslung the water canteen he had around his shoulders and handed it to Thorn. Stig and Lydia did the same, then Lydia stepped forward wordlessly to hug Ingvar close to her.

"Thanks," said Thorn. "We'll see you in two days."

Then he grasped hold of Ingvar's waist and led the injured lad off into the side gully.

chapter twenty-eight

The Iberians moved slowly through the ravine, staying to the sides of the narrow track as they went, hoping that the overhanging boulders either side would shield them from further missiles hurtling out of the night sky.

The one called Juan led the way, stopping at every twist or turn in the track to make sure the shadowy figure ahead of them wasn't waiting in ambush at the next stage. When he was sure the way was clear, he signaled for his men to follow and stepped out, nerves tingling, eyes straining to pierce the shadows.

He realized that this enforced slow pace was giving the party ahead of them time to make their getaway, but he wasn't going to try to move faster and risk losing another man to the dart thrower.

Nor did he want to risk himself.

As a result, Hal and his two companions had stretched their lead considerably. With Lydia bringing up the rear, constantly stopping and checking the trail behind them, they moved at a half run, winding their way toward the far side of the ravine.

Thorn and Ingvar moved more slowly, hobbling along the narrow side trail they had taken, searching either side for a good hiding place. Both were aware that this slow pace was letting their pursuers close the gap. They had only minutes to find a suitable spot.

They rounded a sharp turn in the trail and Ingvar lurched to a stop, pointing at a dark opening among the boulders ahead.

"How about there?" he said.

Thorn peered suspiciously at what appeared to be a cave among the rocks. He pursed his lips in a negative expression. "It's a bit obvious," he said. "They'll be sure to check it out when they see it."

He was assuming the worst case possible—that the Iberians would turn off the main trail to follow him and Ingvar. If they did, the cave would be not so much a hiding place as a trap. He felt Ingvar's shoulders slump in disappointment

"You're right," Ingvar said. "Let's keep moving."

"At least it'll slow them down when they do check it," Thorn told him and they edged their way past the slit in the rocks. As they came closer, they could see that it was little more than a meter and a half high and a meter wide. Behind it, the shadows were deep and impenetrable. Thorn hesitated, bringing their stumbling progress to a stop. Maybe it might be a good spot after all, he thought. If they were in the darkness inside, they could ambush their pursuers as they came through that low opening. And so far, they hadn't seen any other likely spot to hole up.

He turned to make this suggestion to Ingvar when, suddenly, his blood froze.

A deep, threatening rumble sounded from the darkness inside. He felt Ingvar tense and stand straighter.

"Is that what I think it is?" Ingvar asked, the fear obvious in his voice.

Thorn nodded. "It sounds like that bear Lydia was talking about," he said, keeping his voice low. Even so, the sound of it reached to whatever was inside the cave, and once more, the blood-freezing growl echoed from the darkness.

Thorn, his arm around Ingvar's waist, backed away from the opening, moving farther along the track. Ingvar hopped with him, the scuffling sound of his boots on the rocks drawing another threatening rumble from the cave.

A thought struck the old sea wolf and he began to search the rocks around them.

Finally, his eye fell on a low fissure in the shape of an inverted V, where two slabs of rock had slipped from the rim of the gully and come to rest against each other. They reached the narrow opening and Thorn gestured for Ingvar to drop to his knees.

"Crawl on through," he ordered. The gap wasn't tall enough for them to pass through any way other than on hands and knees. Ingvar scrabbled his way through the narrow space, turning his shoulders to give himself room. Thorn, waiting anxiously, could hear vague sounds behind them—low voices and the footfall of boots on the uneven rock surface of the track. Finally, Ingvar's feet disappeared from sight.

"It widens out behind here," Ingvar called back.

Thorn dropped to his hand and knees and hurriedly crawled in after Ingvar. There was an open space beyond the two fallen slabs, as Ingvar had said. It was barely three meters by two, but there was room for the two of them to crouch out of sight. It was also, he noted uneasily, a blind alley. There was no way out other than the way they had come in.

The same thought must have occurred to Ingvar. He gestured around the rock walls that contained them. "Is this any better than the cave?" he asked. "If they look for us here, we'll be like rats in a trap."

Thorn nodded. "There's one advantage," he said. "To look for us here, they have to get past that very bad-tempered bear. I doubt they'll be keen to do that. She'll keep them out."

Understanding dawned on Ingvar's face. Then it was replaced by doubt. "One question . . . When we decide to leave, won't she also keep *us* in?" he asked.

Thorn regarded him with some exasperation. "We'll worry about that when we decide to leave," he said.

With no sign of their dart-throwing quarry for some time, the Iberians had begun to move with greater confidence. Juan, leading the way, was now moving at a swift walk, although still pausing at every bend to check the way ahead. His men bunched up behind him, their equipment and weapons rattling and their footsteps echoing off the rock floor. Juan considered ordering them to move more carefully, but discarded the idea. There were a score of them and they were all sailors, not hunters or stalkers. It was inevitable that they would make noise on a rough and rock-strewn track like this.

He stopped at yet another twist in the track and peered around, showing as little of himself as possible. Behind him, he heard several of his men collide as the line of men telescoped and those at the rear failed to stop in time. He muttered a curse as he studied the track before him.

This was a relatively long, straight section. He heaved a small sigh of relief as he saw no sign of the dart thrower. Signaling for his men to follow, he stepped out into the open and advanced once more.

After several meters, he stopped, holding up his hand and gritting his teeth as he heard the inevitable exclamations behind him as his men ran into one another.

The track ahead of him forked, with one section angling to the right and the other turning sharp left. He started forward, moving more swiftly as he came to the division.

Which way, he wondered. The path to the right was wider. It was the main track, leading toward the far side of the ravine. Logically, that was the way the strangers would have gone. He studied it thoughtfully. It led over hard rock and there were no footprints to be seen. But on the left, there was a patch of coarse sand a few meters past the division in the track. He moved toward it and dropped to his knees for a closer look.

There were definite footprints here, although they were scuffed and indistinct, making it difficult to see how many people had passed along the track. In some places, the footprints overlaid each other, and one track was indistinct, as if the foot had been dragged through the sand, rather than stepping evenly on it.

The sandy patch lasted only a few meters before giving way to broken rock. Juan was no tracker, but it was obvious to him that people had passed this way. And from the clear, sharp-edged imprints that accompanied the indistinct dragging track, they had been here recently.

He rose and gestured down the side track. "This way," he said.

Conscious now that they must be close behind their quarry, he reverted to his previous cautious pace, his eyes searching the shadows ahead of him for any movement.

His men stumbled and clattered behind him, their noise and clumsiness setting his teeth on edge. In deference to his constant orders for silence, those nearest him refrained from talking. But from farther back down the small column of armed men, he could hear comments being made in lowered tones—as if those making them assumed that they were inaudible.

And so he moved on, accompanied by incautious footfalls, the rattle of equipment and weapons, and indistinct, mumbling voices. He shook his head in frustration. Discipline among the pirate crew was regrettably slack—understandable when one considered the nature of their chosen profession. Pirates tended to ignore authority and to behave as they wished, which was why they were pirates in the first place.

At least, he thought, that same disregard for discipline and order made them fearsome fighters. If and when they caught up with the group ahead of them, he had no qualms about the result of the fight that would ensue. This noisy, shambling rabble he was leading would fall on any hostile group with quick and merciless force. He could think of no enemy that would stand up to them.

Except Skandians, he amended. But then, there were no Skandians within a hundred leagues, and he was grateful for the fact.

And then he saw the cave.

chapter twenty-nine

Hal, Stig and Lydia reached the foot of the track leading up the western side of the ravine. Lydia called a halt and then gestured for silence as she listened for any sound of pursuit. She didn't want to be halfway up the path and exposed to view if the pirates arrived.

"I think we've shaken them off," she said.

Hal frowned. "Which means they've gone after Thorn and Ingvar," he said unhappily.

Stig disagreed. "Not necessarily. We've been moving quickly and they would have slowed up after Lydia hit a couple of them. Maybe we've just got ahead of them. If they'd caught up with Thorn and Ingvar, we would have heard them."

Hal nodded reluctantly. "I suppose so," he said. He had hated to leave his two shipmates behind, but the choice had been forced on him.

Sensing his skirl's feelings, Stig dropped an understanding hand on his shoulder. "Don't blame yourself," he said. "You made the right decision—and Thorn will make sure they're not taken."

Lydia looked gratefully at Stig. She had hated deserting Ingvar and she had experienced the same foreboding feeling as Hal. She studied the track behind them, then urged them toward the path up the cliff. "Let's get back to the ship," she said.

Hal started up the steep path, Stig close behind him. Lydia waited a few seconds until the shower of rocks and pebbles dislodged by their feet had died away, then followed them swiftly. Practiced in moving stealthily over rough ground, she made little noise. She paused halfway to the top, turning back to look down into the ravine, searching along the narrow track they had taken. There was no sight of the pursuing Iberians, although her view of the track only extended for a hundred meters or so. More significantly, there was no sound of them approaching either, and she knew that such a large party moving over the rough ground would be unavoidably noisy. Satisfied, she started up the path again. Like Hal, she felt a twinge of concern about the fate of Ingvar and Thorn.

Shaking her head, she pushed the thought away. There was nothing she could do now, she realized. Thorn and Ingvar would have to take their chances. She reached the top of the cliff and found Hal and Stig waiting for her. Casting one last glance into the shadowy depths of the ravine, she led the way toward the little bay where the *Heron* was waiting for them.

"What's happening?" Ingvar whispered. Although he kept his voice low, it sounded deafening to Thorn, who was crouched, peering out through the narrow slit in the rocks. There was only room for one of them at a time to observe the track and the cave. He twisted awkwardly and crawled back to Ingvar, who was crouched farther back in the narrow, cramped space. Placing his mouth close to Ingvar's ear, he said in a barely audible voice:

"They've found the cave. They're checking it."

Ingvar turned his head and met Thorn's gaze. There was an expectant smile on the older man's face. Then Ingvar pushed past him and crawled to the opening to watch what was about to happen.

The track widened a little outside the mouth of the cave and Juan signaled half a dozen of his men into a curved line, surrounding the low opening. The rest of his men stayed back, jammed together by the rock walls, crowding up on one another to watch. He drew his sword, and there was a rustle of steel on leather as his men did the same. He moved forward, toward the mouth of the cave, and the line moved with him, drawing closer together as they advanced. He stopped a few meters from the cave mouth, conscious of the men either side of him jostling him.

He turned his head to listen, dropping to one knee so that he could hear more clearly any sound that might emanate from the low cave mouth.

He fancied he could hear a vague movement coming from inside the cave—something heavy moving across the rock-and-sand floor. He recalled the blurred, dragging footprint he had seen in the sand where the track had forked and felt a surge of expectation. Maybe one of the people they were pursuing was injured and moving awkwardly, he thought. His heart rate accelerated. He glanced to either side, making sure his men were ready. Then he called out.

"In the cave! Whoever you are! Come on out."

Silence from the cave.

In the heightened tension, he could hear the ragged breathing of the men beside him. He clenched and unclenched his hand on the sword grip, holding it forward, point lowered. He rose slowly to his feet and called again, louder this time.

"In the cave! Come out now!"

"Show yourself!" yelled one of the other men, unable to stay silent. Juan glared at him. He was about to tell him to shut up when the silence from the cave was finally broken.

A low, rumbling sound, full of threat and menace.

Juan felt the hairs on the back of his neck stand on end. That was no human sound, he realized. In fact, he had no idea what it was—he had never encountered a bear before. But superstition was rife among the Iberians, and he wondered if such an unearthly sound might come from a djinn or a demon.

Instinctively, he backed up a pace. The line went with him, and for a moment, he feared the men might panic. If they ran, he realized, they would become tangled up and jammed together in the narrow track, at the mercy of whatever was inside the cave.

"Hold your line," he ordered, struggling to keep his voice even. He leveled his sword at the cave, noticing that his hand was shaking so that the tip of the blade trembled.

Again, the sound boomed out of the cave, louder this time—and this time with a definite note of threat in it. Juan sensed rather than saw one of his men backing slowly away.

"Stay where you are!" he ordered, and the movement stopped. But his voice had risen in volume when he gave the order and that seemed to anger the source of that threatening rumble even more. Now he heard a blood-chilling, full-throated roar from the cave—a sound that rose in volume and extended for what seemed like minutes.

One of the men in the line let out a yelp of fear, calling on his gods to protect him. Like Juan, his men had decided that the sound came from something supernatural, something terrifying and ghastly to behold.

"Shut up!" hissed Juan. This time, he kept his own voice down, as his previous shout had seemed to anger the creature even more. But the damage was already done. He saw movement in the shadowy darkness of the cave mouth, and a dark shape began to emerge.

Juan may have been frightened, but he was no coward and he was an experienced fighting man. Instinctively, he realized that retreat would be a mistake. The way was blocked by his own men, huddled together on the track, and he would be exposing his back to the creature if he turned and ran. Besides, now he could see that he was facing some kind of animal, big and heavy, but not a supernatural being.

It was brown and shaggy, but it was barely a meter and a half tall as it shuffled out of the cave mouth. And as he realized that, his confidence surged.

"Come on!" he shouted to his men, and he stepped forward, drawing back his sword for a killing blow.

And then the beast stood up.

It seemed to rise up forever, until it was well over two meters high, towering above him and roaring with defiance and rage. He saw the dim light in the ravine reflecting off huge, sharp teeth, and saw the immense claws on the end of its massive forepaws.

He froze. Dimly, he was aware of the cries of terror and alarm from his men, and realized that the line had broken and they were scrambling back to escape from the horror that confronted them. Then the bear moved forward, with startling speed.

One massive, claw-laden paw swiped at him before he could bring his sword forward in defense. The huge claws opened four red weals across his face. But it was the force of the blow that did the real damage. Juan was hurled back across the narrow clearing, smashing into the rock wall behind him. His limp body slid slowly to the ground.

Then the bear set about the other men standing facing it. Snarling and roaring with hatred, it lunged forward, snapping at the men with those terrible, powerful jaws. At the same time, it smashed to left and right with its massive paws, the claws rending and tearing flesh, sending men flying out of its way.

Helpless to defend themselves against the rampaging monster, the line broke and the survivors fell back, desperately trying to find some way of escape.

But Juan's earlier prediction was born out now as the men scrambled and fought against one another, trying to force their way back down the narrow track, but becoming hopelessly tangled in a mass of bodies and arms and legs.

And all the while, the terrible bear snapped and smashed at those nearest it, leaving a trail of broken bodies.

Juan and five of his men paid the ultimate price, their bodies hurled to the rocks either side, or lying still where they fell. But eventually, the logjam cleared, and the survivors ran, screaming, back down the track.

The bear pursued them for a short distance, reared up on its hind legs, towering over the men that it caught up with. Then, sensing victory, it dropped back to all fours and, with a final devastating bellow of rage, shambled back to the cave and went inside to its cubs.

Thorn and Ingvar had crowded together to watch the attack. As silence fell over the track once more, Ingvar turned to his companion.

"What now? Should we make a run for it?"

Thorn shook his head. "I'm not going anywhere till that bear has calmed down. Her blood's up now, and any noise is likely to bring her storming out of that cave again."

Ingvar nodded agreement, then frowned. "But what about the Iberians? They're gone now."

"And they won't be back in a hurry. They won't stop running until they reach their camp. No, we'll wait it out and give the bear a chance to settle down. May as well make ourselves comfortable."

chapter thirty

Stefan was on lookout duty when the small party reached his position at the top of the cliff overlooking *Heron*'s mooring. He tilted his head curiously when he saw their diminished numbers.

"Where are Thorn and Ingvar?" he asked. He couldn't believe that two of the fiercest warriors in the crew had been killed or taken by the Iberians.

Hal quickly reassured him. "They'll be along," he said. "Ingvar hurt his ankle, so they're hiding up until we go back for them." He glanced around the little bay below them. "Anything happening here?"

Stefan shook his head. "Not a thing. Haven't seen or heard anyone. It's getting pretty boring, as a matter of fact. Did you find *Wolfwind*?"

"Found her. Got to work out a way to take her. There are too many men around her for a simple attack." Hal looked away, distracted. Already an idea was beginning to form in his mind—just a hazy thought for the moment. He knew he had to sit down and clear his mind of other matters so he could put flesh on the bones of his nascent plan. He turned toward the path leading down into the bay.

"I need coffee," he said. "Coffee, food and a few hours' sleep."

But sleep didn't come to him. He lay on his back, staring at the roof of the tent close overhead, his thoughts racing. And slowly, his plan developed.

He rose from his sheepskin and crept out the door of his tent, stooped double. Once outside, he stood erect and studied the campsite. Edvin and Stig were sitting opposite each other across a small fire. The rest of the crew were relaxing or resting on the sand.

Erak was a few meters away, his head nodding as he dozed. Kloof lay on her belly in front of him, her chin on her paws, the eyes fixed on the ebony shaft of his walking stick where it lay on the sand beside him. Sensing that he was asleep, she wriggled forward on her belly, coming closer to him by a few centimeters. When he didn't react, she repeated the movement.

"Put that thought right out of your head," Erak growled, without opening his eyes. Kloof's tail thumped twice on the hard sand and she wriggled forward again, eyes fixed on the gleaming black-and-silver prize.

Hal grinned at the ongoing contest. He glanced up to the rim of the cliff. Stefan had completed his turn as sentry, and Wulf was now on duty. Hal sat down beside Edvin and Stig.

"Break camp and get the gear back on board," he said. Then he glanced around. "Where's Lydia?"

Edvin gestured to the top of the cliff. "She went hunting an hour or so ago," he said. "She should be back soon. Are we leaving?"

Hal nodded. His plan entailed partially disabling *Heron,* and he had no wish to be discovered by a search party while she was in that condition.

"Now that they know there are strangers in the vicinity, the pirates may well send out search parties. I'd rather put some extra distance between us and them if they do," he explained.

Edvin turned away. "I'll get things ready to go," he said.

Stig glanced up at Hal, curiosity on his face. "I take it you have an idea?"

Hal nodded, dropping to the sand. "As I told Stefan, there are too many men for us to make a direct assault on the pirates' camp," he began. "We're going to have to lure *Wolfwind* out to sea, where we can take advantage of our speed and maneuverability—and the Mangler," he added, after a pause.

Stig grinned. "Erak will love that part."

Hal regarded him seriously. "Erak will have to put up with it. He shouldn't have let his ship be captured in the first place." Which was a little harsh. Erak wasn't solely responsible for the loss of *Wolfwind.* The blame could be shared by the entire population of Hallasholm, Hal included.

Stig poked a charred stick into the embers of the fire, raising a small shower of sparks and bringing the flames to life once more.

"*Wolfwind*'s not going to come out after *Heron,*" he pointed out. "They know we can outsail her."

"She won't come after *Heron*," Hal agreed. "But she might come out after a clumsy trading coaster."

"*Heron* in disguise?" Stig asked.

Hal nodded. "Exactly."

His friend considered the idea. It was simple—but most good plans were. And it would give them an element of surprise when the enemy realized what they were chasing. Surprise could well counterbalance the discrepancy in numbers between the two crews. The Iberians would expect the crew of the "trader" to surrender meekly when they discovered they couldn't outrun the raider. They wouldn't expect them to fight back with the ferocity of a wounded tiger.

Stig nodded thoughtfully. "Just get us close to *Wolfwind*'s crew," he said. "And leave the rest to us."

"I'll see what I can do," Hal told him.

An hour later, their gear was packed back aboard the *Heron*. Lydia had returned, with the skinned, gutted body of a small deer slung over her shoulder.

Edvin eyed it appraisingly. "I take it we'll be camping farther down the coast?" he asked Hal. When the skirl agreed, he rubbed his hands together with pleasure. "We'll eat well tonight then," he told Lydia.

They boarded the ship and launched her from the beach. There was a favorable wind and Hal didn't waste any time rowing out of the bay. He ordered the sail up and sent the trim little ship gliding out to sea, heading east.

As she swooped and cruised over the evenly spaced rollers, he experienced his usual pleasure at the feel of the ship—taut, responsive and perfectly in tune with her element. A frown crossed his face as he cast his mind forward to the way he knew she would feel when he had finished the planned alterations. She would be clumsy and wallowing, he knew.

And slow. Desperately slow.

They sailed down the coast for a further eight kilometers before Hal was satisfied that they were far enough from the pirates' base. Sighting a narrow beach where a small stand of pines crowned the headland, he brought the ship in until its bow grated on the sand. As ever, Jesper dropped over the bulwark and carried a sand anchor up the beach some twenty meters.

"Set up camp, Edvin," Hal ordered. Then he beckoned Stefan and Jesper to him. "See that growth of pines?" he asked, pointing to the top of the headland. They looked up and nodded. "Go find me a sapling—say three meters long and straight enough to use as a yardarm. Strip it and bring it back down here."

The two nodded. They showed no surprise or curiosity at the unusual order. They were used to Hal's ideas by now, and the strange commands that often accompanied them. Hal ordered Ulf and Wulf to rouse out the tarpaulin that was used to shelter the deck of *Heron* in bad weather, and had them bring it to him on the afterdeck, where he sat with his sail-needle, palm and heavy thread, waiting for them.

He spread the tarpaulin out on the deck and quickly marked out a rectangle, three meters by two, and began cutting it out with a pair of heavy shears. He marked reinforcing and shaping seams in the rectangle of cloth and stitched them neatly, so that the canvas puckered and would pull the sail into a more efficient shape.

Then he began sewing loops made from broad strips of the leftover canvas into the top of the sail, ready to slip over the yardarm when Stefan and Jesper delivered it. He had finished the last of these, fitting the two end loops with wooden pegs to hold them in position, when the two arrived with the pole. He nodded in satisfaction when he saw it. It was almost perfectly symmetrical, without any undue bends or irregularities. It would serve ideally for his purpose. He slipped the loops over the trimmed pole, fastening the end loops into place with the wooden pins, and studied the result.

"Hold it up," he ordered.

Stefan and Jesper hoisted the spar off the deck, holding it up so that the roughly formed sail dropped below it, stirring slightly in the soft breeze. Hal studied it and nodded approval.

"That looks fine," he said, and gestured for them to set it down.

It took a little longer to rig the halyards and lashing that would hoist the yard up the mast and secure it there. Hal worked busily, his head down and his tongue protruding slightly from his teeth. Stig and Thorn, well used to watching him at work on the ship, refrained from asking the many questions that ran through their brains. Hal worked on in silence until, late in the afternoon, he sat back, rubbing his aching back but regarding his handiwork with some satisfaction.

"All right," he said. "Let's get her hoisted."

Jesper shinned up the bare mast while the others rigged halyards and hoisted the new spar into position. Once it was at the top of the stumpy mast, Jesper set about lashing the cradle of ropes into position, so that the yardarm was held firmly in place, but free to swing toward either side of the mast. They fitted ropes to each extremity of the yardarm so that the sail could be hauled into position, depending on the wind. Further ropes attached to the two lower corners of the sail would act as sheets, pulling it tight against the wind.

A gust of wind blew in from the sea and the sail bellied out before it. Hal signaled for the twins to haul on the sheets and the sail filled, billowed out, then collapsed as the wind gust gave way.

Hal smiled. "I think that'll do very nicely," he said.

chapter thirty-one

It was too late in the day to try to lure *Wolfwind* from her lair. They camped for the night, feasting on the meat of the young deer that Lydia had shot. Erak patted his stomach in appreciation, having had two helpings of roast venison with vegetables. He leaned back against a log and gave a contented sigh.

"You Herons live well," he said to Hal.

The skirl smiled agreement. "Edvin is a good cook. And Lydia often provides fresh meat. It's the advantage of having a hunter as part of the crew."

In Erak's day, shipboard meals had usually consisted of salted meat or dried fish. And the preparation had been rough and ready. He'd never had a ship's cook with the skill that Edvin had developed.

"So what's the plan for tomorrow?" he asked.

Hal paused, gathering his thoughts, then replied. "We'll pick up Thorn and Ingvar first," he said, "then we'll cruise up the coast past the pirates' camp. Once we see them, we'll turn out to sea, as if we're trying to escape."

Erak snorted. "Not much chance of that with that blown-out sail rig you put together this afternoon."

"That's the general idea," Hal replied. "*Wolfwind*'s skipper will see how slow and clumsy we are and she'll come out after us. Once we've lured her far enough out to sea, we'll drop that rig and hoist our proper sails. And then the fun starts."

Erak's eyes narrowed. "You're not going to damage my ship with that overgrown crossbow of yours."

Hal shrugged. "We may have to, Erak. Face it. We'll be seriously outnumbered so we'll have to do something to compensate. I'm afraid you'll just have to get used to the idea. I'll try to keep the damage to a minimum, but if things get tight I can't promise you anything."

The Oberjarl assumed a glum look. He knew Hal was right. "I understand," he said. "But I don't have to like it."

It had taken a day for the bear to settle down. Obviously, the disturbance caused by the pirates' approaching her lair and threatening her cubs—as she saw it—had set her on edge. During the day, she emerged several times from her cave, prowling around the clear space outside the entrance and sniffing at the bodies of the Iberians she had attacked.

Thorn and Ingvar remained hidden in their own cramped niche among the rocks. Fortunately, they had water in their canteens, although they had nothing to eat—a fact that Ingvar bemoaned. Thorn was unsympathetic.

"It won't hurt you to skip a few meals," he said.

Ingvar turned a pained look on him. "I'm a growing lad."

Thorn raised his eyebrows at the thought. "Gorlog's beard, I hope not," he said. Ingvar was already taller and broader in the shoulders than anyone else in the crew. "How's the ankle?" he asked.

Ingvar rotated the injured member gingerly. "Seems to be freeing up a little," he said. "But it's still painful." He rose carefully to his feet and tested his weight on the ankle, grimacing in pain. "Another day should see it right."

As the day wore on, the bear spent more and more of her time in the cave, emerging infrequently and for only a short duration each time. Encouraged by the fact, Ingvar suggested that they might leave their hiding place, but Thorn vetoed the idea.

"There's no need to rush. Hal said they'd come back for us in two days. Let's give it another night and let her settle down even more."

Ingvar agreed, albeit reluctantly. "Whatever you say. It's just there's nothing to do but sit around."

"There'll be plenty to do if we go out there and disturb her," Thorn told him. "Let's let her go back to hibernating before we try to leave."

The following morning, they watched for an hour after first light for any sign of the creature. There was none, and Thorn stood, brushing the sand off his clothes and offering a hand to Ingvar to help him to his feet. The big warrior shifted from side to side, wincing slightly as he set his weight on the injured ankle. Thorn had bound it tightly with strips cut from Ingvar's jacket to support it.

"That's much better," he said, in reply to Thorn's inquiring glance. He limped toward the narrow entrance to the fissure. "So what do we do if she comes after us? Run?"

Thorn shook his head. "I doubt that you're up to running yet," he said. "You saw how fast she can move when she went after the Iberians. If we do disturb her, we'll have to fight her, so keep your weapon ready."

He gestured to the voulge Ingvar carried. It was a long-handled weapon, with a combined spear blade, ax and hook as its head. If there was an ideal weapon for facing a bear, the voulge definitely qualified.

They crouched at the opening leading out to the track, watching the cave mouth with intense interest. Thorn turned his head slightly to listen, but there was no sound from the bear. He indicated himself with his thumb.

"I'll go out first," he breathed.

Ingvar nodded agreement. It made sense for Thorn to go first. He could move faster and easier than Ingvar in the event that the bear heard movement and came to investigate. Ingvar stepped aside to let Thorn past. The one-armed sea wolf dropped to a crouch and went through the narrow gap on his hand and knees, rising quickly to his feet as he reached open space, his left hand dropping to the hilt of his saxe.

No sound came from the cave.

Thorn bent down again and gestured for Ingvar to follow him.

Ingvar scrambled through the narrow gap, turning his shoulders sideways as he went. In the last meter, as he emerged, his voulge caught against the rock slab that formed part of the entrance to the fissure where they'd sheltered. The spearhead rang against the rock with a metallic clang and Ingvar froze, halfway to his feet.

They both stared fearfully at the dark semicircle of the cave entrance. For a moment, there was no sound. Then they heard a low rumble from within. Thorn threw up a warning hand to tell Ingvar to remain still.

Seconds passed. They heard the faint sound of snuffling, and a heavy body moving inside the cave. Ingvar realized that the bear was settling down, turning in a circle and scratching at the sand floor of the cave with her claws to make a spot to lie down.

Just like a big dog, he thought. He had seen Kloof go through a similar routine countless times.

There was a lighter sound—a higher-pitched growl that was almost a squeak—as one of the cubs reacted to the mother's movement. She growled back, although this time the sound was less threatening and more reassuring. Then there was silence.

Thorn counted slowly to thirty, then gestured for Ingvar to start moving again. Ingvar complied, rising to a standing position and taking infinite care this time not to knock his voulge against the rocks. He took a limping pace toward Thorn, who glared at the voulge and shook his head at Ingvar.

Ingvar shrugged. *I didn't do it on purpose,* he thought.

With Thorn leading the way, they moved slowly and carefully back along the track, hugging the far wall as they passed the cave. They reached the narrower section of the track without further incident and paused to take stock. Ingvar wrinkled his nose at the torn and scattered bodies of the five Iberians who had fallen prey to the bear. Then Thorn touched his arm and led the way back down the track. The farther they went from the cave, the faster they moved as the immediate threat of the bear receded.

Hobbling swiftly, Ingvar caught up with Thorn and touched his arm to stop him.

The sea wolf regarded him curiously. "What is it?" he asked, in a lowered voice.

"Maybe we should take it easy," Ingvar suggested. "We don't want to run into the Iberians again."

Thorn gave a short laugh. "There's no fear of that," he said. "They probably haven't stopped running yet. After the way the bear went for them, they won't be hanging around anywhere here."

Ingvar realized he was right. Reassured, he let Thorn lead the way, half running and hopping on his aching ankle, using his voulge to support some of his weight.

In no time, they reached the fork in the track where they'd parted company with Hal, Stig and Lydia. They turned left and headed west.

They mounted the steep path leading to the top of the western side of the valley. Thorn paused to take Ingvar's arm as the going became harder. By the time they reached the top, they were both breathing heavily. They stopped to rest and a broad smile broke out on Thorn's face.

In the distance, he could see Hal and Lydia trotting toward them. As the two parties sighted each other, Lydia broke into a run.

chapter thirty-two

Once Thorn and Ingvar were back on board, the crew launched *Heron* and hoisted the clumsy replacement mainsail to the top of the mast. Hal had explained the essence of his plan to the two new arrivals, and Thorn looked scornfully at the loose, billowing sail.

Without proper shaping or reinforcing seams, it sagged loosely in the wind. Unlike *Heron*'s normal sails, it wouldn't hold a firm curve, so in spite of Ulf's and Wulf's best efforts—and they were expert sail trimmers—the sail alternately billowed and collapsed, billowed and collapsed as the gusts varied. As a result, their progress was measured in a series of surging, lurching rushes.

With each new gust, the rope harness fastening the yardarm to the mast would stretch out, then fall loose with a dull thud that resonated through the hull.

Thorn gripped the edge of the chart table to steady himself against the lurching, plunging movement.

"This is terrible," he said.

Hal nodded agreement. "That's the way I want it to be," he told the old sea wolf. "I don't want *Wolfwind* to feel threatened."

"Threatened?" Thorn scoffed, as the sail flapped loosely and half collapsed once more. "They'll probably die laughing at the sight of us."

They proceeded to lurch and plunge their way up the coast toward the pirates' encampment, although the journey took much longer than *Heron* had taken under her normal sail plan. As the wide bay drew closer, Hal studied the headland where the watchtower had been built. He could see small figures moving, climbing the ladders that led to the observation deck. Faintly, he heard the sound of the alarm horn.

"They've seen us," he reported. "Check your weapons."

It would be some time before they came into contact with the pirates manning *Wolfwind* but the crew members proceeded to draw their weapons—axes and swords as their individual fancy took them—and unhooked the distinctive round shields from the railing. Nothing would identify *Heron* as a fighting ship faster than those. Stig passed Hal his triangular metal-and-wood shield, and the skirl nodded his thanks, leaning it against the bulwark beside him. Then Stig fetched the rectangular wooden shield designed to protect the steering position and slotted it into place.

"Better get the Mangler ready," he said. Even though they still had time up their sleeves, it was better to make their preparations without any sense of urgency. Stig headed for'ard and unlashed the tarpaulin protecting the big crossbow from spray. He eased the weapon back and forth a couple of times, making sure it traversed smoothly. Ingvar joined him and they checked the ready ammunition locker, selecting two of the heavy bolts that the weapon shot. Satisfied that all was ready, Stig turned and, leaning under the sail, gave Hal a thumbs-up.

As *Heron* sailed clumsily past the eastern headland, the bay opened up before them and they could see the camp, with *Wolfwind* moored at the far end. The alarm had already been sounded from the headland and men were running in all directions. The camp looked to all intents like a disturbed anthill, and Hal could make out a line of Iberians hurrying to board *Wolfwind*.

"Time we weren't here," he muttered and swung the tiller over to head the ship south and out to sea. The wind, now almost dead astern, bellied the sail out, pulling the yardarm clear of the mast. The little ship surged unevenly forward, then lost way as the wind fell momentarily, only to lurch once more as it picked up and the sail filled again.

"Do we look as if we're panicking?" Hal asked Erak, who, without a set battle station, had joined him by the tiller.

"I don't know how I look, but I am panicking," the Oberjarl replied grimly.

Hal smiled. "Let me know when *Wolfwind* clears the bay," he said. Then he returned his attention to the tiller. The unbalanced sail made *Heron*'s steering awkward and erratic. She tended to yaw off course, requiring constant correction.

Several minutes later, Erak pointed astern. "She's out," he said. "She's under oars but they're raising the sail now."

Hal glanced over his shoulder. He could see the white rectangle of *Wolfwind*'s sail blossoming just above the horizon. He nodded to himself in satisfaction. Even at their current slow speed, they had traveled a considerable distance from the coast. He estimated that it would take *Wolfwind* another quarter of an hour before she was in striking distance.

They plunged and rolled on. The Sonderland coast was now a thin gray line on the horizon. *Wolfwind* was edging closer. Initially, only her sail had shown above the horizon but now, as they rose on each successive roller, they could make out her hull as well.

"Jesper!" called Hal. "Up into the cross-trees. Get ready to cut that sail loose when I give the word."

Jesper nodded and swarmed up the mast, hand over hand, settling himself on the yardarm, close to the mast. Hal checked the wind telltale. The wind was still coming from the shore, but was at a slight angle to their stern, coming over the starboard quarter.

"Ulf! Wulf!" Hal called. "We'll go with the port sail first."

"Port sail," Wulf called in confirmation, and he and his brother scrambled into the starboard rowing well, where they crouched ready by the halyards and stays.

Wolfwind was now fully visible behind them, and coming closer. They could see her even when *Heron* sank into the troughs of the waves, and Hal could begin to make out details. In contrast, the coastline was now below the horizon, out of sight.

"Where do you want me?" Lydia asked quietly.

Hal glanced at her and saw that she had two quivers of darts slung over her shoulders. The atlatl itself was ready in her right hand. He gestured for'ard.

"Move up by the mast," he said. "It looks as if they have archers and spearmen in the bows, ready to shoot at Stig on the Mangler. See what you can do to discourage them."

She nodded that she understood and made her way for'ard, moving smoothly in time to the lurching, rolling deck.

"You'll be turning back into *Wolfwind*?" Thorn asked.

Hal nodded, looking over his shoulder and judging the relative speeds of the two ships, and the angle between them. "Any minute now," he said, his eyes narrowing as he measured the distance to *Wolfwind*. With the wind behind her, she was bearing down on them, her bow plunging into the waves, sending showers of white spray high on either side. There were men crowded into the bow section, waving weapons and yelling threats at the little ship.

Erak grunted. "Now I know how people felt when they saw *me* coming," he said.

"It's not a pleasant sight," Hal agreed. Then he turned and shouted to Jesper. "Cut loose the sail. Ulf, Wulf, send up the port-side sail as soon as it's clear."

Jesper didn't bother to acknowledge. The blade of his saxe flashed in the sun as he drew it. Then, stepping onto the bracket that held the fore and aft yardarms in place, he swung the razor-sharp knife at the rope cradle supporting the square sail. They heard two loud thumps, then the long yardarm fell away as the twins released the halyards that secured it.

The sail collapsed, folding up under the falling yardarm. There was a moment of confusion as Stefan and Ingvar gathered it in, clearing it out of the way. Then the port yardarm soared up the mast as Ulf and Wulf bent to the halyards. Jesper stepped off into the rigging to clear the way as the yardarm thunked solidly into the bracket at the masthead. Then the twins cleated off the halyards and hauled in on the sheets, and the triangular sail hardened to the wind, bellying out, then settling into a smooth, firm curve. At the same time, Thorn, waiting behind the mast, shoved the fin keel down into its recess, providing the ship with a firmer grip upon the water.

Hal felt the difference through the tiller almost immediately. The little ship steadied, then thrust ahead with new energy, shedding the rolling, lurching motion and accelerating smoothly.

During the changeover, *Wolfwind* had drawn almost abreast of them, some thirty meters off their starboard quarter. But now, as *Heron* showed her true performance, the bigger ship fell rapidly behind.

Faintly, above the hiss of their passage through the water and the groaning of the rigging and sails under the new pressure, Hal could hear *Wolfwind*'s helmsman shouting instructions to his sail handlers as they hauled desperately on the sheets, trying to match their quarry's new burst of speed.

But *Heron* was now the faster of the two ships and she drew ahead with each passing second. Hal watched as the big wolfship fell astern, still on their starboard side.

"Stand by to wear ship to starboard!" he shouted. "Ready on the Mangler!"

He planned to cross *Wolfwind*'s bow and turn 180 degrees so that *Heron* was heading north, giving Stig a clean shot at the other ship.

"Wear ship!" he yelled, and threw the tiller over. Instantly, Ulf and Wulf let the port-side sail come sliding down and hauled up the starboard sail. Edvin and Stefan gathered in the lowered sail, leaving it ready to be raised again as needed.

Hal had hoped the helmsman on *Wolfwind* would try to match their maneuver, turning to starboard and presenting Stig with an easy, close-range shot. But the Iberian was an experienced seaman. He could see that *Heron* was the more agile of the two ships and wasn't prepared to indulge in a turning duel with her. Instead, he swung his bows to port, away from the little ship, and the huge weapon that threatened him from its bow, gaining sea room from her.

"Gorlog bite him!" Hal exclaimed. "I hoped he'd let us get close."

chapter thirty-three

Now the two ships circled away from each other, *Heron* wheeling to starboard and *Wolfwind* turning to port. Hal glanced at Erak, crouching beside him, shield on his left arm and his huge battleax ready in his right.

"He's no fool," Erak said, through clenched teeth.

Hal nodded. "More's the pity," he replied. He checked the wind once more, and the set of the sail. *Wolfwind* was far out to starboard now but *Heron*'s superior speed and agility were starting to take effect. As *Wolfwind* came round to complete her turn, *Heron* was already ahead of her, sailing on a parallel course.

"Going about to starboard!" Hal yelled, and put the tiller over. There was no need to change the sail. The starboard sail, now let out to its fullest extent, drove the ship through the turn. The *Heron* wheeled around to face the wolfship, bearing down on her, port side to port side. *Wolfwind* was now heading into the wind, and as they turned, Hal saw her big square sail shiver, then disappear as her crew let it slide down from the mast. At the same time, oars appeared on either side and began to stroke powerfully.

It was all done smoothly and quickly and it bespoke an experienced and well-practiced crew. Hal frowned. That wasn't going to make matters any easier, he thought. He'd hoped the Iberians would be clumsy and unused to their new ship. Obviously, that wasn't going to be the case. After all, he realized, they'd had plenty of time to get used to her.

In spite of that, the maneuver presented *Heron* with an opportunity. If he could catch the enemy skipper napping, he might be able to sweep down *Wolfwind*'s port side, smashing and splintering the oars with *Heron*'s sharp, reinforced stem. He angled the little ship to port, hoping to close with *Wolfwind*. If he could smash her port-side bank of oars, she would be seriously disadvantaged when it came to traveling upwind. In addition, the impact of *Heron*'s bow on the oars would cause havoc on board, with the butts of the oars swinging wildly in the collision, injuring the oarsmen, breaking limbs and knocking them unconscious.

He heard the familiar thump of the Mangler as Stig sent a projectile hurtling toward the enemy ship. Vaguely, he realized that Stig had been shooting while the two ships headed for each other.

Out of the corner of his eye, he saw Lydia step clear of the mast, a dart poised over her shoulder, then saw her release. The missile flashed across the intervening space, and one of the pirates fell back from the railing of the bigger ship.

But that momentary distraction was enough to cause Hal to misjudge the angle. As *Heron* swung in toward *Wolfwind*, the opposing helmsman yawed *Wolfwind* to starboard, so that *Heron*'s knifelike bow missed the row of swinging oars by a wide margin. *Wolfwind*, oars beating the water to foam, was able to accelerate clear of her smaller harasser and head north at high speed, putting more distance between them as *Heron* sailed through her wake, plunging and rocking as she crossed the disturbed water left behind the wolfship.

"He's too good," Hal muttered to himself. Then, realizing that he was losing ground, he yelled to the sail handlers. "Wear ship!"

Ulf and Wulf crouched over the sheets as the ship came round. The wind was now coming from over her starboard quarter, and as they turned and headed upwind, it shifted to her port bow. As before, the wind drove the sail across during the turn, so they lost no speed. But now they had a lot of distance to make up before they could attack the wolfship once more.

Stig, realizing that it would be some time before they were in contact with *Wolfwind* again, ran lightly back down the deck to report to Hal.

"I got three shots away," he said. "That cleared out a good dozen of her crew. And Lydia hit two more."

Hal gave him a satisfied nod. They were still outnumbered, but the odds were definitely improving. That left fourteen fewer men to deal with. But he needed to damage *Wolfwind* seriously. If possible, he needed to disable her by raking her oars or damaging her rigging. And he had to do it before the bigger ship escaped back into her haven. They wouldn't get another chance to surprise her.

"I'm going head to head with her again," he told Stig. "As we get close, aim for her chain plates. I want to disable her."

The chain plates were the timber-retaining panels that anchored heavy rope cables supporting the mast on either side—fastening the mast to the ship's bulwarks and holding it erect. If Stig could smash them, the mast would be unsupported on one side.

"I'll bring her down our port side," he added. Stig nodded, turning to make his way for'ard again. As he went, Hal shouted, "Thorn!"

The one-armed sea wolf looked back from his position by the mast, then hurried to make his way aft. When he was within earshot, Hal quickly laid out his plan.

"I'm going to head her again. When we turn south, bring up the fin keel. But be ready to put it down again the minute I call for it."

Thorn frowned at the instructions, wondering what Hal had in mind. But he knew the young skirl must have his reasons—and past experience told him they'd be good ones.

"Fin up once we've turned south, then down again when you call. Got it."

And he turned and ran back to his battle station by the mast.

Hal checked the telltale once more. The wind was holding true, and *Heron* was butting through the waves as close to the wind as she would lie. *Wolfwind* was ahead and out to port, oars still thrashing the water. If her skipper wanted to fight, Hal thought, he'd turn her south again and raise her sail. But the pirate helmsman obviously wasn't interested in continuing the contest. He had little to gain by doing so and he risked having his ship badly damaged. He could only avoid *Heron*'s attacks for so long. And now he had a better idea of her capabilities—and her armament. He'd seen how the Mangler could decimate his crew while *Heron* stood off at a relatively safe distance, where he had no chance of retaliating. And her superior agility and speed nullified his best tactic—to close with her and ram or board her.

Slowly, *Heron* crept past the wolfship, steadily increasing her lead while maintaining a parallel course. But the time wasn't right to turn in yet. Hal was going to need a substantial lead over the other ship so that he could angle in and cross ahead of her, then have time to turn south onto his ramming course.

The minutes passed. *Heron* swooped up and over the smooth rollers, gradually overtaking *Wolfwind*. And the longer the race continued, the more ground she would make up as the oarsmen on board *Wolfwind* tired. Already, they had been maintaining a cracking pace for some time. Hal knew that an experienced crew could row for hours at a time—but not at this muscle-wrenching pace. Full speed like this could only be maintained for a matter of minutes.

Already, he had seen telltale signs that the rowers were changing over. From time to time, a pair of oars would rise clear of the water while the rest of them continued to stroke. In that interval, a fresh pair of oarsmen would take their place on the benches. But it was done at a cost. As the oarsmen changed over, the ship's speed necessarily dropped off. And by the time the changeover was completed, the rowers who had already changed would be beginning to tire.

He smiled grimly. In this race of sails against oars, the odds were all in *Heron*'s favor.

Heron continued to increase her lead, and now *Wolfwind* was well behind them, and out on the port quarter.

"She's slowing," said Erak, and Hal nodded as his previous thought was confirmed. Kloof, forepaws braced on the ship's port railing, barked defiance at the other ship. Hal's eyes shifted constantly between the enemy ship, the sail and the wind telltale at the top of the mast, ready for any change in the conditions that might affect his plan. *Heron* was traveling at close to her top speed now and he could sense the slight hum that reverberated through the sound box of the hull. He smiled grimly to himself.

"That's my girl," he whispered.

Erak glanced at him curiously. "Did you say something?"

Hal merely shook his head, continuing that pattern of watchfulness: sail, telltale, *Wolfwind*. The other ship was well astern, but still on their port side. As they sank into the trough of each successive wave, her hull was hidden from sight for several seconds at a time, only to reappear as the two ships climbed to the next wave's crest.

"I think the time might be about right," Hal said, more to himself than to Erak. Then, raising his voice, he shouted to the twins. "Coming about to port!"

He put the tiller over and watched the starboard sail slide down, to be replaced instantly by the port-side sail. The maneuver was carried out smoothly and efficiently, and *Heron* was quickly headed on her new course, angling across the bow of the distant wolfship as it continued to beat its oars into the water either side.

Hal wanted to cross her path completely, so that he would be able to approach her downwind, port side to port side. He saw movement on the foredeck, where Stig and Ingvar were preparing the Mangler for the attack he'd ordered. It was a pity, he thought, that they couldn't use one of the exploding warheads he had developed when they were fighting the Temujai in the high mountains above Skandia. But such pyrotechnics were too dangerous to use on board ship. There was always the risk that they could cause as much damage to *Heron* as to an enemy.

He was past *Wolfwind*'s course now, peering back at her over the port quarter of the ship. A few more meters, he thought. A few more . . . now!

"Coming about!" he yelled, and swung the tiller until the wind was over the starboard quarter. Ulf and Wulf let the sail out to its fullest extent and *Heron* accelerated once more.

"Thorn," Hal yelled. "Fin keel!"

But there was no need to remind him. Thorn was already hauling the fin keel up into its recess behind the sail.

chapter thirty-four

Instantly, Hal felt the difference in *Heron*'s response. As the fin keel was raised, the ship lost much of its grip upon the water and began to drift downwind to port, even as she surged forward.

Hal kept her bows pointed at the enemy ship, but he could see the sideways drift taking effect. He tweaked the tiller so that *Heron* was pointing well to the right of the other ship. But the lateral movement meant that, no matter where she was pointed, she was drifting downwind to the left, failing to hold her course.

Stig could see the same thing from his position for'ard. He turned and shouted to Hal in the stern. "Engaging to port?"

"Port side," Hal shouted back. He smiled grimly in satisfaction. If Stig could see the drift was taking them across the other ship's path, it was highly likely that *Wolfwind*'s helmsman would see it too. When he did, his obvious course would be to bear straight ahead, with *Heron*'s vulnerable forepart exposed to a ramming attack. Even if *Heron* could turn back and face her bow to bow, *Wolfwind* was bigger and heavier and would crush the smaller *Heron* underfoot.

"Let's see if you're as good as we think," Hal said, and at that moment, he was gratified to note the slight alteration in *Wolfwind*'s course as she angled round to allow for *Heron*'s lateral movement.

"He's fallen for it!" he exclaimed triumphantly to Erak, who was watching *Wolfwind* bearing down on them with increasing concern. As an experienced helmsman himself, Erak could see that *Heron* was sailing into danger, her fragile sides exposed to the reinforced bow of the wolfship.

"That's good," he said doubtfully. "If you say so."

"Thorn!" yelled Hal. Thorn leaned on the raised fin keel, driving it down into the water beneath *Heron*.

Again, the effect was instantly obvious. The big fin increased *Heron*'s grip on the water, halting the leeward drift immediately. She steadied, then answered to the helm as Hal brought her bows back to starboard. Now, instead of simply yawing awkwardly as she continued to drift to the left, she shot smoothly and powerfully to the right, crossing back in front of the oncoming *Wolfwind*, then swinging to approach her, port side to port side.

Wolfwind tried to match the maneuver but there was not enough time. Hal had judged his move perfectly, swinging the ship just as *Wolfwind* had begun to bring in her starboard bank of oars to protect them from any attempt Hal might make to rake them. Confusion reigned on the larger ship as she tried to run out her starboard oars and withdraw the port-side ones at the same time. She slowed and hesitated in the water. Hal heard the distinctive *slam!* of the Mangler in the bows.

"Hang on!" Hal yelled in warning to his own crew, then brought *Heron* smashing into the oars along *Wolfwind*'s port side.

The air was filled with the splintering, cracking sound of the oars being smashed and shattered. Lethal splinters of white oak flew above the two ships, rattling against the raised shields of the *Heron*'s crew. The Iberians, with no prior warning, were not so lucky. Several of them fell, struck by sharp daggers of white oak.

Others were hit by the butt ends of the oars as they swung violently out of control under the impact of the speeding Skandian ship. Other than a direct ramming, nothing could wreak more havoc than having the oar bank raked in this way. The fact that the two ships were heading in opposing directions doubled the force of the impact. Within seconds, a good half of the rowing crew were injured or disabled, lying groaning or unconscious on the rowing benches of the big wolfship.

With a final grinding crunch, *Heron* tore herself free and sailed clear of the stricken wolfship.

No longer under control, *Wolfwind* drifted in her wake, turning slowly into the wind, the sea around her littered with smashed timber and even several bodies, caught by the violently flailing oars and hurled clear of the ship to lie facedown in the sea.

The crew of the *Heron*—those not involved in the sail trim of the little ship—crowded aft along the port bulwark to stare back at their damaged enemy, cheering and raising their weapons in defiance at the stricken ship as she drifted downwind.

Hal called to his tall second-in-command, beckoning him over. "Did you hit her chain plates?" he asked.

Stig grinned in confirmation. "I saw splinters fly," he said. "They're definitely weakened." They both looked aft, to where the crew of the drifting wolfship, with half her oars smashed and out of commission, were struggling to raise the big mainsail and bring their ship under command.

"We'll soon see," Hal said, then called for the crew to return to their posts.

"Going about to port!" he called to Ulf and Wulf, and swung the ship back toward the floundering *Wolfwind* once more.

They had gone well downwind of her as they turned. Now they surged back at her, sails taut and the rigging humming in the wind. The wolfship's crew saw them bearing down on her and redoubled their efforts to get their ship underway. Jerkily, the big square sail began to rise up her mast, pulling the ship across the wind as it went. When it was fully hoisted, the sail handlers hauled in on the sheets to tighten it and it filled, bellying out. Slowly, *Wolfwind* gained steerage way and began to gather speed.

But *Heron* was still faster and the distance between them was closing. In the bow, Stig crouched over the sights of the Mangler, then let fly with the usual resounding *slam!* Hal crouched at the tiller, peering under the sail to watch the flight of the giant bolt. It smashed into the men crowded round the mast, cleaving a deadly path through them, throwing bodies to left and right before it sailed clear over the side into the sea.

"That's a few less we have to worry about," said Erak. He hadn't seen the Mangler in action before and he thought now how it was living up to its gruesome name.

Then disaster struck *Wolfwind.*

They heard a grinding, cracking noise from the bigger ship. The sail, drawing fully, had put an immense strain on the chain plates, already damaged by Stig's earlier shot. Now, the three-meter length of timber fastened to the ship's bulwark gave way with a splitting crack, releasing the port-side rigging from its tension. The tarred stays recoiled, the ropes flailing the air like giant whips. The mast, losing all support on one side, tilted wildly to starboard, then came crashing down, bringing the big sail and yardarm with it to lie over the side of the ship, which was brought to a halt as the mass of timber, canvas and rope dragged in the sea alongside.

Erak, seeing the damage to his beloved *Wolfwind,* gave an agonized groan as she drifted, listing to one side, badly damaged and out of control.

"Get ready to board her!" Hal shouted. There would never be a better time. *Wolfwind*'s crew were busy hacking at the stays and halyards that held the mast, yardarm and sail fast to the hull. The ship and her crew were in total disarray.

Erak heard him and dashed forward into the bows. Kloof, barking wildly, followed him. The rest of the crew assembled calmly, with Thorn and Stig at the front and the others in a tightly organized group behind them. There was no jostling or pushing. They had done this many times before and each man knew his position and his task. Lydia stayed back, finding a vantage point in the bows from where she could cover the crew once they boarded the enemy vessel. She had her atlatl in her hand and two quivers of darts slung over her shoulder. Only Ulf and Wulf remained at their sailing positions. They would join the boarding party once the two ships were tethered alongside each other and the sails had been lowered.

Hal would remain on board. With Stig and Thorn leading the boarders, there would be no need for him to join in.

Heron sped forward, arrowing toward the stern quarter of the bigger ship as it turned and twisted out of control—hampered by the dragging wreckage beside it.

So far, nobody on board had noticed her silent approach. There was no shouting or clashing of weapons from the Herons as they waited to board *Wolfwind*. They had been well taught by Thorn and they knew that such displays were a waste of energy, usually performed to bolster the courage and confidence of the boarding party. *Heron*'s crew, highly trained as they were, felt no need of such false displays. They would go about their work with silent efficiency.

Ulf and Wulf crouched over the sheets and halyards, their eyes fixed on Hal, awaiting his signal. When *Heron* was fifteen meters away from her quarry, Hal made a chopping motion in the air and the twins released the sheets, letting the air spill from the sail, then brought the yardarm and sail sliding down to the deck.

As the mass of timber and canvas settled, the two sail trimmers grabbed their swords and shields and raced to take their positions at the rear of the boarding party.

Hal watched, eyes narrowed with concentration, as the two ships slid together, *Heron* carried on by her momentum. At the last moment, he twitched the tiller so that *Heron*'s bow turned away from a direct impact and slid alongside *Wolfwind*'s stern quarter, grinding the two hulls together as she slid alongside the bigger boat.

Perhaps it was due to the slight impact, which set the wolfship rocking, but for the first time somebody aboard *Wolfwind* noticed *Heron*'s approach. There was a warning shout from the group amidships, desperately working to untangle *Wolfwind* from her shattered mast and rigging. The Iberians turned to look for their weapons.

Thorn checked his boarding party, making sure everyone was ready, and bellowed the time-honored battle cry of the Herons.

"Let's get 'em!"

An instant before he did, Erak had leapt up to the rail at the very prow of the ship and hurled himself across the gap onto *Wolfwind*'s deck.

chapter thirty-five

In stark contrast to Erak's impulsive, wild attack, the Herons advanced steadily and remorselessly, in a disciplined, coordinated group. They had practiced the maneuver repeatedly under Thorn's leadership and direction and had used it in a score of sea fights over the years. It was now virtually second nature to them.

Thorn led the way, at the point of the wedge they formed. His massive club-hand smashed out to left and right, shattering shields, breaking limbs and fracturing ribs among those who opposed him.

Slightly behind him and to his left was Stig. His battleax whirled in a constant, glittering arc. The power and speed of his blows was phenomenal—very nearly as devastating as Thorn's club. Men fell back or fell before him. No armor or shield seemed capable of deflecting or stopping his blows. The huge ax head sheared through breastplates and shields as if they were made of light wood.

To Thorn's right, and once again slightly behind him, was Ingvar. Massive and implacable, he hacked at the pirates closest to him with the ax head on his long-handled voulge, dropping them like flies. Those farther away were subjected to savage thrusts of the spearhead, or were caught on the sharp hook opposite the ax blade and jerked forward off balance, to be finished off with either the ax or the spear.

The three warriors formed a wedge shape and they were the shock troops of the boarding party, armed with weapons designed to batter and smash the enemy line and force a way forward, scattering those who didn't fall before their onslaught.

Widening the wedge were Jesper and Stefan, armed with swords that darted in and out from behind their shields like serpents' tongues. Thorn had schooled them long and hard in the technique to employ in a close-in fight on board an enemy ship.

Don't swing wildly, he had cautioned them. *You'll expose yourself and your comrades to return thrusts. Use your shields for cover and thrust, thrust, thrust.*

Now, his dictum was proving itself once more. The glittering blades darted in and out from behind the big, round shields, stabbing at arms, legs and torsos that were left unprotected by the pirates' wildly swinging weapons, which for the most part clattered harmlessly off the metal-rimmed wood and ox-hide shields.

In the fourth rank, and again spreading the wedge farther, were Ulf and Wulf. Armed with swords and shields, they continued the deadly thrusting and stabbing that had already taken such a toll on *Wolfwind*'s crew.

Finally, Edvin brought up the rear, finishing off any wounded enemies who had fallen and were trying to rejoin the battle, and ready to step in and take the place of any of his comrades who might be wounded and forced to retire.

Lydia, from her vantage point on board *Heron*, stayed out of the close combat, but stood ready to deal with any enemy who might avoid the forward thrust of the fighting wedge and try to approach from the side or the rear. Already, she had launched three darts with deadly effect.

So the fighting wedge advanced steadily across *Wolfwind*'s crowded deck, forcing the frantic, panicking Iberians back into an increasingly smaller space as they went. The pirates could find no effective counter for them. They fought wildly but their own superior numbers were a hindrance. They got in one another's way as they alternately tried to fight back or retreat from the lethal Skandian wedge. By contrast, the Herons were efficient, deadly and disciplined.

Less so was Erak. He had landed on *Wolfwind*'s deck several meters ahead of Thorn and Stig, and plowed instantly into the mass of Iberians before him. Many of them were still intent on clearing *Wolfwind*'s deck of the shattered mast and rigging that lay across her, causing her to list dangerously in the water. They looked up too late at the infuriated Oberjarl as he charged down on them, his massive battleax smashing left and right, cutting them down like wheat before the scythe.

His huge shield was no less a weapon, hurling enemies to one side like a battering ram.

Several of them fought back, inflicting wounds on the raging

Oberjarl. But he seemed impervious to them, ignoring the blood streaking his arms and legs, dealing out quick vengeance to any who struck at him. The pile of fallen pirates grew around him as he battered and smashed his way along the blood-streaked deck. Those facing him began to fall back from the terrifying sight, crowding into their comrades behind, shoving and pushing to escape. And still Erak charged into them, creating havoc among them, dealing death and destruction to either side.

It was his own momentum that nearly led to his downfall. The farther he advanced, the more he became isolated and exposed as the milling crowd closed in behind him. Whereas the Herons' formation and training allowed them to cover one another's backs, Erak was alone, pushing forward into the Iberian crew, leaving more and more of them behind him, ready to attack.

One, bolder than his comrades, rose to his hands and knees from the deck, where a glancing blow from Erak's shield had thrown him several minutes before. He saw his own sword lying on the deck nearby and reached for it. Coming fully erect, he advanced on the back of the Skandian warrior, drawing back his sword for an overhand blow to Erak's exposed neck, above the edge of his mail shirt.

On board *Heron,* Lydia was temporarily unsighted as Erak had plowed into the Iberian crew, surrounded as he was by the surging, struggling mass of men. Then, too late, she saw the Iberian rise behind Erak, his sword drawn back for a killing blow. Desperately, she drew back the dart she had already mounted in her atlatl. But the surge of struggling men closed again and blocked her shot.

Then a huge black-white-and-tan shape soared over *Heron*'s railing, its hind legs thrusting against the rail for a huge leap that carried it over the gap between the two ships to *Wolfwind*'s bulwark. It gathered all four paws beneath it for an additional leap and soared into the middle of the desperate struggle around the Oberjarl.

Massive jaws clamped shut on the hand holding the sword that threatened Erak's back. Kloof dropped to the deck, her fifty-five kilograms of weight dragging the shocked pirate down with her, her head shaking violently as she sought to rid the man of his weapon.

The Iberian screamed in pain and shock and released his hold on the sword, which spun high into the air, landing among his shipmates. But Kloof retained her grip on his arm, dragging the pirate back as he rolled and twisted in agony, trying to free his arm.

Sensing the conflict behind him, Erak glanced back briefly, took in the scene and slapped the flat of his ax against the side of the man's head, knocking him unconscious. Then he turned back to the battle before him.

Satisfied that the pirate was hors de combat, Kloof backed away and crouched, ready to spring into action once more if the Oberjarl was threatened. One Iberian, who had been crawling along the deck to a spot behind Erak, saw the sequence of events and hurriedly reversed his course.

Erak sensed the crowd around him was beginning to melt away. Turning briefly, he looked over his shoulder and saw that Thorn and his fighting wedge had finally cut their way through the enemy to stand by his side. He allowed himself a ferocious grin.

"Where have you been all this time?" he demanded of Thorn.

"Saving your neck," the grizzled warrior replied, bringing his club down on a pirate who was threatening Erak with a spear. The pirate lost all interest in proceedings and fell senseless to the deck. Erak shoved him aside with his foot.

The remaining pirates were backing away fearfully. Having faced Erak's berserker rage, they were now confronted by the Herons' deadly fighting wedge. There seemed to be axes, clubs, spears and swords on all sides, ready to deal swift vengeance to any further attempts at resistance.

After the devastation caused by the Mangler, Hal's oar-shearing collision and Lydia's darts, *Wolfwind* had started the hand-to-hand battle with twenty-five of her original crew of forty. Now there were fewer than a dozen left standing, cowering away from the weapons of the Skandian warriors advancing on them. The rest of their comrades lay, either groaning and nursing their wounds or, more ominously, in silent heaps on the deck. Those among them who were inclined to notice such details saw that there were more of the latter than the former.

One man threw his weapon down on the deck with a resounding *clang*, and fell to his knees in surrender. That started a hail of dropped weapons and calls for mercy as the rest of his comrades followed his lead.

Erak straightened from his battle crouch and lowered the head of his ax to the deck, resting on the upturned handle. He surveyed the surrendering crew with contempt.

"They're not up to much, are they?" he said.

And in truth, he was right. The Iberians were used to attacking relatively unarmed and untrained sailors on trading ships. Habitually, they had used their superiority in numbers and their ruthless ferocity to capture or kill the crews they had preyed on.

Facing a disciplined, well-armed and well-trained fighting force like the crew of the *Heron* was a different matter altogether. The Iberians had little stomach for an encounter where their opponents not only fought back, but fought back with the sort of savagery and skill that the Herons had shown. The Herons' training and tactics had nullified the pirates' superior numbers, and Erak's berserker rage had been something they had never before encountered.

Thorn surveyed the cowering pirates with equal contempt. Then he turned to Ulf and Wulf. "Gather up their weapons. Stefan and Edvin, tie them up before they get any ideas about starting the fight again."

As the four of them moved to obey his orders, Stig, Ingvar and Jesper stepped forward, weapons at the ready. But there was no resistance left in the Iberian survivors. Meekly, they allowed themselves to be tied up. As Jesper approached the first of the pirates, he turned to ask Thorn.

"Hands in front or behind?"

Thorn paused to consider, then answered. "In front. They can row us back to Sonderland."

chapter thirty-six

Livosk was the principal city of the Sonderlanders. It lay two days' sailing time to the west, where the coastline curved back northward.

The two ships headed in company toward the city. The damage to *Wolfwind*'s mast was too serious for Hal to repair it at sea, so the bigger ship proceeded under oars. In addition to the dozen Iberians who had surrendered, there were another eight who were only slightly injured in the collision or the ensuing fight.

After the surviving pirates had surrendered, Stig had discovered their chief, huddled under a tarpaulin in the stern, cowering and shivering with fear, and totally unharmed. Upon questioning his crew, Hal found that he was called El Despiadado, the Savage One.

"Doesn't look too Despiadado now," he commented.

The pirates showed their disdain and disgust for their cowardly former leader, snarling insults and threats at him as they realized he had deserted them in the battle, hiding from the vengeful Skandians in the stern sheets.

El Despiadado and the other twenty ex-pirates were chained to the oars. Normally, *Wolfwind* had thirty oars deployed, but many had been damaged or smashed when Hal brought *Heron* raking down her port side. As a result, some of the surviving oars were double banked, with two men chained to each.

"That should keep them out of mischief," Thorn said as he watched the chained men heaving on the oars. It was an effective way of keeping the prisoners subdued. Nobody was likely to start a rebellion while he was tethered to a heavy three-meter oar. Thorn and Stig had stayed aboard *Wolfwind* to keep an eye on the pirates, along with Erak, Ingvar, Stefan and Jesper. In addition, Kloof prowled back and forth along the central deck, peering down into the rowing benches and baring her teeth at the former pirates, who cowered away from her.

Ulf, Wulf and Edvin had returned to *Heron* to assist Hal and Lydia. The smaller ship cruised easily under sail, keeping an eye on her consort, wary of any sign of uprising from her former crew. At night, they closed in to the coast and beached the two ships, leaving the prisoners chained, and feeding and watering them where they sat.

They arrived at Livosk in the early afternoon. The city was situated on a wide bay—too wide to be protected by a boom or other defensive device. The two ships sailed into the harbor and Hal could see an immediate stirring among the people on shore.

Heron was flying the Skandian flag—a gold wolf's head on a blue background—and *Wolfwind* bore a similar ensign, flying above the Iberian red-and-gold flag, a sign that the ship had been captured at sea. Both ships had a green leafy branch at their bow posts, signifying that they wanted to parley.

Wolfwind anchored in the bay, some distance away from the shore. *Heron* nudged alongside her and they tethered the two ships together.

"After all," Erak observed wryly, "we don't want to frighten them."

Word had obviously reached Livosk of *Wolfwind*'s depredations, which explained the signs of alarm on shore when they arrived. But the wolfship was obviously damaged and half her mast was missing. She didn't seem to pose a threat to the town, anchored as she was in the center of the harbor, and the initial panic quickly died down.

Nevertheless, a guard boat was soon heading toward them. It was a large rowing boat, crewed by some twenty armed men in addition to the ten oarsmen aboard her. It circled the two anchored ships warily, then moved into hailing distance.

"What ship is that?" the officer on board called to them.

Erak stepped up onto the steering platform and replied. "This is the Skandian ship *Wolfwind*," he called in a carrying voice. "And I am Erak, Oberjarl of the Skandians. I want to speak to your Hierarch."

Sonderland was ruled by a triumvirate, three men who had gained their positions by scheming, bribing and, in some cases, murdering their way to power. They rotated the position of

Hierarch, or ruler, every two years. Erak had no idea who the current incumbent might be. Nor did he care. He simply wanted to establish that *Wolfwind* was back in the hands of her rightful owners.

His demand obviously caused some consternation on the guard boat. There was a hurried consultation between the men on board, then the spokesman called again. "Who did you say you are?" he asked. There was a doubtful tone to his voice.

Erak erupted. "I'm Erak Starfollower, Oberjarl of Skandia, and I'm getting tired of sitting here in the middle of your harbor answering your mindless questions! Now take me to the Hierarch! At once!"

There was a long pause, then the officer replied, even more uncertainly, "Your ship . . . it's been accused of acts of piracy against Sonderland . . ."

"It was stolen by Iberian pirates, and I've just taken it back from them!" Erak bellowed. "Now I'm going to ask one more time: Take me—"

He got no further. The officer seemed to come to a decision. He gave an order to his men and then waved to Erak as the guard boat began to pull for the shore. "Follow us," he called.

Erak stepped aboard *Heron* as Stig and Jesper cast off the lines securing the two ships together. As the sail filled, *Heron* curved smoothly away from the wolfship and headed after the guard boat.

The guard boat pulled in alongside what appeared to be the official government wharf. *Heron* moored behind it, and Erak, Hal and Thorn stepped ashore. The commander of the guard boat was waiting; he gestured for them to follow him.

The Hierarch's headquarters was a short walk from the waterfront, in a large open square. It was a squat and graceless monolith of a building, constructed from sandstone and standing over two stories high, dwarfing the single-story buildings around the edges of the square. Its walls were stepped in twice, ending in a shallow dome. Three wide steps led up to the main entrance—a massive pair of ironbound doors. Their guide signaled to the soldiers standing guard at the doors, which were opened, admitting the visitors to the vast chamber inside.

Hal looked around as they entered the dim interior. *Empty* was the word that sprang to mind. There was little furniture, and although the building was very tall, there was no upper floor. One vast room dominated the space, although, as his eyes grew accustomed to the dim light, he could see several other chambers at the rear of the building. The Hierarch sat on a massive wooden chair—a virtual throne, although it was devoid of any gold leaf or jewelry embellishing it. It was placed two-thirds of the way down the chamber, in the center, and it stood two steps higher than the floor around it. Several wooden benches were arranged on the marble floor in front of it, and at the foot of the stairs. Presumably, these were for supplicants who had gained an audience with the Hierarch.

The man himself was short and squat. His feet barely touched the ground in front of the chair, giving him a comical, childlike appearance.

But there was nothing comical about the expression on his face. He was olive skinned; with a fleshy face and neck, a heavy, beaklike nose and beetling eyebrows over black eyes. There was a permanent frown mark between his eyes and it deepened as he glared at the new arrivals before him.

"Yes? What do you want?" he demanded roughly.

Beside him, Hal felt Erak tense. The big Oberjarl stood a little straighter at the surly, unwelcoming tone.

"You are the Hierarch?" Erak asked.

The frown on the Sonderlander's brow deepened. "Yes. I am the Hierarch! Did you think I was the court jester?" he demanded.

Erak shrugged. "That was always a possibility," he declared calmly.

The Hierarch's swarthy face now suffused with rage. He stood from the throne, pointing an angry finger at the burly Skandian. Even with the advantage of the two steps, he was still almost on the same eye level as Erak.

"How dare you! Who do you think you are?"

"I *know* I am Erak Starfollower, Oberjarl of the Skandians and your equal in rank. I am not going to be browbeaten by the likes of you," Erak replied forcefully.

His hand dropped to the head of his battleax, slung from his belt. Perhaps unwisely, the Sonderland guard had neglected to relieve the Skandians of their weapons.

The Hierarch noted the movement and swallowed nervously, measuring the distance between Erak and himself, and comparing it with the distance between his guards and the angry Skandian. The advantage was with Erak, he noted, and Skandians did have a reputation for sudden acts of violence when annoyed.

The Hierarch made a placatory gesture. "Forgive me, Oberjarl. I spoke in haste. I had no idea of your identity or your rank. Please, what can I do to help you?" He sank back into the chair, but remained tense, his hands grasping the wooden arms on either side.

"For some days now, one of our wolfships, crewed by Iberian pirates, has been raiding shipping and coastal towns around the Stormwhite," Erak began.

The Hierarch nodded. "Yes. I'd heard that the Skandians were raiding again," he said.

Erak frowned. "I *said,* the ship was crewed by Iberian pirates. It was stolen from Hallasholm harbor some time ago."

The Hierarch allowed himself a sarcastic smile. "That was careless of you," he said.

Erak paused, took a breath, then continued deliberately. "The ship was used to plunder and kill, in an attempt to discredit the Skandian navy and disrupt the treaty between Skandia and the other Stormwhite states. We have been in pursuit of her for the past eleven days."

"And now my men tell me you've caught her," the Hierarch said. Then he shook his head and pursed his lips. "But I fail to see what this has to do with Sonderland. Surely it's a Skandian problem."

"It's a problem for both of us," Erak persisted, "because the pirates have been operating from a base on your coastline, some fifteen leagues west of Malmet."

The Hierarch shrugged. "I wasn't aware of this."

"Perhaps not, but it could be held that Sonderland was providing shelter and aid to the pirates, even supplying them with a base and provisions." As he said the words, Erak suddenly wondered whether there might not be more than a grain of truth in them. Sonderland had a murky reputation when it came to international law. The country was notorious for providing mercenary troops to other nations where civil war had broken out.

The Hierarch shifted uncomfortably in his seat, and Erak became convinced that his suspicion might be correct.

"I knew nothing of this," the Hierarch repeated.

Erak paused, his eyes boring into the Hierarch's. Eventually, it was the Sonderlander who dropped his gaze.

"Of course, I believe you," Erak said. "And that belief will be confirmed when you supply troops to wipe out that base and capture the remaining pirates so they can face justice in your courts. I'm sure your neighbors round the Stormwhite will see things in the same light. Otherwise, you may find your country facing trade embargoes and sanctions."

The Hierarch could see that he would have to submit. But he tried to bluster. "Are you threatening me?"

Erak smiled. "Yes," he said.

The Hierarch tried one more time. "What makes you think you can make threats like this and simply walk out of here?" he demanded.

Erak's hand dropped to the head of his ax again. "What makes you think I can't?" he asked.

The Hierarch's gaze dropped away from Erak's. He was not a man of action. He had gained, and kept, his position by dint of intrigue, dishonesty and underhand means. In the course of this, he may have had men assassinated, but he had never participated in the act himself. Now, faced with Erak's powerful personality and physical confidence and aggression, he felt at a total loss. He was uncertain as to how the big Skandian leader might react if he refused to address the problem of the Iberian pirates but he sensed a definite physical threat to himself. For the second time, he cursed his underlings for allowing the Skandians to retain their weapons—and to move so close to the throne.

"Very well," he said in a defeated tone. "What do you need me to do?"

chapter thirty-seven

"Do you think a hundred troops will be enough?" Hal asked Erak as they walked back to the jetty where *Heron* was tied up.

Once the Hierarch had capitulated, he had agreed to everything Erak had stipulated. The Oberjarl had suggested that a force of one hundred men would be needed to clean out the pirate base. He nodded now as he answered.

"There can't be more than fifty or sixty men left at the camp," he said. "And not all of them will be fighting men. One hundred Sonderland troops, with us to back them up if necessary, should be more than enough to get the job done. The Sonderlanders may be a dishonest, underhand bunch, but they're good fighting men."

One of the Hierarch's senior officers had been tasked with

gathering the force. It would take at least a day to gather the men, and to find and provision the ships necessary to take them back down the coast to the Iberian base. Twenty of the troops would travel on *Wolfwind*. In light of the enforced delay, Hal had arranged to pay a visit to the government ship chandlery in Livosk. He needed timber and cordage to repair *Wolfwind*'s rigging and mast, although he knew he wouldn't have time to effect the repair before they left to attack the Iberian camp.

"I'll do it while the Sonderlanders are cleaning house," he told Erak. The Oberjarl nodded. He was keen to see his ship in full fighting trim once more.

They boarded *Heron* for the short trip out to where *Wolfwind* was anchored. Hal dropped Erak off and turned the ship back for the shore.

Two days later, they set off down the coast in a convoy, accompanied by two Sonderland ships. There were twenty Sonderland troops at the oars of *Wolfwind*, with the Iberian captives having been taken ashore to the Livosk prison, where they awaited trial.

"What'll happen to them?" Lydia asked as *Heron* glided out to sea, following the other three ships.

Hal shrugged. "They'll be tried. When they're found guilty, they'll hang," he said dispassionately. "After all, there's no question about their guilt."

As a sailor, he had a distinct antipathy to pirates. They preyed on innocent and vulnerable seamen, striking without mercy, usually in overwhelming numbers, killing their prey and destroying their ships. To Hal's mind, anyone who chose a life of piracy could suffer the consequences. They knew what price they would pay if and when they were caught.

And the Iberians had definitely been caught.

He saw the faint look of distaste on Lydia's face. "Don't waste any sympathy on them," he told her. "They knew the risk they were running and they chose to take it."

She nodded reluctantly. "Still, it seems a little hard," she said.

He shrugged. "It's a hard life," he told her.

By contrast, the attack on the Iberian camp was so easy as to be anticlimactic. The four ships swept into the bay, *Wolfwind* in the lead. The Iberians in the camp, seeing her returning—albeit with her mast and sail down and traveling under oars—made the understandable mistake of thinking that the other three ships were prizes she had taken after sinking the clumsy little square-rigger she had set out to pursue.

As a result, there was no defense organized, and when *Wolfwind* led the way to the shore and ran her prow into the sand, a small group of Iberians made their way down the beach to welcome her back. The others in camp went on about their normal daily business.

They realized their mistake when fifty fully armed Sonderland troops rapidly disembarked and deployed on the shore, accompanied by another fifty from the two supporting ships. There was a hurried rush for weapons but it was too late. The Sonderland formations advanced rapidly up the beach, shields up and weapons ready, striking down the fleeing pirates to left and right.

Thorn watched from the deck of *Heron,* beached alongside her larger consort.

"I don't think we're going to be needed," he said, with a tinge of regret. Like Hal, he had little time or sympathy for pirates.

A small group of a dozen pirates managed to make a stand in front of their tent lines. The Sonderlanders, who outnumbered them by four to one, quickly swept their defenses aside and smashed into their line, sending the few survivors reeling, trying in vain to find hiding places in the tents.

A few more, including those manning the clifftop lookout, managed to escape into the hinterland, leaving behind the bulk of their weapons and possessions.

The captain commanding the Sonderlanders let a squad of his men pursue them for some minutes, but the attackers were hindered by their heavy armor and the rough ground, and the pirates showed them a clean pair of heels. After a short pursuit, the captain had his trumpeter sound the recall and his men made their way back to the beach.

"They won't last long," he told Erak. "The locals here don't like strangers. They'll give them short shrift."

The surviving pirates were rounded up and herded aboard the two Sonderland ships to be taken back to Livosk, where they would face the Hierarch's vengeance. The captain paused before he boarded one of the ships.

"Are you coming back to see them hang?" he asked.

Erak shook his head. "I've seen all of them I want," he said. "I'll head back to Hallasholm. Remind your leader that he agreed to sending out ships spreading the word that Skandians aren't raiding again."

"I'll do that," the soldier agreed. He sketched a swift salute, raising his clenched fist to the brim of his helmet, then turned and marched back down the beach to his ship.

Erak turned away toward *Wolfwind*. He could hear the sound of hammering and he realized that Hal was already at work, repairing the shattered chain plates so he could raise the mast once more.

While Hal worked on the repair to *Wolfwind*, Stig, with Ulf, Wulf and Stefan as crew, took *Heron* back to Hallasholm, to bring back a crew for the refurbished wolfship.

Thorn, Ingvar and the rest of the Herons stayed with Hal, along with Erak, helping with the repair work and guarding against the possibility that the escaped pirates might return. Hal detected a slight air of disappointment from Thorn when they neglected to do so.

The work progressed well, and in a week, *Wolfwind* was re-rigged, with a new mast and rigging, and the original yardarm and sail. Erak surveyed the result with a smile of satisfaction. He had hated seeing his beloved *Wolfwind* so badly injured. Now she was complete again.

"I could have given her a fore and aft rig like *Heron* if you'd wanted one," Hal said, working hard to keep a straight face. "That way she'd be much handier sailing upwind." He knew the Oberjarl loved *Wolfwind* as she was, in spite of her old-fashioned square rig.

Erak had sniffed at the idea. "She does fine into the wind as she is," he replied, conveniently ignoring the fact that *Heron*'s superior upwind performance had contributed significantly to their victory over the Iberians.

They had sufficient crew to take *Wolfwind* on short runs to sea to test her new rigging and mast. Hal deferred to Erak when it came to taking the tiller, and he enjoyed seeing the contented look on the Oberjarl's face as he put his ship through her paces. Kloof crouched at Erak's feet, watching him avidly, and constantly looking at the polished walking staff that he kept by his side.

"Leave it, Kloof," Hal warned her.

Kloof thumped her tail on the deck at the mention of her name, but continued to look from Erak to his walking staff and back again.

"This won't end well," Hal cautioned her, but she ignored the warning.

Ten days after Stig, Ulf and Wulf left for home, *Heron* and another wolfship swept round the headland and came ashore. Both ships were crammed with men, as they were carrying a full crew for *Wolfwind*, under Svengal's command. They examined the refurbished ship, studying the graceful new mast and the freshly tarred standing rigging.

"She looks as good as new, boss," Svengal told Erak, with a broad grin. Like his skirl, he valued *Wolfwind*'s traditional rig.

"And she sails the same way," Erak told him, adding in a lowered tone, "The boy has done a good job on her."

Erak never liked to hand out praise too freely, particularly to the younger men under his command.

The three ships set sail the following morning, each now complete with a full crew. They cruised easily along the coastline, heading for Hallasholm. In the middle of the day, the wind backed until it was out of the east. The two wolfships lowered their sails and took to their oars, the crew rowing easily and smoothly, well used to the task. As Hal had noted during their battle with *Wolfwind*, Skandians could row for hours at a relaxed pace. It was only when they went to full speed that the oarsmen would tire.

Nevertheless, he couldn't resist the opportunity to lord it over them, sending *Heron* on long tacks across the wind, leaving the two bigger ships in her wake, then hauling her wind to allow them to catch up.

"Now you're just showing off," Lydia commented, the third time this happened.

He grinned happily at her. "Yes. I am," he said, and since he was obviously enjoying himself, she shrugged and moved away, a slight smile on her face.

Men, she thought. *They're such boys!*

The self-contradiction in that thought totally escaped her.

Hal noted that whenever *Wolfwind* came close, Kloof would stand with her paws on the bulwark and bark enthusiastically at Erak, steering the bigger ship.

Erak would reply, waving the long, polished walking staff at the dog, who barked even more enthusiastically at the sight of it.

"I'll have to keep an eye on you," Hal said.

chapter thirty-eight

The three ships had been sighted sailing west along the Skandian coast. Word quickly spread and an enthusiastic crowd gathered at Hallasholm to welcome *Wolfwind* home. Out of deference to Erak, *Heron* and *Wolfcry,* the other wolfship, hove to off the entrance to the harbor and let the Oberjarl enjoy the moment of triumph alone.

People thronged along the mole, standing three and four deep, whistling, cheering and clapping as the big ship drew alongside. Erak beamed with delight. He was a popular leader and all Skandians understood the bond that formed between a skirl and his ship. Svengal supervised the mooring, then gestured for the Oberjarl to step ashore, where he was instantly mobbed by the crowd.

Erak moved slowly through the surging tide of people, shaking hands to left and right, acknowledging the good wishes of those who couldn't reach him in the press. The people went along with him as he strode down the mole, his walking staff clacking loudly on the stones as he went, measuring his progress.

Svengal, grinning hugely, caught Erak's eye above the heads of the welcoming crowd and shouted, "This is going to call for a party!"

Erak nodded enthusiastically. "A big one!" he agreed.

Not that Skandians ever needed an excuse for a party. But given an excuse, it could be guaranteed that such a party would be a riotous affair and would involve the entire town. This meant several days would be needed to organize the event, and to prepare food and drink for a large number of hungry, thirsty and, most of all, noisy Skandians.

In the meantime, Erak had something to take care of. The following morning, he summoned his hilfmann—his private secretary and administrative assistant—to his lodge.

Viktor Svenson, the current incumbent in the position, sat down opposite the Oberjarl and arranged his papers and writing materials on the table in front of him. Experience had taught him that whenever Erak was absent from Hallasholm for an extended period, there was always a lot of routine paperwork to catch up on. This time, however, Erak had something in mind that was definitely non-routine.

"I want you to draft a letter to the Iberian ruler—what's he called?"

"El Déspota," Viktor told him promptly. His job meant that he had to have such diplomatic minutiae at his fingertips, which also meant that Erak didn't.

"Yes, him," the Oberjarl replied. He paused while he thought for a few seconds. Viktor waited expectantly, his stylus poised over a wax note tablet. "It's an official warning, from one head of state to another," Erak continued.

The hilfmann raised his eyebrows. "A warning?" he said. This was definitely not a routine piece of correspondence.

"It's about this business in Sonderland," Erak explained.

Viktor inclined his head curiously. "You think he had something to do with it?"

Erak nodded emphatically. "I'm sure he did. We both know that nothing, nothing, gets done in Iberion without his knowledge and tacit approval. So, yes, I'm sure he had plenty to do with it. Just as I'm sure he took a share of the loot."

The Iberian ruler was well known for his propensity to levy taxes and imposts on everything his subjects did.

"He'll deny it, of course," the hilfmann said, half to himself, and Erak snorted in disgust.

"Of course he'll deny it! He's an underhanded, devious, untruthful swine who's as crooked as a dog's hind leg."

"That's all true," said the hilfmann mildly as Erak warmed to his theme.

"He's a thieving, conniving scoundrel who couldn't lie straight in bed! He's . . ." The Oberjarl paused as he sought more words to describe the perfidious nature of the Iberian despot.

"Mendacious?" Viktor suggested.

Erak agreed immediately. "Exactly! *Mendacious* is the word for him!" He paused and frowned. "What does that mean, exactly?" It definitely sounded derogatory, but he wanted to be sure.

"It means he's a compulsive liar," Viktor explained.

Erak slammed a fist down on the table, setting the hilfmann's pens and inkwell rattling. "Exactly! He's mendashey!"

"Mendacious," Viktor corrected him.

Erak pointed his forefinger at his assistant. "What you said. You can put that in the letter if you like."

"I may do just that," said Viktor, making a note on the wax tablet in front of him. He paused, waiting for the Oberjarl to elaborate, then prompted. "What else?"

"What else what?" Erak asked. He thought he'd covered everything, but Viktor pointed out the need for further content.

"You said this was to be an official warning. A warning denotes consequences."

"Exactly! And there will be some! Plenty of them!"

"Perhaps we could spell them out a little more specifically," Viktor suggested.

Erak paused to think. "Tell him . . . ," he said eventually, "that if any of his people engage in piracy against Skandia or any of our treaty partners, or if they attack and steal Skandian property—specifically ships—I will hold him personally responsible."

Erak paused while Viktor's stylus raced across the tablet. Then he continued. "And tell him that no matter how much he might deny any involvement or knowledge of such behavior—"

"Complicity," muttered the hilfmann to himself.

"Gesundheit," Erak said automatically. The hilfmann decided to let it pass. "I will once again hold him personally responsible . . ."

"And?" prompted Viktor.

"And I will bring a fleet of wolfships to blockade Zidac harbor—"

"The Iberian capital?" Viktor interjected.

Erak nodded. "Exactly. I will blockade his harbor so that no ship can enter or leave. I will cut off his international trade and the taxes he imposes on all ships that come and go in Zidac. And I will continue to do so until his people are starving, his businesses are ruined and his personal fortune is reduced to a handful of copper pennies."

Viktor wrote swiftly, nodding his approval of the threats. They were forceful and realistic. The Skandian navy was more than capable of maintaining such a blockade.

Erak noted the quick head movement and queried him. "Are they enough consequences?" he asked.

Viktor immediately confirmed that they were. "They're excellent. There's nothing that'll frighten the Despot more than a threat to his ongoing income." A large part of the Despot's personal fortune was made up of payments he levied on ships coming and going from Zidac harbor, and he was reputed to spend the money very nearly as fast as it came in. Any disruption in the flow would quickly leave his personal fortune in tatters.

Erak waved a dismissive hand. "Good, good. Then draft that up exactly as I said it . . . in your own words, of course. I want it to be diplomatic."

The hilfmann pursed his lips thoughtfully, wondering how a threat to starve the Iberian people, destroy their trade and impoverish their ruler could be phrased diplomatically. Then he shrugged and dismissed the thought. A threat like this needed to be blunt and unequivocal and that was the way he would phrase it—exactly as Erak had spelled it out. Erak was, after all, the embodiment of blunt and unequivocal.

"I'll write that up straightaway for your seal," he said.

"Good. Then arrange for a fast courier ship to deliver it to Zidac and the Despot as soon as possible."

The hilfmann nodded and gathered up his materials, preparing to leave. But Erak held up a hand to stop him.

"Not *Heron,*" he stipulated. Normally, Hal's ship would be the first choice for such a mission. "I want them here for the party."

chapter thirty-nine

A beef carcass and two large boars were turning on spits over massive fire pits. The fat and juices sizzled as they were released from the meat. The fires had been set hours before and the masses of hardwood fuel had burned down now to deep beds of glowing, red-hot coals. The air above them shimmered with the heat they released, and the men turning the handles on the iron spits were dripping with perspiration.

Eager helpers plied them with tankards of ale to keep up their energy. The spit turners accepted them equally eagerly.

Baskets of fresh loaves were piled high on the trestle tables set up in the town square, before Erak's official offices and residence. Huge platters of steamed and roasted vegetables were brought in a constant stream from the town's kitchens and laid out on the tables.

As the outer layers of beef and pork were cooked, kitchen hands sliced off portions and piled them high on platters. The townsfolk helped themselves, transferring meat, vegetables and torn-apart bread loaves to their own plates and retiring to convenient spots to sit and devour the feast.

The cold night air was redolent with the smell of wood smoke and roasting meat.

Large barrels of ale and smaller casks of wine were placed on trestles around the outer edge of the square. The men and women attending them doled out brimming tankards and glasses of each to those who approached them. In between, they sampled the contents of the barrels and casks, just to make sure, as they put it, that the drinks hadn't spoiled.

Judging by their satisfied expressions, they hadn't.

Ulf and Wulf were at the center of an admiring group of the town's younger women. Word had gone around the town about their appointment as Lydia's bridesmen in the upcoming wedding. Most of the town's prospective brides had been fascinated by the idea and wanted to know more. Several had already decided that they, too, would be happy to be attended by two handsome and dashing young men as they made their way down the aisle to their respective husbands-to-be.

The twins had decided to come in their official bridesmen's regalia, designed and crafted by their doting mother. They wore soft green-leather vests over white linen shirts. The vests sported a silver Heron motif on the left breast and were gathered at the waist by well-polished black-leather belts, each supporting a silver-hilted saxe.

Thick black woolen tights covered their legs, reaching down to soft knee-high sealskin boots.

On their heads, they wore their distinctive Heron watch caps, and over their left shoulders each wore a short green-velvet cape, which was trimmed with white ermine and draped to leave their right shoulders and arms free and unimpeded.

All in all, they were a dashing sight. Hal watched from the edge of the square, where he was nursing a cup of hot, sweet coffee. He smiled indulgently at his sail trimmers. He was delighted that they had chosen to honor Lydia in this fashion, and equally delighted that she had accepted their offer. Now, he was enjoying listening to them fielding questions and requests from the young attractive women who crowded around them.

"Can anyone be a bridesman?"

Both twins shook their head solemnly. "No-o-o," Ulf said judiciously.

Wulf elaborated. "Bridesmen have to be identical. That's the whole point."

"I want bridesmen for my wedding!" said Birgitta Holsdottir, one of the leading lights of the Skandian social set.

Two others turned on her, scandalized. "But you've already asked us to be your bridesmaids!" one said.

The bride-to-be shrugged carelessly. "I can change my mind. I'm a bride," she replied archly. She turned to Ulf and Wulf. "You'll be my bridesmen, won't you?" she asked, confident that their reply would be in the positive. She actually recoiled a pace when Ulf answered her.

"No. We can't do that."

Wulf completed the answer. "We can only be bridesmen for our brotherband member. You'll have to find someone else."

"And they'll have to be identical, like Ulf and Wulf!" said one of her deposed bridesmaids triumphantly.

"But they're the only identical twins in Hallasholm!" Birgitta protested.

Her second ex-bridesmaid added slyly, "There's always the Follskirk brothers."

Helmut and Arnett Follskirk were identical twins. In addition, they were identical sixty-five-year-olds, identically bald and running to identical fat. Their personal hygiene was also identically less than might be desired. They lived in a falling-down hovel on the outskirts of Hallasholm and made their living picking over rubbish discarded by the townsfolk. Anything less like the two handsome *Heron* crewmen was difficult to imagine.

"I can't have them!" Birgitta wailed. Then, making the best of it, she turned back to her two former bridesmaids. "Very well. I'll have you two back," she said magnanimously.

"In a pig's ear!" said bridesmaid number one indelicately. Then she linked arms with her counterpart, and the two of them flounced away, noses in the air, leaving Birgitta to ponder the ruin of her upcoming nuptials.

Hal smiled and turned away, looking for a refill of coffee. He nodded to Erak, who was striding in the opposite direction, circulating among the happy revelers. The Oberjarl had a huge tankard of ale in one hand and his shining black walking staff in the other. Three paces behind him, moving like a wraith, the black-white-and-tan shape of Kloof slunk through the shadows. Erak beamed at Hal as they met.

"Enjoying the party?" he asked.

Hal nodded. "The town's done you proud," he said. In truth, he wasn't totally at home in noisy, populous events like this. He preferred to stay on the sidelines and observe.

The Oberjarl looked around at the throng of people. "Haven't seen Jesper," he said. "I hoped he might be doing a saga for us."

"Gorlog forbid," Hal muttered, then, in a louder voice, he said, "I wouldn't be surprised. I saw him yesterday trying to think of a rhyme for 'pirate.'"

"Good! Good! We need more culture!" Erak enthused, waving his tankard and sloshing ale over several passersby. He moved on, beaming to left and right, trailed by the ominous shape of Kloof.

Hal saw a coffeepot on one of the serving tables at the edge of the square and moved to fill his mug. He looked around for a bowl of honey but there was none. Frowning, he turned and saw the door to a storeroom a few paces away. He strode over and was about to go in when he heard a voice mumbling inside. Easing the door open, he peered into the little room, crammed with sacks of flour and grain, sides of bacon and various condiments ranged on shelves around the walls. In the far corner, he saw Jesper, sitting on a flour sack, pencil and paper in hand, mumbling to himself.

Jesper looked up as his skirl eased himself into the little room. He smiled a greeting.

"Hal! Just putting the final touches to my new saga!" he said. "I needed a beginning but I think I've cracked it."

Hal saw a pottery jar of honey on the shelf and reached for it. Jesper arranged the sheets of parchment where he'd been jotting down his verses and began.

"I'll tell you a saga,

should you require it,
of how Hal and Erak
defeated the pirates . . ."

He paused and looked to Hal for approval.

Hal nodded as he backed out the door. "Very good," he said.

Jesper smiled proudly. "Just a few more lines to add at the end and I'll be done," he said, bending over the work once more.

Hal closed the door behind him, still hearing the mumbling voice inside. He went to turn away and bumped into something. It was a chest-high barrel of ale standing ready to be served. He tested the weight of it. It was full, and he could barely move it. An idea came to him and he set down the coffee mug and honey pot. Then he put his shoulder against the barrel and tilted it onto its rim. That way, he could move it by rolling it. He gently rolled the barrel until it was against the door, effectively locking Jesper inside. Satisfied, he retrieved his coffee and the honey and went back into the town square. He decided he'd release Jesper later, when the party was dying down, and Hal could decently head home for the night.

He saw Erak some meters away, talking to a group of smiling townspeople, still gesturing with his tankard, still spilling ale onto those around him. Hal noticed that Erak's other hand was empty and looked around in panic.

From beneath a table, he heard an ominous crunching sound. Bending down to peer under it, he was horrified to see Kloof, with the polished walking staff held firmly between her forepaws, her eyes closed and her head tilted to one side for better purchase. The massive jaws were crunching the shining wood. Half its length had already gone, scattered around her in small wood chips.

Hal winced. These were the same powerful jaws that had clamped down on the Iberian's sword hand as he prepared to attack Erak's unguarded back.

"Kloof! Bad dog!" he hissed in a horrified whisper.

Kloof's eyes opened and she thumped her tail on the ground. Hal felt a hand on his shoulder and turned to see the Oberjarl looming above him.

"Leave her be," said the Oberjarl, smiling fondly at the big dog. "She earned it."